D0885553

PALM
BEACH
NASTY

PREVIEW EDITION

304 pp.   ISBN: 978-1-57962-414-9

Pub. Date: January 2015 $29 cloth

PALM BEACH NASTY

TOM TURNER

THE PERMANENT PRESS
Sag Harbor, NY 11963

ACKNOWLEDGMENTS

I have many people to thank for helping make *Palm Beach Nasty* a reality.

First, and foremost, are Susan, Serena and Georgie. Susan, I couldn't have done it without your support and patience. Serena and Georgie, you are the best . . . oh, and DFUY.

Then, in no particular order, come my readers. Some of them couldn't hide from me and my dog-eared manuscript because we were onboard a boat or on an island—so thank you Liz Berens, Eduardo and Gillian Mestre, Bridget and John Macaskill and Loic de Kertanguay. Others who volunteered to read it—often after a cocktail or two—were Robin Senior, Doug and Ali Milne, Julia Ireland Randall, Chris Kirk, Laura Swiggett, Kathleen Rivers, Caroline Coleman and Marcie Barnhill. Still others felt obligated to read it because they're family—so thank you John Turner and CeCe Haydock.

Lastly, I want to thank Ed Stackler, who has gone above and beyond a million times. Consummate editor, best eye and ear around, incredibly good guy.

Thank you all so much.

ONE

It turned out Crawford really missed the murder and mayhem up in New York. Which was weird, since the whole reason he'd gone south was to get away from it all.

At age thirty-six, with a bad case of acid reflux, chronic cynicism and acute burn-out, Charlie Crawford had packed up his Upper West Side apartment and headed down to the Sunshine State. He decided on the Keys, the plan being to take up surfing, give the Jimmy Buffett thing a shot. But after three months of listening to stoned-out beach bums in lame Hawaiian shirts oohing and aahing pretty average sunsets and duding each other to death, Crawford was ready to move on.

So he'd reached out to a handful of Florida law enforcement agencies, and when the Palm Beach Police Department made him an offer, he grabbed it. But almost a year into the job, *no one* had come close to getting knifed, shot, garroted or even banged up a little. Christ, what he'd give for a face-down stiff, a little rigor setting in. Crawford was drawing a bunch of nowhere cases, which could best be summed up by the one he was writing up now.

※ ※ ※

It was late afternoon on Halloween, and a call had come in about a possible trespass up on the north end. The north end of Palm Beach was really two places, depending on the exact location. Obscenely rich and doing just fine, thanks. Spectacular houses on the ocean and Intracoastal that started at $10 million and went up from there. Or fixer-uppers, on postage-stamp lots at around a million. Even in the depressed 2008 market, some Russian fertilizer billionaire had just plunked down a shade under $100 mill for Trump's monumentally ugly, but colossally huge, ocean spec house.

Despite being a homicide cop, Crawford was pinch-hitting on a routine call, because several uniforms were out with the flu. He pulled into the driveway of the address the dispatcher had given him and parked next to a big-haired blonde in a black Jag convertible. She smiled at him as he got out of his Crown Vic.

"Hi, I'm Detective Crawford."

"Rose Clarke," the woman said. "Place is one of my real estate listings."

It was a two-story yellow stucco house with oversized columns.

"You put in the call?" Crawford asked, looking through a big picture window for signs of life.

"Uh-huh." Beautiful smile, teeth like Colorado snow behind pouty lips.

"You think someone's in there who's not supposed to be?"

"Think?" she said. "I just saw a naked woman through the slider in back."

"Who's the owner?"

Crawford started toward the house. She followed.

"Willard Gregg was," she said, "but he died six months ago."

"Couldn't be a relative you saw, could it?"

"No way . . . I'd know about it."

Crawford started walking. "I'm going to try round back."

Rose nodded and Crawford went toward the side of the house, she a step behind him.

He pressed the back-door buzzer, shaded his eyes and looked through the slider. Nothing.

He felt Rose's eyes on him.

"You look like that polo player . . . in the ads," she said, "guy with the brooding eyes. Taco or something."

He pretended to be absorbed in his work. He'd heard it before and wasn't flattered. Crawford was six two, 180 pounds and had thick brown hair he wore a little longer than his boss, the chief of police, liked. He had hazel eyes and above his right eyebrow a thin scar zigzagged across his forehead.

"You have a key, Rose?"

She handed him one.

"Thanks."

He keyed the lock and thought he heard footsteps inside.

It crossed his mind to call for backup, but he nixed it. He was pretty sure the Manson family wasn't waiting in ambush.

"Stay here, please."

"Okay," Rose sighed.

He walked in. There was a torn rubber carpet mat on the living room floor and holes on the walls where paintings had hung.

"Palm Beach police," he said, pulling out his Sig Sauer semiautomatic, "whoever's in here, come on out."

Nothing.

He inched toward a closed door and turned the knob. An air mattress lay on the floor with sheets and a puffy comforter on top. Men's and women's clothes hung on doorknobs.

"I don't want to say it again . . . come on out *now*."

He pushed open a door to a bathroom and saw tooth-brushes, cosmetics, a man's razor with shaving cream on it. He backed out and spotted a yellow Lacoste shirt hanging on a closet door. He opened the walk-in closet and saw shadowy shapes behind the clothing.

"Okay," came a man's voice, "we're coming."

"Slowly, hands up."

First, came a man in blue boxers, then a woman in red, lacy panties and a black push-up bra.

"Who are you?" Crawford handed the woman a terry-cloth bathrobe that hung from inside of the closet door.

"We're the Kazmeyers, I'm Dick and my wife, Jan," the man said, like he was making introductions at a cocktail party.

"Hi," Jan said, knotting the sash on her bathrobe.

Crawford heard steps behind him.

Rose walked in and her eyes popped.

Crawford holstered his gun. "What are you doing here?" he asked the couple.

Jan glanced at her husband. "Just kind of . . . crashing."

"Wait a minute," Rose said, "you were at my open house here a couple of weeks ago."

Jan nodded sheepishly. "We . . . hid in the garage after—"

"—actually that little room with the hot water heater," Dick corrected her.

Rose's mouth dropped.

"When the open house was over and you left, we came out," Jan said.

"Got our mattress and stuff from the car," Dick said, like describing a camping trip to Yellowstone.

They still had their hands up.

"Winters up in Buffalo get really long," Jan said. "This is our fourth season down here."

"Rent free," Rose muttered.

"Okay," Crawford said, "you can put your hands down."

"Thanks," Dick said, then to Rose, "We kept our stuff in that little crawl space . . . in case you showed the house."

"How very thoughtful of you," Rose said.

"You hardly ever showed it, though," Jan said.

"'Cause it's way overpriced," Rose said. "Besides nothing's moving in this market."

"Get dressed, please," Crawford said, "we're going down to the station."

Dick started to panic. "Can't you just give us a ticket?"

"No," Crawford said. "We don't have tickets for something like this."

"Isn't it breaking and entering?" Rose asked.

"We didn't break anything," Dick said, suddenly indignant.

"And we entered perfectly legally," Jan added.

"Let's go," Crawford said.

Rose, by his side, nudged him and whispered, "Only in Palm Beach."

✳ ✳ ✳

IT WAS six thirty now and Crawford was at the station writing up the incident, wishing the crashing Kazmeyers had come on someone else's shift. Half listening to his radio, he thought he heard the dispatcher say the code for homicide.

No way. Yesterday's big investigation had been a socialite's poodle getting pancaked by a Lamborghini. Day before had been a blue-haired lady who sideswiped a mailbox after happy hour at Ta-Boo.

"Say again," Crawford said into his radio.

"Call from a jogger," dispatch said, "reporting a young white male, down at Mellor Park"—then a long pause, as if he couldn't quite process it himself—"hanging . . . from a banyan tree."

TWO

Crawford flipped on his strobes as he turned left onto Brazilian and floored the Vic. He figured it was a ten-minute drive to the park in South Palm Beach he could do in five. He eased up to South Ocean, looked both ways, flicked his siren, punched the accelerator and made a skidding right turn heading south. He stepped on it again and heard the delayed roar of the Crown Vic's 405. A cluster of trick-or-treaters on the sidewalk was a purple and black blur as he blew past them.

He fished his cell phone out of his breast pocket and, doing seventy in a thirty-five, dialed his partner, Mort Ott. Ott was in West Palm, interviewing a witness on a mail-fraud case.

"Yeah, Charlie?"

"Got a seven down at Mellor Park."

A long pause.

"You're shittin' me?"

"No," said Crawford, and clicked off.

That would be the end of Ott's interview, since the two of them were the only homicide detectives on the Palm Beach force. There were six other detectives and seventeen uniformed cops, nicknamed "bags."

Crawford was first on the scene. He heard sirens off in the distance. As he pulled up to the park, he clicked on his high beams, grabbed the Maglite on the front seat and jumped out of his car. The first thing he saw was a small neon circle floating at eye level fifty yards ahead. Then, after a few more steps, he realized the reflective circle was on the back of a sneaker.

The sneaker was on the foot of a body dangling from the thick, shiny branch of a banyan tree.

Then he heard short breaths and flicked his Maglite to his left. A woman in her fifties, black spandex tights and a white baseball hat was staring up at the body, her mouth slack, her expression frozen.

"I'm Detective Crawford. You the lady who called?"

She nodded.

"Stay right here, please," he said, sweeping past her and aiming his Maglite up at the body. The victim, wearing black jeans, a faded red T-shirt and a hoodie hiked up over his stomach, looked to be around twenty. Crawford reached up and checked his pulse, even though he knew there was no point.

The vic's head was tilted forward, purple and swollen, a lime green rope cutting into his neck. Crawford recognized it by the material: paracord, a type of rope used by the military.

The vic was around six feet tall, weighed probably close to two hundred. Had to be at least two perps, Crawford figured. One to pull up the rope, the other to lift up the body. Too much for one guy to do alone. Might have been a third on lookout.

He flicked the flashlight up and noticed the kid's bulged-out eyes, a trace of ruptured blood vessels on his lids.

He reached into an inside pocket of his jacket, pulled out a pair of vinyl gloves, put them on, then shined his Maglite on the kid's jeans. He reached into the back pocket and pulled out a lumpy wallet. He opened it and saw a Florida driver's license. His name was Darryl Bill and he looked way better in the picture.

Bill had turned nineteen three days before.

Crawford looked around and saw the woman jogger hadn't moved. He wondered if she was in shock.

"Ma'am, you all right?"

She nodded.

"How 'bout I take you over to that bench?" he asked, pointing. "I need you to stick around awhile, ask you a few questions."

He led her to a park bench.

"I got a bottle of water in my car."

"That's okay, thanks."

He walked back to the crime scene, got out his cell and dialed as he saw a squad car pull up and a tall uniform hop out.

"This is 211 at Mellor Park, South Palm," Crawford said into his phone. "Confirming dead white male, nineteen years old. Notify brass, the ME and crime scene techs."

He clicked off and scanned the area, looking for a public restroom or other buildings where security cameras could have picked up something. Nothing. He retraced his steps toward the park's entrance gate, still looking for cameras, but saw none. Then he remembered that all four bridges over to Palm Beach had cameras specially installed to read license plates. Tag readers, they called them. He'd get a copy of the day's recording from the south bridge and ID every plate that had come and gone since morning.

The tall uniform, Ramsey Steer, walked up to him. Crawford told him to watch where he stepped, tighten up the perimeter and tape off the scene. A few more cars rolled up.

He went back and studied the kid again. He had short blond hair, a two-inch mullet in back, and was wearing a cheap beaded necklace.

Crawford shined his flashlight on the sand and saw several sets of footprints. One set caught his eye. The toe of the shoe print looked like it had really dug in. He couldn't see any heel mark that went with it. Like someone had his weight forward and was swinging hard, trying to knock one out of the park. He pictured one of the perps holding the kid's arms behind his back while the other one whaled away on him.

Kid probably was out cold when he got lifted up. No way he was conscious or he would have been fighting for his life—kicking, biting, whatever it took. Crawford was surprised there wasn't more blood on the sand below.

He saw the white EMT truck with the yellow stripe pull up. Two guys came running toward him, one with a trauma kit, the other a Zoli resuscitator.

Crawford caught one of their eyes and shook his head.

They were ALS—Advanced Life Support—a hospital on wheels. The truck carried everything a sick or injured person would ever need—ventilators, triage cardiac systems, defibrillators and more meds than a Rite Aid. But there was nothing they could do for Darryl Bill.

"ME on his way?" one of the ALS guys asked.

Crawford nodded and went to his car to get a camera.

Just as he got there, his partner wheeled up.

"Trick or treat?" Ott asked, as he got out.

The knock on Ott was that he was not the most sensitive guy around. Maybe it was the twenty years in Cleveland homicide.

"A kid . . . nineteen, hanging from a tree."

"Fuckin' A," was all Ott said, taking long, deliberate strides toward the crime scene.

Ott had come down about two years ago. So far he and Crawford had a mostly good relationship. Ott had a go-with-the-flow attitude, didn't get too ripe after eight hours in a car, and never sucked up to Chief Norm Rutledge, the way other guys did. The Palm Beach cops looked at Ott as a throwback. A guy who said "fuck" every third word, drank at the low-life cop bar in West Palm and still used Ten-Code even though the Palm Beach department had switched over to "plain talk" five years before.

Some of them called him "Sip," after Andy Sipowicz, the bald, cranky cop in the old TV show, *NYPD Blue*, but most of them just called him "F-bomb."

Ott walked up to the body, too close for the EMT supervisor's liking.

"You mind?" the EMT said.

"Not if you got a way to bring him back." Ott pulled on his gloves and looked up at the kid.

"Two perps, I'm guessing," Crawford said. "Maybe three."

Ott nodded as two uniforms came up behind them. "Really put the wood to the poor fucker," Ott said.

"Yeah, wearing gloves."

"Why you say that?"

"Noticed a couple fibers—looked like leather—on his lips. Left cheek, too."

Ott moved closer to the body and nodded.

"Guy I took in once, just offed a bunch of hookers," Ott said, "used these high-tech ski-racer gloves. Real light padding. Told me he got a nice bone-on-bone crunch."

The young EMS guy glanced over, caught Crawford's eye, and shook his head.

Ott was looking up at something over the kid's head. "Check out that knot," he said, pointing. "A sheep shank. Military. Maybe one of our perp's some psycho just back from Iraq."

Ott theorized a lot, but was more often right than wrong.

A uniform, his flashlight shining down, was about to step on a shoe print.

"Hey, dipshit, not 'til we cap it, huh," Ott said, then to Crawford, "Fucking guys tryin' to fuck up our crime scene. ID him yet?"

"Name's Darryl Bill, from somewhere in West Palm," Crawford said. "I'm gonna diagram the scene and make sure Steer doesn't let anybody unauthorized get through."

Ott nodded. "I'll put placards down. Cutter on his way?"

Crawford nodded and smiled at Ott's dated reference to the ME.

"It's all comin' back, huh Mort?"

"Just like ridin' a Schwinn."

Crawford turned away and started snapping pictures of the footprints in the sand. Then he walked a little farther and spotted the kid's other Nike over by a swing set. He noticed the shoelace was broken, as if the kid's foot had been twisted violently to one side. Ott came over for a look.

Crawford saw someone approaching; he flicked his flashlight in their direction.

It was a woman in a blue jacket that said Crime Scene on the back.

"We got the cute one," Ott said.

Crawford had heard about her. A crime scene tech named Dominica McCarthy whose bulky nylon jacket and polyester pants did little to flaunt a figure everyone agreed was way above average. The Crime Scene Evidence Unit techs were the fingerprint and DNA analysts. Their TV counterparts got a lot of face time on the tube, but in real life, they mostly crawled around on their hands and knees with tweezers and baggies.

McCarthy looked over at them, holding her gaze on Crawford for a second, then looked up at the body.

The ME came next. George Bullen was an egotistical showboater with thirty years on the job. He'd walk around a crime scene grabbing his chin and striking poses, then answer all questions the same way: "You'll get all your answers in my write-up."

Crawford decided to steer clear of the great man.

He and Ott spent the next forty-five minutes combing the scene and questioning the jogger, who had little to tell beyond recounting her grisly discovery.

"I don't see 'em coming up with any good prints," Crawford told Ott. "Best shot's probably DNA off that hoodie."

Ott nodded. "Guys were pros. Nice clean job."

Crawford walked toward the cars and went past Dominica McCarthy, who had just finished bagging the hands of Darryl Bill. She was even better looking close up.

He nodded.

She nodded back.

Crawford took down the license plate number of a Mitsubishi two-door that he'd seen when he first pulled up. It looked like a nineteen-year-old kid's car. It was black with bald tires, low to the ground. He took off a glove and touched the car's hood with the back of his hand, not wanting to get his fingerprints on it. It was warm. Maybe been there an hour and a half. He shined his flashlight inside. The car was surprisingly neat except for one Magic Hat beer in the cup holder. Then he walked back to the crime scene and approached Dominica McCarthy, who was bagging the hoodie.

" 'Scuse me," he said.

She looked up. Big emerald green eyes and sharp, high cheekbones.

"You might want to dust that black car over there," he said, pointing. "The Mitsubishi."

"Thank you, Detective . . . already did."

Crawford nodded and walked over to his car.

On the ride back to the station, he was amped up. He was leaving white-collar crime and Mickey Mouse bullshit in the rearview mirror. Dick and Jan from Buffalo bunking for free in some dead guy's house . . . that was someone else's job.

He finally had himself a murder.

He'd never admit to anyone he'd missed it.

But he had.

THREE

Todd Tropez sized up her net worth. Somewhere in the $8–$10 million range, he figured. Conservative stock portfolio. J.P. Morgan. Smith Barney maybe. Probably had an ivy-covered white brick colonial up north, ocean-front condo down here, owned both free and clear. Nothing conservative about her clothes, though, or the bling. Manolo shoes, flashy designer dress, giant rock on her finger. North of three hundred K easy. A triple string of Wilma Flintstone-sized pearls and diamond earrings dangling from her mushy earlobes. It crossed his mind to just follow her out and roll her.

But he wasn't into that anymore.

Todd looked around the darkened bar for younger options. He saw a few but no one looked anywhere near as rich. Keep your eyes on the prize, he reminded himself. The woman took a long pull on her drink, then smiling at him, fluttered her glued-on lashes.

"So I'm guessing . . . twenty-eight?" Her orange corduroy throat waggled along with a small fortune in facial reconstructive surgery.

"Twenty-*six*," Todd said, raising his hand to the bartender.

"Oh, God," she said, "I was twenty-six when you were born."

Sure you were, he thought. She'd shaved off at least fifteen years. Who was she kidding? Even in the dimly lit Leopard Room, designed to shroud crow's feet, wrinkles and pouches, the woman had to have at least one foot into her seventies.

The Leopard Room at the corner of Peruvian and Cottage Row in Palm Beach was owned by an astute Cuban businessman who built his business on the sound concept that even septuagenarians get horny.

Todd smiled at her the way Amory Blaine would have. He was going through his F. Scott Fitzgerald phase now. That was the way he did it: picked an author and read everything the guy ever wrote. John O'Hara had been before Fitzgerald and before O'Hara was a more obscure guy, Boston writer by the name of J.P. Marquand.

Margo, the bartender, brought over his Mount Gay. "Here you go, Todd."

"Put the gentleman's drink on my tab, please, Margo," the woman said.

"Will do, Mrs. Schering."

"Thank you." Todd raised his glass to her.

"It's Janet," the older woman said, flipping her long platinum wig the way women half her age did.

Todd could tell being called Mrs. Schering made her feel old. He also knew his drink would have been on the house, since bartenders took care of their own.

When Margo said his name, he realized again how much he hated it.

Todd. Should have changed it, too, back when he jettisoned his last name Gonczik? Tough enough making it in Palm Beach, but with the name Gonczik? And Todd, he thought, such a mama's boy name.

He thought about going with Trent. It had a sort of Waspy ring to it.

But Trent Tropez? Nah . . . that was lame, too. A guy in a soap opera with capped teeth and blond flecks in his hair. Plus Trent was one of those Brant, Brent, Brett kind of names. Phony as Janet Schering's age . . . and nose, for that matter.

Todd took a big slug of courage. The Mount Gay went down easy.

"Would you like to dance?" he asked.

"Love to," Janet Schering said, eagerly sliding off the zebra-skinned bar stool.

Todd had weighed his options and decided on a slow dance. It was a toss-up which would be worse, pressed up against the old bag or doing some spazzed-out version of the twist with her.

He put his left hand in her right and his arm on her shoulder and smiled down at her wizened four foot eleven. Her back was bare, her expression eager. His hand slid along the flank of her shoulder, then down her back. He could feel goose bumps spring up at his touch. Then his hand snagged on something. He realized in horror it was a mole. A mole the size of a blueberry. He slid his hand back to her bony shoulder.

"You know, you are a *very* handsome man," she said.

"Thank you."

Well, truth was, he wasn't. His looks were perfectly adequate, nothing special. Five eleven, thick blond hair with a nice wave and a very straight part. His eyes were a little too close together and if he was a woman, he would have gotten some collagen pumped into his thin, prissy lips. Done something about his nose, too. In fact, as soon as he had the money, he'd take his face into the shop.

But for now he made the most of what he had. He worked hard at maintaining a perpetual tan and dressed like a preppie, a look you could never go wrong with in Palm Beach.

Janet suddenly started thrusting up against him like a sexed-up bulldog. He fought the urge to bolt. The song ended, but she didn't break the clinch. Then the band launched into a Rod Stewart standard, which seemed to plunge her even deeper into the mood. She moved her right hand from his shoulder up to the back of his neck.

Oh, Christ . . . please, no. She started to caress his neck, then slid her hand into his hair.

Todd soldiered on, grinding into her gently, knowing he'd need a bucket of Viagra to get it up. Then, oh my God . . . she moaned. More like a bleat. She pushed into him and his hand slipped back down onto the blueberry. He gasped unintentionally.

"What, honey?" she whispered in his ear. "I turn you on, don't I?"

"Oh, yeah," he whispered back.

"Want to come back to my house?" She wheezed, apparently tuckered out by the fox trot.

He pulled his head back and smiled down at her.

"I'd follow you anywhere, babe."

Please . . . just put one between my eyes, right now, he begged silently. What pathetic third-rate ham had invaded his body? As they headed outside, walking down Peruvian, Todd had a strong urge to just roll her, snatch her jewelry, be done with the whole sorry mess. Then he reminded himself again.

He wasn't into that anymore.

FOUR

Crawford had written up his report in his car at the crime scene. Then he'd stopped off at Dunkin' Donuts on his way back to the station.

He flashed back to Dominica McCarthy at the crime scene. First woman he'd ever seen look good in baggy, blue polyester.

Ott had gone straight back and was on the computer in his cubicle when Crawford got there. That was one of the many things Ott grumbled about—his cubicle—since he had had four walls and a door up in Cleveland. Even when the chief, Norm Rutledge, pointed out it was bigger than most of the others, Ott just shrugged. Said he was a corner-office kind of a guy. Crawford knew he really didn't give a damn. He just liked busting Rutledge's balls.

Ott looked up and chuckled.

"You look like a new man, Charlie."

"The hell you talking about?"

"Don't bullshit a bullshitter, finally got something with a little meat on it."

Crawford just walked away, knowing Ott could read him like he had subtitles.

He went down to dispatch, where the Veriplate tag recognition system was.

"Mind if I get on your machine?" he asked the dispatcher.

"All yours."

"Thanks."

He backed the machine up to four in the afternoon and watched the procession of cars on tape coming onto Palm Beach via the south bridge. It was amazing how clear he could read the plates. After forty-five minutes he saw the black Mitsubishi. He stopped the machine. He moved closer and backed the machine up again. He decided to run plates on cars that came over the bridge an hour before and an hour after the Mitsubishi came over. Somewhere around a hundred fifty cars, he estimated.

A half an hour later he was looking down at a fire engine red Ferrari with the license plate, Rainmkr. No shortage of asshole rich guys with massive egos in Palm Beach, he thought. Thirty cars after that came a blue Ford Explorer SUV. He looked at the plate, but couldn't make out anything. He backed it up again and froze it. Still nothing. No numbers, no letters, not even blurry ones.

Then it hit him. The possibility that whoever was in the Explorer could be his guys. Back about fifteen years ago some outlaw Einstein had come up with a special gelatin substance that bad guys, particularly bank robbers, sprayed onto license plates to obscure their letters and numbers. When the gel had been sprayed onto a plate, you could read it clearly with your eyes, but a camera couldn't make out anything.

Ott came bursting into the dispatch area.

"Let's take a ride out to the kid's place," he said. He lived way out on Paladin."

Paladin Road was in the West Palm boonies. Not a lot of $20 million spec houses out that way.

"Gimme a minute," Crawford said, then filled in Ott about what he had seen on the Veriplate.

"Fuckin' guys know what they're doin'," Ott said. "Like some of your mutt buddies up in the Deuce."

Crawford slouched down in his chair, and looked at more plates.

The Deuce had been Crawford's turf for eleven years. The district between Sixth and Ninth Avenues on Forty-Second Street—essentially Times Square—a neighborhood that was cleaned up by one of Giuliani's squads, but still had a nasty underbelly of seediness and sleaze.

After another twenty minutes taking down plate numbers, Crawford went in and got Ott.

They went out to the back of the station, got into Ott's white Caprice and headed west on Okeechobee.

Crawford's phone rang just past the Florida Turnpike. He looked down at the number. It was Lil Fonseca. They'd been going out for two and a half months. It fell short of boyfriend-girlfriend status in his mind, but she felt otherwise.

"Hey, Lil."

"You okay?"

"Sure, why wouldn't I be?"

"I heard about the murder, the shoot-out and—"

"I'm fine, but, sorry . . . no shoot-out."

It amazed him how fast the word traveled in Palm Beach, how distorted things always got. Like everyone had to twist, tweak and add their own spin to whatever story was currently making the rounds. Like that game Telephone.

"Does this mean I get to see you even less?"

"I'm gonna be flat out 'til we solve this."

"Well, then, what are you waiting for," she said, "solve it."

"I got a feeling I'll be hearing that a lot."

They flashed by a broken down Pentecostal church. Nothing but churches and cows out this far.

"Don't forget dinner next Tuesday," she said, like ducking out wasn't an option.

"I'll try."

"Pine Island Grille, seven thirty."

"I'll try," he said again.

"Bye, honey. Be careful."

He cringed a little. First time she'd said, "honey."

Ott looked over and smiled, left hand on the wheel. "How's little miss smokin' hot?"

"Keep your eyes on the road."

Lil Fonseca was definitely "smokin' hot." Throw in wild, enigmatic, a woman with her own agenda and, he suspected, eager to give him a make over. Turn him into a guy who wore red pants, used words like "iconic," and said "at the end of the day" a lot.

They had met a few months back while they were in line to get overpriced sandwiches at a place a block from the station.

Last time he was with her, she tried to take him shopping on Worth Avenue after describing his tie selection as "Russian mafia circa 1990." He told her every store on Worth was way north of his budget. She ended up taking him to an upscale thrift shop on South County. Most of the ties she favored there were either pink or lime green. Or had furry little Hermès animals on them. Worst part was that they started at forty bucks apiece . . . for a used tie. He told her he hardly spent that much on a brand new suit. They walked out empty-handed.

The thing Crawford didn't get about Lil was that for a woman with undisguised social ambitions, what was she doing with him? A lowly cop. For that matter, what was he doing with her?

He looked over at Ott, one hand on the wheel, the other flossing his teeth with a plastic dental pick. Ott's story was as straightforward as Lil's was complicated.

Bald, lumpy and physically unprepossessing, Ott was a first-rate detective. He'd spent twenty-three years on the Cleveland force staring down at stiffs. Dutch on his father's side—originally Van Ott—and Jewish on his mother's, Ott was easy to underestimate. Part of it was because at age fifty-one, he looked ten years older. He stood just five seven and weighed in at over two thirty, but despite the donuts and Checkerburgers, he was in shape. Spent an hour a day in the gym before work and could bench three hundred pounds. He had no problem mixing it up either, a solid wingman.

He had told Crawford that it had gotten old—dead people on the Cleveland pavement—and the fact that Palm Beach probably had fewer than twenty homicides in its entire recorded history was a big plus for him. Not that people didn't die all the time in Palm Beach—just not from TEC-9 drive-bys.

Twenty minutes later Crawford and Ott pulled up to a rundown bungalow on a dried-out, dirt road. The grass was brown on both sides of the house and a Chevy Z/28 was up on blocks in the back. A tar-paper shack would have been an upgrade.

"Like the goddamn Dust Bowl out here," Ott said.

A tall girl answered the door dressed in short cut-off jeans and a bathing suit top. Crawford guessed sixteen or seventeen, a brunette with dark, striking eyes, bare feet and a body that had ripened early.

"Are you . . . related to Darryl Bill?" Crawford asked, showing ID.

"I'm his sister, Misty," she said, stifling a yawn. "What'd he do this time?"

"I'm Detective Crawford, my partner, Detective Ott, can we come inside?"

"Okay . . . is this serious?" She scratched her cheek.

"Yes," Crawford said.

"Tell me," she said.

The house was hood rich—Salvation Army-furnished—except for one expensive-looking sofa and a huge hi-def Sony. On its screen, guys on dirt bikes were jumping fifty feet in the air off built-up mounds.

"Can we sit down?" Crawford asked.

Misty gestured to a sofa. Her eyes were flitting from side to side, jumpy now.

Crawford and Ott sat down in the red leather sofa that looked brand new.

Misty sat on the arm of a love seat, one leg on top of the other, jiggling nervously.

"How do we reach your parents, Misty?" Crawford asked.

"You don't . . . my father's in jail, my mom—" she raised her arms, "who knows?"

Crawford leaned forward.

"I'm sorry to have to tell you, Misty but . . . Darryl was killed."

She jumped up and put her hands to her mouth.

"Oh, my God, no."

Then she started screaming "no" over and over.

She put her hands over her eyes, tears flooded through them.

She bumped into a coffee table, then kicked it with her bare foot.

Crawford looked at Ott knowing he was thinking the same thing. Notifications . . . by far the worst part of the job.

"I'm very sorry for your loss," Crawford said.

Misty walked to her kitchen, tore a few paper towels off the roll and wiped her eyes. Crawford glanced around and noticed a shopping bag from Saks, another from Nieman Marcus, and an elliptical exercise machine, unused and unsweat upon.

Misty came back over. She looked older than when they walked in.

"What happened?" she asked, mopping her eyes with a paper towel.

"He was beaten and . . ." Crawford hesitated.

"What? Tell me."

"Hanged," Crawford said.

She screamed "no" again, this time raking her cheeks with her nails.

"What do you mean?" she pleaded. "Who . . . who *hangs* a person?"

"We are very sorry," Crawford said again, then looked at Ott.

"Misty," Ott said, "any idea who coulda done this? Anybody your brother—"

"No," she screamed again, "this can't be real."

She put her hands on her head and slammed her eyes shut.

Crawford and Ott just sat there.

Then she opened her eyes and reached for two shiny, pink seashells in a straw basket on the table in front of her. She played with them like they were worry beads. Tears streamed down her cheeks. After a moment, she put her head in her hands, letting the shells drop silently to the carpet.

Crawford went and got some more paper towels.

She took them and looked up at him.

"I want you to leave now," she said.

"I understand," Crawford said.

She walked over to a window and looked out.

"We need to ask you to do something very hard. We need you to come down and ID—"

Misty burst into loud sobs, her whole body shaking.

"It can wait 'til tomorrow morning, if you want," Crawford said. "We could pick you up."

"I want to go do it now. In my own car."

She said she wanted to change first. Clean up.

She wanted to look her best for her dead brother, Crawford could tell. He gave her directions, then he and Ott walked out to their car.

"Christ," Crawford said, opening the door, "sure as hell doesn't get any easier."

"No kiddin'," Ott said, starting the engine and turning to Crawford. "You check out those shopping bags? That TV? Guarantee you that sucker was five grand."

Crawford nodded. "Like she's got herself a sugar daddy or something."

"Yeah, and it sure ain't dear old Dad."

FIVE

Nick Greenleaf, briefly Todd Tropez and before that, Todd Gonczik, was shaking a drink called a Bahama Blast at Viggo's in Citiplace. It was for Cynthia Dexter who had become one of his regulars. The place was just starting to fill up. It was Happy Hour.

Since his rutting session with Janet Schering a few nights back, Nick had come to the conclusion that marrying a rich woman—two, maybe three times his age—might indeed be possible, it just wasn't something he had the stomach for. He'd also faced the reality that snagging a well-off, slightly used, forty-something woman was just not in the cards. Because, for the most part, their skin was still reasonably tight, their legs toned and their breasts hadn't toppled over yet. Truth was, they had a fair amount of playing time left and had way better options than a somewhat charming bartender, capable of the occasional literary allusion. Nick grudgingly accepted his place in the hierarchy: a notch below a tanned, handsome golf pro, nip and tuck with a dashing Latin waiter.

Three days after the one-nighter with Janet, Nick was still having painful flashbacks about that night with her. It was a screaming nightmare, still raw. The third and final sweat 'n grunt session took place in the morning when he was completely sober. It was light in her bedroom under the huge canopy bed that was straight out of a thirties B movie. It was like he was in bed with Gloria Swanson, forty

years past her prime. Or maybe one of the Gish sisters—
all cottage-cheese skin and mushy anatomy.

He shuddered at the memory.

But Cynthia Dexter, taking a healthy pull on her Bahama
Blast, had possibilities. Not as a marital candidate, because
clearly she was not a product of a trust fund or lucrative
divorce. No, Cynthia was simply a nice, lonely forty-five-
year-old woman who could educate him to the facts of
Palm Beach life, thanks to her job as social secretary at
the prestigious Poinciana Club. Nick had heard all about
the Poinciana, famous for its exclusive membership and
impressive Mizner buildings, and knew it was like one of
those eating clubs at Princeton that Fitzgerald could never
get into. Waspy, patrician and completely inaccessible,
particularly to someone of Nick's lowborn status.

This was Cynthia's third time at Viggo's in less than a
week. As a bartender, he heard a lot of biographies, way
more than he wanted, but hers was one he could learn
from. Listening to Cynthia was like reading an instructional
manual.

All drinkers had patterns, and Cynthia's was to get
seriously loquacious halfway through her third Blast.
Nick was steering the conversation around to the Poinciana's membership which, she had told him—perhaps
indiscreetly—was about 70 percent inherited money, much
of it greatly diminished in the brutal economic downturn
of the last two years. The other 30 percent was self-made—
new money—which, she reported, seemed to be holding
its own in the "great recession" they were going through.

Nick loved listening to Cynthia talk about rich people
at the Poinciana because he had visions of one day stepping into that life. In fact, he felt it was meant to be, it was
his destiny, just a question of when.

Cynthia was complaining about a woman who had
called to bitch about an eight-dollar overcharge on her

Poinciana bill. Her hedge-fund husband, Cynthia said, had made $200 million two years before the crash.

"Jesus, these people," . . . she kept saying.

"Wait? Two hundred million a year?" Nick said, practically crushing the wine glass he was washing in the bar sink.

"Yes, that's what these guys make, some even more."

"So who's the richest member?" Nick asked, leaning forward eagerly, ignoring a customer trying to flag his attention.

"Oh, probably Andres Castronuevo—or Ward Jaynes." The last name seemed to contort her mouth into a frown. "Or maybe Spencer Robertson, but he's close to a hundred."

"A hundred million?"

Cynthia laughed.

"No, silly . . . his age. In terms of net worth, it starts with a 'b.'"

Now we're talking, thought Nick.

"And this Mr. Castronuevo," said Nick, noticing a guy who looked ready to hop over the bar and mix his own drink, "where's his money come from?"

"Sugar," said Cynthia, "every time you eat something sweet, a nickel goes into his pocket."

Nick made a Dewar's and soda for the guy about ready to jump the bar and another for a customer shooting daggers into his skull. Then he went back to Cynthia.

"Can I get you another?" he asked, and gave her a smile he practiced in the mirror. "It's on the house."

"Sure, thanks," she said, all fluttery eyelashes.

"So tell me about Mr. Jaynes," Nick said.

"I'd rather not," she said, with a frown.

"Okay . . . then Mr. Robertson or is he off-limits, too?"

He saw her disappointment. That she wanted him to focus on her instead of some hundred-year-old man.

"Why are you so interested?" she asked, resting her elbow on the bar.

"Oh, no reason, just a little hobby of mine."

"What is?"

"The other half . . . how they live." Nick mopped the bar to her left with a white bar towel.

"Half? Try like . . . one twentieth of 1 percent?"

Nick smiled and persisted.

"Where's Mr. Robertson's money come from?"

"Plastics."

Nick knew it was supposed to be a joke, but the reference escaped him.

"Before your time," she said. "I really have no clue . . . neither does he probably."

"What do you mean?"

"Guy checked into la-la land a couple years back. No clue what day of the week it is."

It was a classic light bulb over the head moment for Nick. Smacked him like an ocean wave you never saw coming.

"So, ah, this Mr. Robertson . . . who takes care of him?" Nick yawned, his casual interest default.

"Some old guy, I heard," Cynthia shrugged. "Supposedly he goes through help like . . ."

You go through Bahama Blasts, Nick thought.

Another guy, three seats down, was frantically waving his empty glass.

Nick shot over and made him a drink, then beelined back.

He was glad Cynthia couldn't hear his brain whirring, clanking and ca-chunking away.

"I bet he's got relatives lined up around the block . . . just waiting," Nick said.

"Who?"

"Mr. Robertson."

She took another sip of miracle tongue loosener.

"Far as I know, he only has one grandson, who he doesn't even speak to."

Nick leaned closer. The woman was a gold mine.

He flashed to an image of himself in an expensive foreign car driving up a long, crunchy driveway to a red brick Mediterranean.

Nick looked up at Cynthia and smiled, trying to disguise the rush of excitement washing over him, an idea slowly taking shape in his mind. He imagined rubbing shoulders with the Poinciana patricians. One day breathing the same air that Andres Castronuevo, Spencer Robertson and Ward Jaynes did. He snuck a look at his watch. Two more hours. He wanted to be done for the night. He wanted to go home, be by himself to think. Outline his plan of attack on a yellow lined pad, the way he always did.

He still had a lot more questions, but he had to go slow. Be patient, he admonished himself.

"Do you have a girlfriend?" Cynthia asked, getting braver by the sip.

"No."

He started to say he liked older women, but caught himself.

Cynthia did something with her tongue on the rim of the glass. It reminded him of Janet Schering and was not pretty. He pretended not to notice.

"So . . . you ever go to the movies?" he asked.

Cynthia perked up.

"Yes, I'm a regular at Muvico." That was the sixteen plex at Citiplace.

He pictured her. All alone in the middle of the movie theater jamming Milk Duds and popcorn into her mouth.

"How 'bout we go see something? Thursday maybe?"

"I'd love that," Cynthia said and eagerly gave him the address of her condo.

He knew he better lay off the Spencer Robertson questions for a while. Change his Q & A a little.

"So let me ask you . . . how does it work, getting into the Poinciana?"

"You plan on joining?"

He laughed.

"First, you need to know a lot of members," she was slurring now.

"Keep going," he said, leaning forward, avoiding her aggressive cleavage.

"Then, someone proposes you, says you're a really swell guy, how lucky the Poinciana would be to have you, where you work, what your handicap is—"

"You mean . . . that thing in golf?"

"Exactly, the lower the better."

Nick remembered that Jordan Baker, his favorite character in Gatsby, had a really low one. Cheated, too. He loved that about her.

"Okay, so what happens after that?"

Cynthia straightened up and looked very earnest.

"I really can't tell you anything else. I get into the secret handshakes and they fire me on the spot."

Nick forced a laugh.

"Hey, buddy . . . you mind?" said a voice, halfway down the bar.

He realized he was seriously neglecting his other customers. A woman was waving and pointing at her empty glass. He saw a guy at the far end, stabbing a finger at his mouth, like in five seconds he was going to die of thirst. He was sure the patrician patrons at the Poinciana weren't ill-mannered like these louts.

"Be right back."

In a whirl of glasses, ice cubes, bottles, olives and lemons, Nick made four drinks, then returned.

"Back to my favorite customer."

She gave him a cockeyed grin. The fourth Blast had kicked in.

"Fanghu . . . Nig."

Christ. She better not be driving.

He realized there was so much more he needed to get out of her. He decided to call her a cab. It would be a terrible thing if she stumbled out of Viggo's, got into her car and plowed into a ficus tree.

Once he got everything out of her that he needed . . . she could slam into a brick wall going a hundred, for all he cared.

SIX

Crawford was at the station house at six the next morning. He usually punched in at eight. But he knew that in Palm Beach you caught a case like this once in a lifetime and damn well better make the best of it.

A half hour later, Ott walked into Crawford's office.

"So this guy who works in my building knew all about the crime scene, like he was there," Crawford said, putting his lukewarm Dunkin' Donuts down on his desk.

Ott nodded and plunked himself down opposite Crawford.

"I get the idea Rutledge never taught his bags to keep quiet about crime scene shit," Ott said.

"I hear you," Crawford said. "Or much of anything else."

✳ ✳ ✳

THE NIGHT before, Misty Bill had ID'ed her brother.

The three had gone to the Criminal Justice Complex at Gun Club Road, and met with the forensic investigator, who had given her the option of identifying Darryl from a picture. But Misty insisted on seeing her brother. They had cleaned up Darryl as best they could, but his face was bloated, discolored and bruised on the left cheekbone, a towel covering his chest. A signboard with a case number was on top of the towel.

Crawford saw a few tears fall onto the towel, then watched as Misty slowly bent down and kissed her brother on the cheek. A second later as she straightened out, her legs buckled and Crawford stepped forward quickly and caught her before she fell. She smiled at him, said "thank you" and walked out the door.

Crawford and Ott started going through databases, seeing what they could dig up on Darryl Bill. Ott had logged on to one known as Autotrac and was now on another called DAVID, which stored records of everything from shoplifting and moving violations on up to misdemeanors and felonies. Crawford was surfing a site called Florida Crime Information Center. Judging by Misty's reaction to cops showing up on her doorstep, they were pretty sure they'd find a sheet on Darryl. And just to cover their bases, Crawford decided to add Misty to their search. Something told him she might be a few merit badges shy of Girl Scout.

Crawford was on his second Dunkin' Donuts coffee when he heard a knock on his office door. Before he had a chance to say "come in," Norm Rutledge did. Rutledge, who'd been chief of police for twelve years, was a relentless badger who had a reputation for riding his men twenty-four seven when they were on a big case. Crawford had no firsthand experience, since there had been no big cases since he'd been there. He'd heard, though, of a vice cop who'd gotten so incensed for constantly getting yelled at and second-guessed by Rutledge, that the guy had totally lost it and punched him out in his office. Dropped him like a sack of rocks. Rutledge, the story went, felt his face for blood, then got up slowly, while a big, toothy grin spread across his face. He had no problem taking one on the chin to get rid of a guy who didn't play it his way.

Rutledge walked into Crawford's office and sat down. Crawford could see immediately it was going to be a double tic day. Rutledge's left eye was batting away like a butterfly's wing and his upper lip jerked up every few seconds like it had a fishhook in it. He was clutching the *Palm Beach Reporter*—nicknamed the *Glossy* because of the shiny paper it was printed on—in one hand. He was holding it, like if he dropped it, it would detonate.

"Hello, Norm," Crawford said.

"We gotta get these fucking guys."

"No kiddin'," Crawford said.

"Bet I got fifty calls between last night and this morning"—Rutledge was world-class at drama—"from every reporter in the country plus the goddamn mayor, you name it."

Ott came barreling through the door like a 'roid-raged linebacker. "Hey, Charlie, look what—"

Rutledge cut him off.

"—Ott, I want you to hear this, too. We made the national media. Not for being the playground of the rich and famous. Not for having the most expensive real estate in the country. Or our low crime rate—"

Crawford got ready for the big windup.

"—but 'cause some guy got strung up on a fucking banyan tree."

Rutledge eyed Ott.

"You got something?"

"Nah," Ott said, shaking his head, "just working a couple things."

Crawford could tell Ott was holding out. His breathing was amped up.

Rutledge gave a long, dramatic exhale.

"So neither of you got squat?"

"Jesus Christ," Crawford said. "It's seven forty-five the morning after. Crime scene was clean. We haven't even heard back from the techs yet."

Rutledge glared at Crawford. He flung the *Glossy* down on his desk.

"And what the fuck is this all about?"

The *Glossy* was 10 percent local news, 50 percent color pictures of formal-clad attendees at charity ball benefits, the rest glossy real estate ads.

Crawford looked down at the headline.

MURDER IN PALM BEACH. MAN HANGED AT SOUTH END.

"What's the question?" Crawford asked.

"Keep reading," Rutledge said.

Crawford looked back down at it. The headline was more like a genteel announcement, rather than something that grabbed you by the throat in one-inch bold—à la the *New York Post*. The typeface was exactly the same size as yesterday's front page, which announced sweeping zoning changes in the R-4 district.

Then Crawford saw the subhead.

'PAGE SIX' DETECTIVE INVESTIGATES

Swell, thought Crawford, just fucking swell. He thought he had left that behind, dead and buried. It referred to a seven-year-old, one-paragraph article that resulted in him taking endless abuse from everyone he knew and quite a few he didn't.

He was surprised the story had never hit Rutledge's radar screen before, since most things had.

"What's that got to do with anything, Norm?"

Ott craned his neck to read the article upside down. Unable to make it out, he grabbed for the paper. Crawford slapped his hand.

Ott reacted like a spanked child.

"Little sensitive there, Charlie," Rutledge said.

It was easy to see why the vice cop had coldcocked him.

"I'm not real happy," Rutledge said, "seeing one of my guys making headlines in that rag, Charlie."

"Hey, that's ancient history, for Chrissakes."

Ott couldn't take the suspense.

"Jesus Christ, what's it say?"

"Glad you asked, Mort," Rutledge said.

Rutledge grabbed the *Glossy* off of the desk.

"This is an article from like seven years back," Rutledge eyed Crawford, "Charlie's swingin' single days, I'm guessing: 'Twenty-six-year-old actress Gwendolyn Hyde was seen yesterday morning leaving the West Eighty-Seventh Street walk-up of one of New York's finest (and luckiest), Detective Charles Crawford—' "

Crawford tried to snatch it out of Rutledge's hand.

Rutledge pulled it back and kept reading.

"The thirty-year-old detective, who broke the Taxidermist serial killer murders, didn't comment but Ms. Hyde said she and the detective were 'just friends.' "

Ott eyed Crawford with profound new respect. He knew about his partner's cases, but had no clue about him dating movie stars.

Crawford had met Gwen Hyde on a set in New York. The director, who was somehow a buddy of Giuliani's, asked if Rudy could spare the detective for a few days. He had seen Crawford's picture in the paper and described him as, "that guy who looks like Bradley Cooper." Giuliani had no clue who Bradley Cooper was, but perked up when the director told him the mayor in the script was portrayed as a vigorous crime buster. Giuliani immediately put the director in touch with the police commissioner.

The director explained that his lead was playing a homicide detective and wanted to pick Crawford's brain. Crawford sat around for three straight days, drinking coffee and watching the actor comb his hair in his trailer while he asked stupid questions. On the fourth day Crawford met Gwen Hyde. They ended up going out for a year and a half. They kept it under wraps for as long as they could, but finally got outed on perezhilton.com. Then a *Post* reporter camped out on Crawford's doorstep and finally got the money shot of Gwen leaving his apartment. From then on it was nothing but paparazzi and aggravation.

"You're a goddamn dog with a bone, Norm," Crawford said. "We got a murder and you're ripping me for this bullshit."

"Yeah, well, tell that to the mayor," Rutledge said.

Fuck the mayor. Why the hell would he care anyway?

Crawford flashed to Lil Fonseca. What she'd have to say about the article. He knew she'd have a strong opinion on the matter. The girl had plenty of the possessive gene in her.

Rutledge shifted in his chair and pitched the *Glossy* back onto Crawford's desk.

"Last thing we need is shit like this."

Crawford turned and looked out his window.

But Rutledge had more.

"You know, you kill me, you come down here, Charlie-the-hero-cop. How 'bout leaving the headlines to people who live here? They like that shit."

Crawford rubbed his eyes. A few minutes of Rutledge gave him brutal migraines.

"Tell ya what, Norm, I'll call my PR guy, tell him to go low profile." Crawford got up and walked around his desk.

"Where the hell you goin'?" Rutledge asked.

"The can . . . that okay, or do I need a slip?"

"Just act like a cop, will ya, not a fuckin' celebrity." Ruttledge shook his head in disgust.

Crawford walked out of his office.

"Who the hell's he think he is?" Rutledge said to Ott.

Ott shrugged. "Come on, man . . . guy was a Gold Shield up there."

Rutledge snorted a laugh.

"You the PR guy he was talking about?"

"Jesus, Norm . . . the guy never blows his own horn about anything. You ever read about any of his cases . . . like that sick fuck Artiste Willow?"

"Who?"

"Papers called him Slash 'n' Burn. Stabbed his vics, then tossed gas on 'em and torched 'em. Real sweetheart.

Six dead by the time Crawford tracked him down in some warehouse. Guy had two kids and their mother as hostages. Molotov cocktail in one hand, knife in another. They would have been numbers seven, eight and nine . . . if Charlie didn't take him out."

Rutledge crossed his arms and narrowed his eyes.

"Sounds like something he told you after a few beers."

Ott shook his head.

"You really don't know him at all, do you? Story was national. All over TV, the papers, everywhere. I read about it when I was up north. Read about another of his cases, too."

Crawford walked back in.

"So Charlie—"

Crawford eyed Rutledge.

"Yeah?"

"Time to go get 'em," Rutledge said with a sneer. "Pretend like you're going after ole Slash 'n' Burn."

Rutledge walked out.

"Upper one percentile of world class assholes," Crawford said. "What was it you didn't want him to hear?"

"Picked up a little item on DAVID," he said, "one Christie Bill, age sixteen, same address as that dump last night . . . solicitation of prostitution six months back."

"Christie, huh?"

"Yeah . . . Misty must be, like . . . her stage name? You know, like a stripper."

"Good work."

"Wait, hang on, there's more. Her brother was in on it, too."

"How?"

"Her pimp."

Crawford just shook his head.

"Sick, huh. But here's the best part."

"What?"

"The guy she got caught with."

SEVEN

Ward Jaynes was not exactly a household name. But you had to be blind and deaf if you lived in New York and had never heard of him.

A rich, single guy, Jaynes got a lot of face time in both the *Wall Street Journal* and, at the other end of the newspaper spectrum, the *New York Post*. He ran a buyout company, a takeover firm or a hedge fund, Crawford knew, but he didn't really know the difference. Jaynes always had the hot model of the moment on his arm. He clearly loved the spotlight.

Crawford remembered there was more to the story. Something to do with a woman or two. A sexual harassment rap maybe. Or a rape charge that went away.

Ott had just dropped the bomb about Misty's prostitution charge and how Ward Jaynes was the john she had gotten caught with.

Crawford looked across his desk at Ott and pushed himself up out of his chair.

"Come on," he said, "it's time to have another talk with Misty."

❋ ❋ ❋

Ott was driving and Crawford saw him glance over a couple of times.

"What?" Crawford said.

"What was she like?"

"What was who like?" Crawford knew exactly who he meant.

"Gwendolyn Hyde? Man, she was really tasty in that flick—"

"Keep your head on the fuckin' case."

"You're startin' to sound like me, Charlie."

"Yeah, it's catching."

Crawford didn't like the pattern. Ott grading his past and present girlfriends as they rode past the churches and cows on the way to Misty Bill's house.

They pulled up to Misty's house and walked up to the front door.

Misty was less than welcoming. She was wearing the same pair of cut-off jeans but a tank top this time.

"How are you doing?" Crawford asked.

She just shrugged.

"We need to ask you some questions," he said, his hands on the doorframe.

"What about?" she asked.

"Can we come in?"

"It's a mess," she said, scratching her head.

"That's okay," said Crawford, brushing past her.

Crawford went and sat down where he had last time. Ott and Misty took their same spots.

"First question," Crawford said, "you like to go by Misty or Christie?"

Misty's leg started bouncing furiously.

"Well, it's actually Misty, Christie's kinda my—"

"Stage name?" Ott asked.

"Yeah, you know, like dancers."

"Misty, we know about your arrest . . . six months back," Crawford said.

"It wasn't like that, I was just going to give the guy a massage at his house. I even took classes for it."

Ott's eyebrows went up.

"That's not what the girl who was with you copped to," he said.

"She's lying," Misty said.

"Tell us about Ward Jaynes," Crawford said, standing.

She tensed up and reached for her cigarette pack.

Crawford had dug around some more. Found out Wardwell A. Jaynes III was much more than a rich guy who went around with models. According to his computer search, Jaynes was number forty-nine on the Forbes list of richest people in America. He had moved down from New York three years ago, bought a brand new office building in Phillips Point, and ran a fund with twenty billion in assets. The headlines he made in both business and his personal life were, for the most part, unflattering.

"Whatever went down at Jaynes's house in Palm Beach is history," Crawford said. "We got no interest in it, just want to know more about him."

Ott leaned forward. "You understand why?"

Misty stopped jiggling.

"No."

"'Cause maybe Jaynes has something to do with Darryl," Ott said.

Crawford watched her eyes closely.

"You thought that, too, didn't you?" he asked.

She hesitated, then, "No."

"That wasn't real convincing," Ott said.

"I want you to listen to me, Misty," Crawford said, taking a step closer to her. "We came here to help you. Your safety comes first. Catching the guys who killed your brother comes second."

"I really thought I was just going to his house to give him a massage. I *really* did."

Ott shook his head. "No sale."

"It's true."

"Start from the beginning. How was Darryl involved?" Ott asked.

She closed her eyes like hearing her brother's name cut deep.

"Darryl was . . . like my manager—" she opened her eyes.

"Okay," Crawford said. "Keep going."

"Drove me places, made the financial arrangements, stuff like that."

"How many other guys were you seeing?" Ott asked, tapping his foot on the thin carpet.

"A few others . . . but mainly Ward."

"You called him that . . . Ward?" Ott asked, tapping faster.

"Uh huh," Misty said, watching his foot.

"How much did he pay you, Misty?" Crawford asked.

"I don't know, he paid my brother."

"Come on, you know," Ott said, "how much?"

"Five hundred," she said, looking away.

"And how much did your brother give you?"

"Not enough."

"Enough to buy you some pretty clothes," Ott said, looking around.

Misty looked away.

"How many times did you go to his house?" Crawford asked.

She twirled a strand of hair, looking like a little girl.

"Ummm, like maybe . . . ten."

"So your brother took the money?" Crawford asked.

She nodded.

"How'd they get along?" Ott asked. "Your brother and Jaynes?"

"Fine," Misty said.

Crawford watched her closely.

"Misty," he said, "if Jaynes had something to do with what happened to Darryl, who do you think he might go after next?"

Her jaw was tightly knotted and her gaze was locked onto a spot on the yellow living room wall. She was starting to shake.

"I don't know what you mean," she said, after a few seconds. "My brother just drove me there, collected the money, then drove me home."

Her cool was back. The little girl gone. Sixteen going on . . . twenty-five.

"So who was it then, Misty?" Crawford asked. "Who do you think killed Darryl? I know you got a theory."

She shook her head.

"Misty, let's cut to the chase. Darryl lived here with you," Ott said. "You knew who his enemies were. He into the drug scene?"

"Never touched 'em, swear."

"No Oxy . . . crystal meth?"

"No."

Ott got up and drilled her with a withering stare. Cops had a name for it. Eye fucking.

"So some guys hung him 'cause . . . what? They didn't like his mullet?"

She glared at him.

"You son-of-a-bitch ass-*hole*."

Crawford caught Ott's attention and flicked his head. He walked out the front door onto the porch, Ott right behind him.

Crawford turned sharply and Ott almost bumped into him.

"Are you fucking kidding me?" Crawford jabbed him in the chest with a finger. "Girl's sixteen years old, for Chrissakes. Don't be such a hard-ass."

"I was just trying to—"

"Well, don't," Crawford said, staring him down. "Girl's not some skagged-out hooker from the crack side of Cleveland."

"Come on, Charlie, I—"

"Just cool it."

Crawford turned and went back inside. Ott followed him.

Misty looked scared. Like she didn't like being left alone.

"I'll say it again, Misty," Crawford said. "Our job is to protect you, make sure nothing happens to you. For all we know, some guys could show up tonight."

That knocked a little color out of her face.

"We need you to work with us."

She started to say something, then stopped.

"What?" Crawford asked.

"Nothing," Misty said.

Crawford knew now was the time to walk out, when her doubts were stacking high.

"Okay," he said, heading toward the door, "we'll be in touch. You need us . . . you call."

They walked out the front door and got into the car.

Ott stuck the key in the ignition but didn't turn it.

"Tough little cookie."

Crawford nodded. "Yeah, who's got a million secrets."

Crawford grabbed the car door, opened it up, got out and went back inside. He told Misty he was taking her down to the station.

When she protested, he said he didn't want to hear it.

EIGHT

For one thing, Crawford wanted to get her out of the comfort zone of her house. For another, he had a genuine fear for her safety. Not that he could keep her at the station, but at least, if she was in jeopardy, she'd be safe for a while.

She followed them in her car and they took her straight into the soft room. It was minimal on interior decoration: a black Naugahyde easy chair, a sofa with foam cushions and plastic flowers. Marginally better than the hard room next door with its stiff wooden chairs, industrial tile floor and forty-watt light. That was where they interrogated the hard-core guys.

Misty sat down in the chair, Crawford and Ott stood. They wanted to have height on her.

"I'm gonna say it again," Crawford said, "whatever you tell us is confidential."

"But you hold back and all bets are off," Ott said.

She eyed him coldly.

"We're going to record this, too," Ott said.

She nodded.

Ott flipped the switch.

"Okay, Misty, we're all ears."

Misty fumbled for a cigarette.

"Can't smoke in here," Ott said.

Crawford overruled him.

"Just one's okay." He handed her an empty Coke can to use as an ashtray.

Her hands were shaking. It took three matches to get her cigarette lit.

"So tell us all about you, Darryl and Ward Jaynes," Crawford said.

She took a drag on her cigarette down to her toes.

"Darryl kept saying Ward was our pot of gold. How we'd never have to work another day in our lives. Corvettes and caviar, he kept saying. Like he had a clue what caviar was."

"So Darryl tried to blackmail him?" Ott asked.

Misty didn't react.

"Is that what happened?" Ott turned up the volume.

She nodded.

"I want the answer in words."

"Yes."

Darryl against Jaynes, Crawford thought, like David versus Goliath, minus the slingshot. He remembered a few more things he'd read about Jaynes, back when he and Jaynes were in the city at the same time. The guy was one of those very visible New York guys you read about. Self-obsessed lords of the teetering Wall Street cosmos—before anyone knew the underpinnings were rusted out and collapsing, back when everyone thought it was balls to the wall . . . up, up, and away.

"How much was Darryl after?" Crawford asked.

"A million dollars."

"I figured," Ott said, eyeing Crawford. "Chump change."

"Misty," Crawford said, "did Darryl have Jaynes on tape? Pictures? Or what?"

She didn't move.

"Tell us," Crawford said.

She squirmed.

"Yes, photos," she said.

Crawford cocked his head and looked over at Ott.

"Of what exactly?" Ott asked.

She sighed.

"I never saw them," she said. "Darryl just said they were enough to put Ward away for a long time."

Crawford moved a step closer to Misty.

"What went on there . . . at his house?"

Misty flicked her hair back and slumped into the chair.

"Well . . . first, it was just me, then my girlfriend came along—"

"So . . . had yourselves a nice little ménage a . . . whatever?" Ott asked.

Crawford gave Ott his "back off" look.

"And where exactly did this take place?" Crawford asked.

"Started out in his indoor pool, sometimes the hot tub, ended up in a bedroom."

"The master?"

"No, that's upstairs, this huge water bed downstairs."

"Didn't know they were still around," Ott said.

"So it was the three of you?" Crawford asked.

Misty coughed nervously.

"Until one of those friends of Ward's showed up," she said.

"Guys, you mean?" Crawford asked.

"No, two women."

"Who were they?" Ott asked.

"I don't know . . . well-dressed, expensive jewelry, older."

"How old?" Ott asked.

"One maybe twenty-five, the other . . . thirty, I guess."

"They come together?" Ott asked, walking behind her.

"I don't think so."

"So, they got there . . . then what?" Ott had his hand on the back of her chair.

"We had some champagne, blew a few lines . . . then you know . . ."

"What?"

"Took our clothes off."

She said it like it was the same as brushing her teeth.

"These two women," Crawford asked, "what'd they look like?"

"Their bodies?"

Ott laughed.

"Faces," Crawford said, "eyes, hair color, distinguishing features . . . you know?"

"Well, first one had kind of reddish hair. Lot of rings. Really pretty."

She lit another cigarette. Crawford rolled his eyes, but let it go.

"The other one . . . even more."

"Even more what?"

"Pretty . . . a blonde, awesome blue eyes, a few freckles here," Misty said, touching below her eye.

"How long ago was this?" Crawford asked.

"Um, eight or nine months about."

"Remember their names, Misty?" Crawford asked.

She bit the fingernail on her right index finger.

"Red-haired one was Nicole."

"Any last name?" Crawford asked.

"No," she said, looking at the tape recorder.

"And the other one?"

"She was only there twice, maybe three times." Misty's eyes scrunched up, "Kind of a funny name."

"Think real hard," Crawford said.

She put her hand on her forehead and closed her eyes.

"I remember now," she said, smiling. "He called her Liliana. That was it, Liliana."

NINE

Nick wished he had watered down the Bahama Blasts because Cynthia was getting less and less intelligible. She had just slurred her way through an explanation of how Spencer Robertson's only living relative was a bad seed grandson named Avery Robertson, who she described as a kind of pudgy, shorter version of Nick. Then she started going on about how handsome Nick was. The Blasts clearly affected her vision. "Sexy" hair and "nice bone structure," she was saying now. Not that he minded hearing it, but he wanted her to stick to the dysfunctional Robertson family. This was business after all.

Then she started blathering on about some incident that took place years before, when fifteen-year-old Avery Robertson showed up out of the blue at the Poinciana. Kid was on spring vacation from boarding school. He and three friends went there to play golf—and unbeknownst to his grandfather—went straight to the Poinciana pro shop and charged up four sets of top-of-the-line golf clubs, along with shirts, hats, sweaters, balls, the works. All totaled the tab was more than $5,000 including guest fees and a $250 lunch.

The shit hit the fan when Spencer Robertson's conservator at J.P. Morgan, Paul Broberg, got the bill and in a rage called the club manager. The manager was no dope and deftly handed the ball off to Cynthia. She listened to a ten-minute harangue as the irate Broberg demanded to know why a fifteen-year-old kid was allowed to just walk into the Poinciana and charge up any damn thing he wanted. It was a very good question. Cynthia said how Broberg told Spencer Robertson all about it, and that Robertson was so furious he basically told the kid to stay away.

"When was this?" Nick asked.

"What?"

He was ready to mainline espresso into her.

"The grandson incident, at the Poinciana?"

She yawned. "Umm, ten . . . twelve years ago."

Avery Robertson would be about Nick's age. The light bulb clicked on again.

Cynthia kept jabbering about how Paul Broberg got all wound up and launched into another tirade about "entitled brat" this and "little bastard" that. Cynthia said she felt like she was not only being blamed for the kid's self-indulgent spending spree, but also his whole reckless, misspent youth. In the course of his diatribe, Broberg mentioned that Avery was an orphan. Something horrible had happened to his parents, Broberg intimated. Cynthia didn't dare ask what.

Nick was hanging on to her every drunken word.

Cynthia's story about Avery Robertson catapulted Nick back to his childhood in Mineola, New York, a down-wardly mobile Long Island suburb of New York City. His childhood was a cliché in many ways. His father was an abusive bully who used to work for Grumman, then when it closed down, had a series of dead-end jobs. The one constant in Sid Gonczik's life was his daily twelve-pack of Pabst Blue Ribbon. It brought out the cruel tormentor in him, which was bad news for everyone in the immediate vicinity. That usually meant Nick and his mother. When Nick turned seventeen and got up to 185 pounds, he decided not to take it anymore. One day his father came at him and Nick beat him unconscious with a brass fire poker. He had to be restrained by his mother or he might have killed him.

Nick had no remorse. After that, his father kept his distance and never laid a hand on him or his mother either. Then later that year, October of Nick's senior year in high school, Sid Gonczik went off to the hardware store one morning and never came back. Neither Nick nor his mother was heartbroken. In fact, they never even mentioned him again.

※ ※ ※

THE MORNING after Cynthia got close to setting the record for Bahama Blast consumption, Nick called her up. He pictured her with an ice bag on her head, sucking down glass after glass of Tropicana. He asked her what movie she wanted to see. Some really lame chick flick, of course.

He had spent several hours after he went home from Viggo's that night, working on a plan about how to mine the Spencer Robertson mother lode. He rejected several ideas and finally came up with one that he thought had merit, though it was still a long way from being fully developed. At its most basic, it was simply to gain entry into Robertson's house. Not to clean out the silverware or make off with a couple flat screens, but just to get the lay of the land. See if he could somehow figure out a way to separate a few million from the second richest man in Palm Beach. He knew there had to be a way, some angle to work, especially since the man was way down the Alzheimer's highway. Surely, once he got inside, Nick could figure out how to divert a sizable chunk of Robertson cash into his pathetically anemic bank account. What made him practically salivate was the fact that, according to Cynthia, aside from some older guy who took care of Robertson and maybe a cook, nobody was minding the store.

Nick knew he'd have to keep an eye out for Paul Broberg, the old man's executor, but except for him it seemed like the place would be easy pickings.

He had already forgotten what movie Cynthia said she wanted to see, and steered the conversation back to where he wanted it.

"You know, I got thinking last night," Nick said. "I didn't put it together, but Avery Robertson . . . he'd be about my age, right?"

Cynthia thought for a second.

"Yes, probably, around twenty-six, twenty-seven. Why?"

Nick laughed. "Because I knew a guy by that name up in New York. A real hell raiser, guy drank more than a whole goddamn fraternity."

"Sounds like him."

"Only thing is . . . I'm thinking the guy up there might have been Avery *Rob-inson*."

"Well, the one here is definitely Rob-ertson."

"Now you got me really curious, can you describe him again?"

"I can do better than that," she said, talking very quietly as if she talked any louder it might shoot dagger-like splinters into her hung-over skull. "Actually I have a picture of him. You won't believe why."

"Why?"

"'Cause Paul Broberg sent it to me. In case Avery ever showed up again at the Poinciana," she said. "Guess I was supposed to tackle him or something, make sure he didn't start charging up stuff."

She guffawed like she had just delivered the world's all-time funniest punch line.

"I'll bring the picture, next time I come, you can see whether it's the same guy you were thinking of. 'Course it is a few years old."

"Thanks, that doesn't matter. So this guy Avery doesn't come around much anymore . . . 'cause of that golf thing?"

"'Much?' Are you kidding? Never. Impression I got was almost like the old man put guards at the bridges to make sure he never set foot in Palm Beach again. Word from my manager was if you crossed Spencer Robertson just once, it was the last time, including flesh and blood."

Nick could barely restrain himself from cartwheeling across the room. He closed his eyes and did a fist pump. A game plan was taking shape.

"Weird thing is, Avery's the old man's primary beneficiary . . . least he was."

Nick practically crushed the phone into his ear.

"He is? Why?" he asked, trying to tamp down his excitement.

"Broberg told me Robertson had a thing about charities. Didn't trust 'em. Thought all the money went to administrative costs, none of it ever got to the actual cause."

"So you're saying he'd rather give his money to his grandson . . . even though he was a complete bum?"

"I guess. As long as he never came around."

Nick did another fist pump.

✳ ✳ ✳

Two nights later, Cynthia came in with the picture of Avery. Nick could see "eager-to-please" written all over her.

"See the resemblance to you?"

He did. But the kid had big fleshy lips and a perfect aquiline nose. Blue eyes, too. Nick's were green. But they did have the same hair. Similar facial structure, too.

Nick put the picture down on the bar.

"That's not the guy I was thinking of, I'm pretty sure the one in New York was Avery Robinson."

Cynthia powered through a few watered down Blasts and after her fourth one excused herself, garbling something about going to the "itta guls room." Nick picked up the picture of Avery Robertson and stuffed it into his wallet.

As far as taking her to the movies on Thursday night, that was not going to happen. He had gotten all he needed out of her. He imagined her showing up at Viggo's on Friday after being stood up the night before, loaded for bear, ready to rip him a new one.

When Cynthia came back from the bathroom, he made her the last Bahama Blast he'd ever make her. Because he had decided tonight was his last night at Viggo's. He made it extra strong—three ounces of rum. Because at this point he didn't much care whether she slammed into a big ficus, a twelve-inch wall or a concrete bridge abutment.

The drink, of course, was on the house. To ensure a big tip.

Even though Nick knew his days of counting on tips would soon be behind him.

TEN

Crawford was still reeling from Misty's little shocker.

Ott had just left his office and Crawford was pretty sure, based on Ott's lack of reaction, that he hadn't picked up on Misty's Liliana reference.

He had heard a few people call Lil "Liliana," mainly people she didn't know that well. He flashed back to what she told him late one night. How she had gone through a "bad patch" right before she met him. A nasty self-destructive run where she confessed to drinking way too much and hitting the drugs pretty hard. Coke, in particular. She had apparently left out a chapter or two.

She told him it got so bad that a bunch of her friends did an intervention on her one time. It got late—cocktail hour—and Lil's friend, Mimi, whose house the intervention took place at, broke out a bottle of Santa Margherita. End of intervention.

Eventually, she got talked into going to one of those dry-out places in Minnesota, but only lasted a week there. She promised him she had cut out the drugs completely. Strictly a social drinker, now, she said.

Crawford couldn't get the image out of his head. The big water bed, women—worse, young girls—coming and going. And Lil, right there in the middle of it, snorting coke and doing God knows what.

He remembered something else Lil told him. About her friend, Nicole—the name of the other woman at Ward Jaynes's house according to Misty. Something about this group of women, who sounded like a collection of rich lost souls, who met a couple times a week to pray and gossip at the old Paramount theater on North County Road. Lil described it as a kind of born-again group that jumped from fad to fad—yoga to Pilates to Facebook to whatever. Lil referred to them as members of The Church of What's Happening Now. The mainstay, apparently, was the socially prominent Nicole, a pharmaceutical heiress.

The common cause of the group seemed to be the pursuit of happiness, which, no one thought, was asking too much. But, thus far, that goal had proven elusive thanks in part to straying husbands, alcohol and drug problems, lack of purpose, or all of the above. As he remembered it, the point of the story was that one of the members was caught naked—legs to the sky—in the backseat of another member's husband's Bentley. Nicole had summarily banished the woman from the group, which seemed somewhat hypocritical, based on Nicole's waterbed activities.

After awhile, Crawford got out of his chair and started pacing around his office. He didn't want to think about Lil anymore.

His mind jumped to Ward Jaynes. He didn't want to let it get personal, but maybe he wouldn't be able to help that.

In any case, it was time to have a little talk with the man.

He walked over to Ott's cubicle and suggested they pay Jaynes a visit a little later. Ott jumped at it. Never interrogated a billionaire before, he said. Weren't any up in Cleveland. Crawford told him to give him an hour. He needed to do what he always did. His Boy Scout routine. Be prepared. Research his subject. He went back to his office and dug up everything he could. He wanted to know Jaynes cold. He always started with Wikipedia, if his subject was a big fish, even though sometimes they got their facts a little screwed up.

Turned out Jaynes grew up in Plattsburgh, New York, went to Plattsburgh High, then Syracuse University. That threw Crawford a little, because Jaynes exuded all the characteristics of a bored, entitled patrician from some really fancy place like Greenwich. The clothes, the hair, the attitude, you could tell a lot from a few pictures in the paper. In Jaynes's case, his eyes said it all. It was like they telegraphed what was going through his head . . . the fools I have to suffer, they seemed to say. The morons I have to put up with.

After graduating from college, Jaynes worked for a year at Manufacturers Hanover bank, then jumped to Goldman Sachs for two years and after that went and got his MBA from Harvard Business School. At age twenty-seven he started Jaynes Funds. At thirty-six, he was a billionaire. Jaynes Funds mainly shorted stocks. So if a company tanked, he did well. Clearly smart, tough and shrewd—he was, now at forty-two, a multi-billionaire and had weathered the 2007–08 crash like it was a mere speed bump.

Crawford Googled him next. The man had amassed more gigabytes than most presidents. He found out Jaynes had scores of lawsuits in the last five years, right up there with the cigarette companies. Crawford navigated his way around and realized it would take weeks to read everything about the guy. Jaynes had some pretty nasty chapters in his life and, it seemed, way more enemies than most. The surprising thing was how many of them were women.

Crawford had seen pictures of Jaynes's house—a word that hardly did it justice—in a Sunday *Palm Beach Press* profile. Crawford had heard that when Jaynes bought the place, it set the record for the highest selling price in Palm Beach. Fifty million. Then a few months ago, Trump sold his humongous beast to the Russian fertilizer king and . . . trumped it.

ELEVEN

$\bigcirc$tt was driving them to Jaynes's house. They were going down South Ocean Road.

"See that place," Ott said, pointing to a big Mediter-rean behind a high stucco wall, "that's the house that Alex Cross built."

"Who the hell's Alex Cross?" Crawford asked.

"Christ, man, you illiterate or something?"

Crawford raised his hands. "Sorry, never heard of him. Who is he?"

"Only the most well-known James Patterson character there is."

Crawford laughed. "Okay, got it, Patterson's house."

"Yeah . . . thanks to Alex Cross."

Ottt hung a left and drove the white Caprice down a long driveway.

Crawford was amazed they could just drive right in. Usually at a place like this there was some massive steel reinforced gate that could stop a tank. Or a manned toll booth-like gatehouse where you'd be eyed suspiciously unless you pulled up in a Maserati or a Maybach. The architectural style was not readily identifiable, just mas-sively, grandiosely big. Municipal building big. Cold, too. Even the majestic royal palm trees, which formed a straight allée to the house, didn't soften its starkness. Or warm up the battleship gray stucco exterior.

Crawford remembered hearing that royal palms like these went for about a hundred dollars a foot. He estimated their height and how many there were, then started to do the math, but gave up. He needed a calculator.

According to the Palm Beach County public records he had read, the mega structure had been built just six years ago. He recalled something he was told, how landscaping could make a house look as though it had been there for-ever. But from the outside of this one, he got the feeling it had never been lived in, everything too clean and new. It looked like a $50 million crash pad.

Its parking court could easily accommodate fifty Rolls-Royce Silver Clouds. But the only car parked there was a fire-engine red Ferrari. 'Rainmkr' boasted its license plate.

"Well, well, now isn't that interesting," Crawford said. "That car left the island right around the time of Darryl Bill's murder on Friday night."

Ott pulled in next to the Ferrari.

Crawford opened his door, got out and looked down at the gleaming red car. Ott climbed out and came around next to him.

"You don't really think that if Jaynes was behind it, he'd do it himself, do you?" Ott said.

"My gut says 'no,'" Crawford said, turning and walking toward the house. "But it's been wrong before."

Crawford and Ott had talked over how they were going to play it on the way over. The pictures that Darryl Bill had taken were their ace in the hole. Misty had brought them into the station house in a sealed envelope, then beat it out of there in a hurry. There was only one that would nail Jaynes, but it would more than do the job. It was of Misty on top of a man with a long, jagged scar on his left shoulder. She was naked except for a blue tank top that had been hiked up over her breasts. She was smiling into the camera. It was pretty sick, Crawford thought, seeing how her brother was snapping the picture.

They decided not to tell Jaynes they had seen the pic-tures. See whether he'd go into full denial mode or just how he'd react. They could nail him for sex with a minor, but they wanted to get him for a whole lot more than that.

Ott was going to lead it off. Crawford just wanted to observe for a while.

The front door looked to be twelve feet high and heavy, like you had to be a weight lifter to muscle it open. Ott pressed the buzzer and waited.

Nobody answered.

"Where the hell's Jeeves?" he asked.

Crawford shrugged and studied the door. It looked like it was imported from some medieval castle in Bavaria.

Ott pressed the buzzer again. They waited a few seconds then walked down the steps.

They walked around the side of the house. Ott shouted "hello" a couple of times, then tried "anyone home?" No response.

They walked along the east side of the house down a cast-stone path and passed through a cluster of podocarpus hedges on one side and ancient-looking trees with gnarly trunks on the other. As they got to the end of it, the view opened up wide and there was a big, eye-popping ocean vista. Crawford stopped to take it in. Now he got what all the fuss was about—living on the ocean—looking out at that jaw-dropping view all day long. Fifty feet away he could see the end of a pool. It was the infinity-edged kind, where the water comes up all the way to the top, flows over the sides, then recycles back into the pool. It created the effect that the pool and ocean were connected—one long, floating body of water. Crawford wondered what the price tag on a pool like it was. His eyes drifted over to the pool house. It had a row of six squatty, powerful-looking columns in front like a miniParthenon.

"Who the hell are you?" a man's voice boomed out as they got to the pool.

Crawford and Ott looked hard left and saw two people at the far end. They were bolt upright in their chaise lounges and wore less than welcoming looks. One was a 90 percent naked woman, wearing a thin yellow strip of cloth around her hips and doing her best to cover her bare breasts, which peeked through her long, tan fingers.

The other one was Ward Jaynes.

Jaynes, in a green bathing suit, was around six feet tall, had dark hair flecked with gray and clenched a cell phone in one hand. Crawford saw it right away—the long scar on his shoulder—but another thing caught him completely by surprise. Jaynes had the muscle definition of a three-hour-a-day gym rat. He hardly thought of guys who shorted stocks as being cut and chiseled. But Jaynes was.

Jaynes came charging at them like he was going to head butt them into the ocean.

"Who the hell are you?" he repeated. He smelled of suntan lotion and sweat.

"My name is Detective Ott, Palm Beach police," Ott said, taking a step toward Jaynes. "This is my partner, Detective Crawford; we're investigating the murder in South Palm."

"You're the guy from Cleveland . . . Mort, right?" A grin spread across Jaynes's face, then he looked at Crawford, "and you . . . the big-time New York hero cop. Went out with that actress . . . well, welcome, boys."

Jaynes nodded like a man quite happy with himself.

Crawford was surprised, but not much. Jaynes had done his homework.

Crawford had read about how Jaynes would tear into a company's books, memorize every figure on the balance sheet, then hire guys to dig up dirt on CEOs who used company jets and secretaries for their own personal use. "Relentless" and "ruthless," were two words that came up a lot in the articles.

"Mind if we ask you a few questions, Mr. Jaynes?" Ott asked.

"Not at all, fire away." Jaynes smiled, like he could use a little amusement.

"We're investigating that homicide. Victim's name is Darryl Bill. He had a sister—"

"Yeah," Jaynes said. "Misty or Christie, depending on the day."

"So you knew her?"

"'Course, I know her," Jaynes said, glancing at Crawford. "You knew that or else you wouldn't be here. You interviewing her other clients, too?"

"Clients?"

"Sure, I'm not the only guy she gave massages to."

Ott looked over at the woman who now had her top back on and pretended to be absorbed in her *Vanity Fair.*

Ott motioned with his hand.

"Would you mind stepping over here, Mr. Jaynes?"

Jaynes hesitated, then followed Ott and Crawford out of earshot of the woman.

"The girl claims you had sex with her on several occasions," Ott said, lowering his voice.

"Really?" Jaynes said, folding his arms over his chest.

"Really," said Ott.

"Well, that's complete bullshit. You wouldn't believe all the shit I get accused of," Jaynes said. "People trying to hold me up for every goddamn thing under the sun. It's a hell of a burden, Mort, being so damn rich."

"I feel your pain, Mr. Jaynes . . . Her brother, you ever meet him?"

Jaynes's eyes drifted over to Crawford.

"I don't remember you being mute, Charlie," Jaynes said. "What? You trying to get a read on me or something?"

Crawford smiled.

"So you can blindside me with a couple tough questions? That it, Charlie . . . that your plan?"

Crawford gestured to Ott.

"My partner asked you a question."

Jaynes smirked and turned back to Ott.

"Yeah, I met the brother. Nice redneck kid, nothing much going on under that John Deere hat. He was his sister's ride, one time he came to the door and I met him. Too bad about what happened."

"So you don't know anything about it?" Ott asked.

"Hey, I'm just a guy who trades stocks . . . not goddamn Tony Soprano."

"Misty's only sixteen, you know," Ott said.

"You gotta be older to give massages?"

Ott stepped into Jaynes's space, then, barely above a whisper: "Got a thing for ponytails and lollipops do you, Mr. Jaynes?"

"You're fuckin' with the wrong guy, Mort," said Jaynes, glaring at Ott, then catching himself. "But I like your interrogational style."

"How many times did Misty come over?" Crawford asked.

Jaynes turned to Crawford, shading his eyes from the sun.

"I don't know. What difference does it make?"

Crawford was watching Jaynes's reactions. He showed as much as a top Texas Hold 'Em player. Crawford glanced over at the woman. Her head was still buried in the *Vanity Fair*, cigarette smoke rising up from behind it.

"Not that you asked, Mort," Jaynes said, turning to Ott, "but a friend of Charlie's came over to my house a couple times, too."

The woman peered up over the magazine, cigarette dangling from the corner of her mouth. She was struggling to hear.

"You *do* know who I mean, don't you . . . Charlie?"

Crawford forced a smile.

"An unpaid masseuse . . . with magic fingers," Jaynes said. "Liliana Fonseca."

Ott's mouth dropped a full inch.

"Yeah," Jaynes said, "girl's just crazy about shiatsu."

Crawford wanted to rip the grin off his face.

Jaynes walked back over to his chaise longue next to the girl and lay down on it.

"All right, we're done now, fellas, I'm bored," Jaynes said, looking up at them. "Time for you boys to run along and chase some real bad guys."

But Ott wasn't done. "

Where were you last Friday afternoon, Mr. Jaynes?"

Jaynes shook his head and looked put-upon.

"Let me get this straight, Mort . . . are you asking if I went down to that park and hung that kid? Is that your question?"

The girl set down her *Vanity Fair* on the pool deck.

"Where were you, Mr. Jaynes?" Ott asked again.

"Mort, just think for a minute . . . if I wanted to do something to that kid, you really think I'd get my hands dirty. I mean, come on, get real."

The girl sat up in the chaise.

"Just for the record, officers," she said, thrusting out her breasts, "Mr. Jaynes was right here with me . . . making mad, passionate love . . . from sunup to past sundown."

Crawford walked over to her.

"Thanks for sharing that," he said, then looked over at Jaynes. "But your little red Ferrari went over the Southern bridge somewhere between seven and eight that night."

"Yeah, well, we had to take some time out from all that passion, Charlie . . . Garibaldi's, seven thirty reservation. I had clams oreganata . . . now get the hell out of here."

Crawford walked over next to Jaynes and blocked his sun.

"Don't worry, we're on our way," Crawford said, reaching into a pocket and handing Jaynes a card. "But just in case you happen to remember anything . . ."

Jaynes took the card from him, sat up and put a hand over his eyes.

"Matter of fact, Charlie, I do remember something," he said, eyeing Crawford's card. "An excessive force complaint brought against you up in New York."

Jaynes reached down on the pool deck and picked up the girl's lighter. His thumb flicked the lighter wheel, the flame shot up and he held the card above it. The card caught fire. Jaynes let it burn for a second, then flipped it onto the lawn.

"Nice to meet you, boys, it's been a real pleasure."

TWELVE

"We really kicked ass, huh Mort?" Crawford said, as they drove down Jaynes's long driveway back out onto South Ocean Drive.

"Yeah, poor fucker was really squirming."

"Guy is one very slick act," Crawford said.

Ott looked over at Crawford. "Charlie, that thing he said—"

"It was bullshit, that excessive force thing was this low-life dealer who said I kicked him in the nuts for no reason. What happened was he was going for his piece and I took him out at the knees."

Ott shook his head.

"No, not that, the thing about Lil Fonseca."

Crawford held up his hands.

"Hey, Mort, it's got absolutely nothing to do with the case, okay?"

"I didn't mean to—"

"End of story, Mort."

Crawford's cell phone rang.

※ ※ ※

"Hello."

"Hi, it's Misty." Her voice was dead flat. "Got anybody yet?"

"Sorry, Misty . . . not yet."

There was a pause.

"I was watching that TV show," she said, "*The First 48.* If they get the killers, it's usually in the first forty-eight hours."

"Yeah, well . . . it doesn't always work like that. I'll be in touch . . . I promise."

Ott dropped Crawford off in front of his car behind the station.

❋ ❋ ❋

CRAWFORD PARKED in a spot just down from the Fonseca Gallery. He walked in, heard the tinkle of the little bell and didn't see anyone there besides Lil.

"I should be really pissed, Charlie," she said, getting up from a little desk and coming over to him, "for blowing me off."

He had canceled their dinner date at the Pine Island Grille.

"Sorry, but like I told you—"

"I'm over it . . . along with the affair you had with that actress. Oh, sorry, I forgot . . . she was just a 'friend,' right?"

"That was seven years ago." He was in no mood for banter.

She was wearing a low-cut silk top and a silver lamé skirt cut eight inches above her knee.

"Come here," she said, beckoning with her finger. "All's forgiven if you take me up on my offer again."

A month ago she'd made him an offer which . . . he couldn't refuse.

❋ ❋ ❋

"YOU EVER get bored on the job, Charlie," she had said one rainy afternoon back in September, "just stop by . . . I'll take you back to the back room."

He laughed it off when she said it, then two days later he was walking by and decided to stick his head in. She was all alone. She gave him her beguiling smile and before he knew it, he was in the back room, getting his clothes ripped off. He decided, what the hell . . . might as well just go with it. He didn't have any pressing business at the time.

She had reached behind him and locked the door, then put her arms around him and kissed him with absolutely no holdback. All of a sudden, he was into it. He pulled her blouse up over her head. She yanked off his shirt and tie, then grabbed his belt and deftly opened the buckle, like she'd had lots of practice. They kissed again as he undid one of the hooks of her bra.

She reached back and unhooked the other in one quick swipe. Her bra dropped to the carpet. He pulled her toward him, her breasts pressed up against his chest. He slid his two hands under her skirt and cupped her tight, round ass. Her hand found its way through the slit in his boxers and brought him out. In one motion he dropped her skirt and underpants and entered her. She grabbed his shoulders, then pulled herself up and put her legs around his hips, leaning back slightly.

He was surprised—not unpleasantly—at how athletic she was.

"Quite the little gymnast," he said.

She smiled up at him, her fierce blue eyes blazing, challenging him.

※ ※ ※

THIS TIME Lil motioned to the back room with her head and fluttered her long eyelashes.

"Whaddaya say?" She grabbed for his hand.

"I say, some other time."

"Come on, you can skip the foreplay."

She came up to him intending to give him a kiss on the lips, but he turned and all she got was cheek.

He went and sat down in a love seat.

"What's wrong, Charlie?"

She came over and sat in his lap.

He looked over at the front door, worried someone might come in.

"Relax," she said, putting a hand on his chest. "You're always so damn uptight, Charlie."

"Okay, maybe so. It's just not a real good idea . . . fornicating on the job."

"Funny how that didn't bother you last time."

He heard the tinkle of the gallery's bell.

A tall, older man with a barbershop quartet mustache walked in.

"Hello, Dixon," she said, "picking up your Botero?"

The man glanced over at Crawford.

"Dixon, this is my friend, Charlie Crawford. Charlie . . . Dixon Fordman, my favorite client."

Fordman's ruddy face beamed.

Crawford stood up and shook his hand.

Lil went to the back room and brought out a large painting covered in bubble wrap.

The man took the painting, thanked her, gave her a kiss on the cheek and left.

Crawford had procrastinated his Q & A long enough. He opened his mouth to ask his first question.

"Oh, hey, before I forget," she cut him off, "will you go with me to the Fall Ball?"

She waved a beige vellum invitation at him.

He had politely said "no" to the Red Cross Ball, the Susan Komen Cancer Research Ball and some other thing. What was she not getting?

"And what exactly is the Fall Ball?"

"This charity ball for bipolar kids, or maybe it's diabetes."

"There's a difference, you know."

"I forget which, doesn't matter, it'll be fun."

"Do I really look like a cummerbund kind of guy?"

"I promise, Charlie, you'll have a great time. Dancing, drinking, bunch of fun people."

The drinking part sounded okay.

"Lil . . . one more time, I'm a cop. I'm what is known as a public servant. Servant . . . as in the cleaning lady. Or butler, if they're still around."

"In Palm Beach? Oh, you bet they are. Tell you what, think about it? You don't have to just turn me down cold."

He nodded.

"Lil, I need to talk to you about Ward Jaynes."

She didn't look quite so tan. "What about him?"

"Tell me what you know about him."

"Ward Jaynes is an occasional client of the gallery. He's not one of my favorite people, but I tolerate him because he's got a lot of money . . . even though he doesn't part with it easily."

Her eyes burrowed into his.

"What are you really asking, Charlie?"

"What do you know about his . . . personal life?"

"Nothing," she said, a little too fast.

The front door bell tinkled again. She got up quickly.

Crawford reached for her arm and held her.

"Tell me what you know about a sixteen-year-old girl named Misty."

She shook her arm loose, walked away and gave the customer who just walked in a dazzling smile.

THIRTEEN

Nick took a cab from his studio condo at the Palm Beach Princess to Spencer Robertson's palatial Mediterranean on El Vedato. The ride had only cost four dollars. He could have taken his old Taurus and saved the money, but that wasn't part of the plan.

As they pulled up, he shuddered when he noticed that Janet Schering's house was next door. The terrifying night with her came rushing back like a rampaging succubus.

He shook it off and gave the cab driver a five-dollar tip, instructing him not to leave until someone answered the door.

He was wearing blue jeans, a sport shirt and carrying an L.L.Bean duffel bag. Sloppy rich boy chic was the look he was going for. He pressed the buzzer on the heavy mahogany door. It was a big, two-story house flanked by statuesque banyan trees, standing tall like Buckingham Palace guards.

A middle-aged black man dressed in gray flannel pants and a crisp white shirt answered the door.

Nick flashed him the biggest smile he could muster.

"Wyman?" Nick asked, thrusting out his hand enthusiastically.

The man looked confused, but shook Nick's hand.

"Ah, no, Alcie."

Nick slapped the man on the back. "Sorry, man, Wyman was way before you. I'm Spencer's grandson, Avery."

"Well, welcome, Mr. Avery," Alcie said, smiling.

"Didn't my grandfather's executor, Paul Broberg, tell you I was coming?" Nick asked, a flicker of annoyance.

"No, sir, but that's okay," he said, reaching for Nick's duffel. "Good to have you here."

Nick thumped Alcie on the back. "Thanks, just flew in from out west."

Nick was relieved to see that it seemed Alcie had never even heard the name Avery before. The old man obviously hadn't regaled him with loving anecdotes about his grandson.

Nick walked into the living room, looking up at the ceiling. "God, it's been years. Where's my grandfather?"

"Mr. Robertson's taking a nap, sir, always does this time of day."

"Man, he'll be surprised to see me," Nick said, looking up at the pecky cypress ceiling looming eighteen feet above his head. He scanned the room—overstuffed club chairs in pastel patterns, paintings in expensive gold frames, the whole place reeked of that WASP understated elegance he had read so much about. There also was an overpowering medicinal smell. VapoRub and camphor, he guessed.

"Ah . . . Mr. Avery, when did you last speak to your grandfather?" Alcie stroked his chin, like something was weighing him down.

"I'm kind of embarrassed to say," Nick said, scratching his head, "gotta be four, maybe . . . five years ago."

Alcie leaned forward and spoke softly.

"Well, this is hard for me to say, but your grandfather's got it pretty bad . . . the Alzheimer's. Might not recognize you. Fact is . . . I know darn well he won't."

Thank God . . . that Cynthia, such a gold mine.

"Oh, my God," Nick said, "I'm so sorry to hear that."

Nick shook his head and dialed up his anguished look.

"Well, I just hope maybe there's some way I can make him feel better. Wish I had come down earlier."

"How long are you planning on staying with us, Mr. Avery?"

"I don't know, think I'll kind of play it by ear. Oh, hey . . . if Paul Broberg checks in, don't tell him I'm here, okay? Guy can be a major pain in the ass. Always trying to teach me how to balance my checkbook, stuff like that."

"I know what you mean." Alcie laughed heartily.

Nick thumped Alcie on the back again.

"I appreciate it," he said and winked. "I gotta tell you, it's great to be back."

"And, sir . . . it is indeed a great pleasure to have you back."

Nick was proud of himself. He was, in reality, the total antithesis of a backslapping, hail-fellow-well-met kind of guy. This was all new to him and, goddamn . . . he was pulling it off like a champ. To the best of his knowledge, he had never once slapped anyone on the back before, and he knew, for a fact, he had never winked at anyone. This was the new Nick, he thought. A regular guy but also a man of newfound substance and class.

He turned and scanned the living room again. He saw a lot of expensive-looking antique furniture. And . . . no, it couldn't be. He got closer and studied it. But it was. Even an art history minor from Hofstra University could recognize it. A large Edward Hopper painting of a house on a dune was hanging crookedly on the far dark wall.

Nick was finally where he belonged.

※ ※ ※

As far as Spencer Robertson was concerned, Nick could have been an upright piano or a two-legged rhino. Because when the shriveled-up, bent-over man first saw him, he greeted Nick with a frail wave, then tried to pat him on the head. Haltingly, he said, "Hello, Oswald," as Alcie suppressed a chuckle.

"Don't worry about that, Mr. Avery," Alcie whispered, "he does that with everybody, gives 'em a nickname. Calls me Zapruder."

Right after the greeting, Robertson asked Nick to join him for a game of backgammon, although he had difficulty coming up with the name, calling it "backhammer" instead. Nick had certainly read about the game, but had no idea how to play. There were references to it in Fitzgerald and O'Hara. Nick had never even seen the board it was played on. The game wasn't exactly a fixture in the Gonczik household.

But it didn't matter in the least, since Robertson didn't seem to have much of an idea how to play anymore. Alcie told Nick he had read the rules once and knew the basics. Nick just winged it and Alcie didn't seem to notice.

When Nick suggested they stop playing and get something to eat, Robertson protested noisily and flapped his arms like a petulant kid, saying, "I wanna play" over and over. They played on for another forty-five minutes. Alcie seemed clearly relieved to have someone else share the burden. Once, Alcie explained, he and Spencer had had a five-hour backgammon marathon.

Nick's initial plan had been simply to get his hands on the old man's checkbook and credit cards. But after having been there two days he dismissed the plan as being the thinking of a small-minded man, one utterly lacking in ambition. It was a quick fix, not a long-term, life-changing answer to his dream of becoming fabulously rich and socially prominent.

As he had envisioned it in that plan, he probably would have been able to cash thousands of dollars of forged checks and go on a spending spree with Robertson's credit cards. But eventually, he knew, Paul Broberg would catch up with him: spot an AmEx bill, a checking account statement, whatever, and the jig would be up.

That plan was just penny ante anyway. After all, Broberg probably didn't leave more than $20,000 in Robertson's checking account. Okay, it was not a bad day's work, but then what? He'd have to hightail it out of Dodge. Another bridge burned. And, fact was, he really liked Palm Beach. Loved it, in fact. Driving around checking out all the big, look-at-me houses. Watching everyone strut down Worth Avenue as if they were models on a runway. Nick was absolutely certain he had a future in the town. It was, after all, the perfect place to reinvent oneself. Plenty of people before him had. The stories were legend.

He told himself again: think big. Think over-the-top, Palm Beach excessive, grandiose, big-ass big.

As he went from one painting to the next in the old man's collection, he began to set a new plan in motion. Because even an art history minor from a third-rate college could recognize the millions—hell, tens of millions—of paintings that hung on the swirled stucco walls of the Robertson living room and library. The Hopper was a big solitary, lonely looking house on Cape Cod. Nick remembered looking at a bunch of slides of the artist's other paintings back in art class. He remembered how the more he looked at Hopper's work back then, the more it tended to bum him out. Those sorry-looking losers in that all-night diner. That same old bleached-out couple in a lot of the paintings—Hopper and his wife—Nick seemed to remember, who looked like they'd rather be somewhere else *with* someone else. He always got the feeling Hopper might be the type of guy to take a header off the Geoge Washington Bridge.

Nick went around from painting to painting, studying them, mesmerized by them. One hauntingly bizarre picture in the den was by Francis Bacon. He'd read something about him in the paper recently. Sounded like a guy who was way out there. But what stuck in his head was an item about how one of Bacon's paintings had fetched the highest price of any living artist. He planned to spend a lot of time surfing the net, becoming an art expert.

There was one painting in the library that quickly became his favorite. It was by Lucian Freud, an artist he had once done a midterm paper on. He chose Freud because a girl in the class he had the hots for said how cool the artist's "retro-Dada slant" was. Whatever the hell that meant.

He circled the painting several times, stalking it almost, eyeballing it from every conceivable angle. It was certainly not your typical pretty picture. It was a woman with dark hair and her white dog, neither one of them looking particularly happy. But something about it hooked him. The woman was in a ratty yellow bathrobe and one of her boobs had popped out. The dog had his head resting on her leg. He thought maybe he liked it because everything about it was so off-kilter.

Alcie had walked into the library when Nick was a foot away from the Freud, mesmerized by the eerie flesh tones of the woman in the painting.

"You like that one?" Alcie said in a tone which thinly disguised his disdain.

"Yes, there's something about it that I connect with," Nick opined.

Something about how much he could get for it.

He wondered whether Alcie had paid any attention to the paintings.

"What's your favorite, Alcie, if you had to choose?"

Alcie had loosened up a lot in these two days, partly because Nick had told him to drop the "Mr. Avery." Way too Stepin Fetchit.

"Tell you the truth, Avery, I like beautiful views and happy stuff."

Nick assumed he meant bad landscapes and Norman Rockwell.

"How 'bout that one in the library . . . the big white house?"

Alcie squinted as he thought.

"You know, the one next to the samurai sword collection," Nick said.

But Alcie couldn't seem to place it.

"I can't say I remember that one."

Christ, how could he miss it? Right in the middle of the goddamn room, above the massive coquina fireplace. Nick was delighted, though. The fact that Alcie was not even slightly observant.

Nick let it go and Alcie quietly excused himself to go polish the silverware.

Nick spent the next hour going from painting to painting.

He was looking at his future and it was very, very rosy.

FOURTEEN

Rose Clarke, the big blonde broker in the black Jag convertible, left a message for Crawford a few days after he rousted the squatter couple from Buffalo. He had no idea why she called, but he called her back and they kept missing each other. They were in the fifth inning of a game of telephone tag.

Rose was in her car showing houses to two men when her cell rang. She looked down at the number.

"Can you excuse me?" she said to the man in the passenger seat.

The man nodded.

"Finally, we connect," she said.

"Hi, Rose, sorry 'bout that," Crawford said.

"No prob, I know you're a busy man. Just wanted to tell you something that might be helpful. About somebody . . . you might have an interest in."

That was a little too murky for Crawford.

"Let's talk now," he said.

Rose checked her watch.

"I can't right this minute, I'm showing houses to a couple of gentlemen. How's one thirty?"

"Perfect. I'll come by your office."

Donnie, the man in the back seat of Rose's Jag, assumed that when she said, "a couple of gentlemen," to whoever it was she was talking to, that was code for a couple of gaybos. Tutti fruttis, Donnie called them. He noticed Palm

Beach seemed to have more than its share. Toned guys with short hair, wearing stylish clothes and fancy shoes.

He listened as Rose hung up, then came back to the two questions that had been bugging him: One, why was this woman—supposedly Palm Beach's most high-powered broker—taking customers around jammed into a space the size of a glove compartment? Not that Donnie minded convertibles. He liked the wind in his face way better than air conditioning. But he was six four. What was he supposed to do with his legs? Amputate the suckers? Of course, his partner, Fulbright—all five foot three of him, got the front seat.

On cue, Rose swiveled and looked back at Donnie.

"You okay back there?"

He nodded. Her lips were like big fluffy pillows.

"I normally take the Range Rover when I have more than one client, but I had a little car trouble."

What did you expect? Donnie thought. It was a goddamn Range Rover. Only cars that had more problems were Jags.

"What was wrong with it?" he asked.

"Something to do with the catyliptic connector."

Donnie's specialties were guns, cars and hookers.

"Sure you don't mean catalytic converter?"

"Yeah . . . I guess that's it."

Donnie's second question was, why was this woman who sold $40 million pads on the ocean, schlepping around a couple of guys looking at fixer-uppers on marginal north end streets? Donnie suspected Fulbright had touched someone up for a favor. The guy liked to exploit the leverage of his profession.

Donnie—the antithesis of a Palm Beacher, if there ever was one—was wearing cargo pants and a blue jean jacket with cutoff sleeves. He was an ex-army sergeant with dirty blond hair that he wore on the slightly long—decidedly unmilitary—side. He thought he bore a striking resemblance to Michael Douglas in his *Streets of San Francisco* prime, but Fulbright told him he was deluding himself. More like Nick Nolte in *Down and Out in Beverly Hills.*

Fulbright, sitting erect in the front seat, was chatting up the broker.

He was a skinny guy, forty years old, with a leather jacket and beady eyes that darted around like rats in a cage. He had a left to right comb-over, a 150 IQ and big feet. His real name was Roy Rozzetti, but back when he and Donnie hooked up fifteen years ago, he told Donnie he was a former Fulbright scholar who had "lost his way." Donnie had no idea what a Fulbright scholar was, but knew all about losing one's way. He liked the name, Fulbright, and from then on that's what he called the squirrelly little guy. The two had been a good team because—as is often the case with partnerships—one was the thinker, the other, the doer.

Donnie listened to Rose go on about how the last house they looked at had really good "bones." To him it was a dump with low ceilings and a lousy kitchen—the whole thing would have cost about $350,000 in his Lake Worth neighborhood, instead of $1.9 million here. No way could he picture Fulbright in Palm Beach anyway, unless there was a section of town for psychotic geniuses in black jeans which ballooned out over toothpick legs. Rose was now on a street about as far north as you could go, telling them there were "better values here due to geographic challenges."

Donnie knew that meant it was a shitty location.

Donnie figured Fulbright's biggest challenge was going to be his bank. It was next to impossible for anybody—in this busted economy—to get a mortgage. And here was Fulbright, a shifty-eyed ferret, who couldn't even show the Wells Fargo banker a pay stub. His only hope was seller financing, even though he probably had a sizable wad of cash stowed away in some can in his backyard. Fact was, Fulbright never spent a nickel on anything except Sudoku books and cheap leather jackets that looked like they were made out of Naugahyde.

Donnie heard Rose ask Fulbright if he was a golfer. He almost lost it. Did the guy *look* like a fucking golfer? Bony, short dude with huge pointy shoes. He made that guy Rodney whatever in *Caddyshack* look like Arnold Palmer. Fulbright resembled an aging jockey who never got out in the sun.

"I don't play much anymore," Fulbright said, straight-faced, to Rose, "used to shoot in the low eighties—"

Right, thought Donnie, you mean your bowling score.

Rose nodded and kept her eyes on the road.

"What is it you do, Mr. Fulbright?"

No hesitation whatsoever.

"I trade futures . . . Chicago Merc."

Donnie loved it. If he didn't know better, he would have bought it. The guy was pretty damn convincing.

Last time someone asked Fulbright what he did, he said he was the southern district sales manager of Dick's Sporting Goods. Went on about the Nike and Body Armor reps always hawking him for better display locations. Guy had a real knack.

Fulbright turned to Rose.

"You trading us in, Rose . . . for some other guy?"

"Oh, no, you got me for as long as you want. Thing is the next house is kind of a dog. I predict we're in and out in two minutes."

Donnie leaned forward from the backseat.

"So who is the lucky guy?" he asked.

"The man who called?" she asked. "Oh, he's a police-man, a detective actually . . . working on that murder on the south end."

"I heard about that," Donnie said, "a guy got *hung*?"

Rose shuddered, then nodded.

"That's a tough way to go . . . can't imagine one human being doing that to another one," Donnie said.

✳ ✳ ✳

CRAWFORD EYED the two guys climbing out of Rose's convertible. That was one thing you had to love about Palm Beach. You could never tell when some bearded schlepper in sandals and bad shorts could turn out to be the owner of a couple hundred 7-Elevens. Or the opposite, when some George Hamilton-looking dude in an ascot and double-breasted blazer might be down to his last stock coupon.

But these two guys . . . like Dustin Hoffman and Jon Voight in that old movie. Or two down-and-out shit bums hitching around the country. Or maybe a couple of homeless guys who wintered in Florida so they wouldn't freeze their asses off in their refrigerator box up north.

He watched them amble off. Christ . . . it was impossible to get a handle on people in Palm Beach. Place sure kept you guessing.

Crawford walked into Rose Clarke's real estate office. She was wearing a shiny silver skirt and a long-sleeved blue shirt and had on big sunglasses with Cs on them, more like goggles. Somehow she pulled it off, though. She took him into the conference room and closed the door. They warmed up with a few minutes of small talk, then she rocked him with her bombshell about Ward Jaynes.

FIFTEEN

Even with everything going on, Crawford had thought about Lil a lot. Her "bad patch." The booze, drugs, sexual decadence . . . things she, no doubt, felt really shitty about. Like maybe a whole year where she'd like to have a complete do-over.

Then he thought about several chapters in his own life he would have liked to edit out. Things he did that he wished he'd never done.

Then he realized it wasn't about what Lil had done at Ward Jaynes's house at all.

No, it was simply that he didn't love her. Never had. Never would.

If he loved her, he could have gotten past the Jaynes stuff because he honestly believed that wasn't really her. That was just her at rock bottom.

Fact was, he was just staying in the relationship because it was easy. And, yes, because the sex was good.

But it wasn't fair to her if the whole thing wasn't going anywhere. With everything she had to offer, she could find a guy who would worship her.

He decided to end it.

✳ ✳ ✳

He called her up and offered to buy her a drink at a place on Clematis in West Palm that night. She accepted but he could tell she knew something was up.

Their drinks came. Lil took a long gulp.

He got right to it.

"Lil, I just don't think I'm the right guy for you."

She took another pull.

"Okay, Charlie . . . so tell me what you *really* think."

This was right up there with death notifications.

"I don't know . . . we're just so different. You should be going out with some guy who's got more time to spend with you . . . who likes to go to parties and stuff."

He was picturing a guy with red pants who said "iconic" a lot.

"That is just so pathetic," she said, killing her drink, then standing and wiping her mouth with the white cloth napkin. "That you think I should be out there chasing party boys with no jobs. I mean, *really, Charlie? Are you fucking serious?*"

"Lil, I just mean—"

"Have a nice life, Charlie." She stormed out of the room.

He had pictured a much longer conversation.

Good job, Charlie, he thought.

Real smooth.

SIXTEEN

"So come on, spill the beans . . . what'd the broker have to say?" Ott asked, across from Crawford in his office.

It was seven forty-five at night. Crawford was still kicking himself about his totally inept handling of the abrupt Lil breakup.

"You almost don't want to know, Mort."

"You kidding? 'Course, I do. Tell me."

"I swear, it's a real kick in the nuts."

Ott looked at Crawford and smiled.

"Hey, Charlie, it's me, a jaded fifty-one-year-old who's fuckin' heard it all."

Crawford got up, closed his door and sat down opposite Ott.

"It's about Jaynes."

"Yeah, I figured."

"That broker, Rose . . . she's like wired into everything."

"Okay, so what'd she say?"

"She told me a bunch of stuff about Jaynes, none of it real flattering. But one thing that happened like five years ago you won't believe. Supposedly Jaynes and a buddy of his went over to Bangkok . . . Thailand."

"Yeah, Charlie, I know where Bangkok is."

"Long story short, they're over there to have sex with girls . . . really young girls."

Ott brushed his nose, like he got a whiff of something rancid.

"Fuckin' sicko . . . but, hey, we already knew that."

"What happens is, he adopts these girls. Four of 'em, to be exact."

Ott leaned forward in his chair, eyes getting bigger. "You're shittin' me!"

"Probably gave the parents a couple hundred bucks. Brings 'em back here, they stay at his house for, like, three or four months."

"So like sex slaves?"

"That's as good a name as any, I guess. After awhile Jaynes gets bored with the whole setup and, just like that . . . ships 'em back."

Ott's face was white, his cheeks slumped into his jowls. "On second thought, maybe I *haven't* heard it all."

The door opened and Norm Rutledge stuck his head in. "Guys got anything yet?"

Ott rolled his eyes at Crawford.

"Working on it," Crawford said.

Rutledge frowned, his head disappeared and the door closed.

"I'm gonna get back on the computer, see if I can get more on Jaynes," Crawford said.

"Just log onto . . . sickfuckbillionaire.com," Ott said. "Hey, how'd the broker know you were looking into Jaynes anyway?"

"I asked her that and she said she just heard something. So I pressed her a little and it turns out Rose knows Jaynes's friend, Miranda, the woman at the pool. She also said something like how Palm Beach would be a much better place without sleazeballs like Ward Jaynes."

※ ※ ※

CRAWFORD FIRED up his computer after Ott left. He Googled Jaynes, trying to add to what Rose told him.

Crawford then pored through dozens of pages of lawsuits against Jaynes. For starters, Jaynes had been charged with sexual harassment, not once but three times, of women who formerly worked for his company. The incidents were a lot more than Jaynes getting them drunk at the office Christmas party and slapping the moves on them in the executive washroom. One of his accusers was a seventeen-year-old from Babson College, working at Jaynes Funds as a summer intern. Reading between the lines, Jaynes had apparently introduced her to the wonderful world of sado-masochistic sex, but the *Wall Street Journal*—not surprisingly—came up short on details. The *New York Daily News* and *Post*, however, got a little more specific and some of the related stories got big, garish headlines. It turned out all the lawsuits were eventually dropped. Crawford came to the obvious conclusion: thick envelopes bulging with cash.

Then Crawford read a *Barron's* profile on Jaynes. The writer was more like a groupie than a reporter. The story detailed how Jaynes made $50 million in a two-month period shorting stocks. Two particular targets had been Bear Stearns, before it crashed and burned just a few months back, and Lehman Brothers, which went up in smoke shortly afterward. Jaynes was also a key player in bringing Freddie Mac and Fannie Mae to their knees before the government bailout. Traders like Jaynes who bet against the market were both feared and despised—but also secretly envied by many. They were the Wall Street grave dancers who'd load up on "put" options on companies, betting the companies would go down the tubes. They bet millions that companies with bloated and overpaid managements, or ones rife with fraud and dubious accounting, would fall hard and make quick windfall profits for the "shorts."

Another article recounted how one of the most powerful tools of someone like Jaynes was rumor. A favorite trick was spreading stories that federal authorities were closing in, about to slap "Giuliani bracelets" on some hapless CEO, then perp-walk him into a police van as the flashbulbs popped. The author mentioned how Jaynes had a multimillion dollar media budget dedicated to trashing wobbly companies. But Jaynes apparently didn't discriminate; he went after perfectly healthy ones, too.

The writer ended his article heavy-handedly, saying, "to Wardwell A. Jaynes, III, the choice between making $50 million in eight weeks or a thousand enemies for life was absolutely no choice at all."

Crawford was about to start on another story when his door opened again and he saw Rutledge's face.

"Crawford, you need extra guys, let me know, we got plenty of manpower."

"Let's not clusterfuck it, Norm," Crawford said, not looking up.

"How 'bout just bringing me a few perps," Rutledge said, and his head disappeared.

Crawford shook his head and understood why guys chose to be vampires, cops who only worked graveyard shift. A veteran with twenty-two years on the job he met once was one of them. He told Crawford he worked graveyard so he'd never have to lay eyes on Rutledge, except at cops' funerals.

Crawford's phone rang.

"It's me," said the expressionless voice. "Anything new?"

"Not yet, Misty. Don't worry, though."

It was like she was on a three-second delay.

"Please," she said and hung up.

Crawford looked at his watch. It was almost eight. He glanced out his window. It was pitch black, time for a change of scenery. Time to put as much distance between him and Rutledge as possible.

He walked out to Ott's cubicle.

"Let's get out of here, I've seen enough of Shithead to last a goddamn lifetime."

Dave Shales, a detective in the cubicle next to Ott's, looked up, caught Crawford's eye, smiled and nodded.

Ott, glued to his computer screen, held up his hand.

"Hold on, man. Just want to read this FCIS thing about Jaynes."

Crawford leaned down to see Ott's screen.

"Oh, yeah, I saw that one."

"Where you want to go?" Ott asked, looking up.

"Hard Case."

They could talk shop in peace at the bar.

So he thought, anyway.

SEVENTEEN

Crawford and Ott were the only Palm Beach guys who went to the Hard Case, a cop bar in West Palm. It was way too downscale for clean-cut, wholesome Palm Beach cops. Palm Beach cops wanted to keep their distance from the dog pound of West Palm mutts—a scraggly lot with Fu Manchus and gaudy tats. Crawford liked the Hard Case because it was nothing like O'Herlihy's. O'Herlihy's was where most Palm Beach cops went. Specifically, Rutledge and his suck-ups. They had long, serious debates there about police procedures and all the latest scientific techniques. None of them took their drinking very seriously either. Especially Rutledge—two beers, home to the wife, lights out.

The Hard Case was in a dicey commercial area that was dead at night, about equal distance from a black neighborhood and a blue-collar white one. It used to be called Black 'n' Blue and catered to African American cops.

That was before Jack Scarsiola, an ex-detective, bought it and changed the name. It looked exactly the same, though. A one-story building painted black outside with a blue door that swung out. A small window on the street side provided very little light mainly because of the heavy steel bars around it and the fact that it was frosted. There was razor wire to protect the satellite dish that pulled in 300 channels when the weather cooperated. Inside, beyond the long wooden bar, were two pool tables, a couple quarters on top belonging to the players up next.

On any given night, the population was 90 percent law enforcement. The male to female ratio was usually about eight to one.

Crawford and Ott walked in.

"Hey, Jack," Crawford said to Scarsiola, who was tending bar.

"P. B. boys slummin' again, huh," Scarsiola said, as he worked the draft stick. "Brought along your roly-poly friend, huh Charlie?"

Scarsiola liked to give Ott shit. They just rubbed each other the wrong way.

"Fuck off," Ott said, "and gemme a Yuengling."

"Hey," Scarsiola said, leaning across the bar, "heard you boys caught the hanging case."

"Yeah," Crawford said.

"Got any suspects?"

Crawford didn't answer.

"Like you'd tell me, right?"

"What do you think?" said Crawford, watching a woman take a drag on a cigarette. He had a strong urge for one, even though it had been two and a half years. It was against the law to smoke in the bar, but what did cops care?

Scarsiola handed Crawford a Budweiser and Ott a Yuengling.

Ott scanned the place.

"Usual bunch of beauties, huh?" Crawford said, looking at a guy with a Harley tattoo on his fleshy bicep.

Ott nodded and sipped his beer.

They went and sat at a table.

"I never asked you," Crawford said, "how's this place compare to Cleveland joints?"

Ott gave the question some thought.

"Unfavorably."

"That it?"

"Yeah."

"The laconic Mort Ott."

"Don't give me that Dartmouth vocab shit," Ott said, taking a swig. "I ain't in the minus-fifteen club."

"The what?"

"Never told you about my minus-fifteen club?"

Crawford shook his head.

"Meaning IQ points," Ott said, rubbing his creased forehead, "the difference between down here and up north."

"Keep going?"

"Okay, so take, say, a landscaper . . . fifteen points more stupid down here than up there. Lawyers here . . . same thing, minus fifteen. Across the board—doctors, accountants, toll booth collectors, you name it—fifteen points more stupid down here."

"More stupid, huh?"

Ott looked at him and screwed up his eyes.

"Yeah . . . less smart."

"Gotcha. You got any more half-assed theories?"

"Fuck off."

"Hey, I didn't tell you, I went out to check on Misty Bill."

Ott looked at him funny. "You did . . . why?"

"What do you mean, why? Kid's brother just got killed. Her father's in jail. Her mother's . . . who the hell knows where."

Ott nodded.

"I just wanted to see how she was doing."

Crawford caught a whiff of cheap aftershave nearby and looked up.

"Hey, Crawford," said a voice, "what's the problem, can't you find the hangman?"

The guy was named Sonny Johnson, a West Palm cop he knew by sight. Johnson was with someone Crawford had never seen before. No question about it, both of them were clearly three sheets.

Johnson was around forty, short black hair, a gold stud in his left ear and wearing a Ramones T-shirt. Crawford figured he dug it out of his kid's drawer, no clue who the Ramones were. The other guy was chinless and wore a do-rag.

"What's the problem," Johnson said again, "can't find the hang—"

"Yeah, he heard ya the first time, genius," Ott said to Johnson, "go get yourself another beer, huh. You sober up, something intelligent might flop outta your piehole."

"You're a real funny fuck," Johnson said, leaning closer to Ott. "How is it anyway, being sidekick to the greatest cop in New York history?"

"A great honor," Ott said, straight-faced, shoving his chair back to get away from Johnson's beery breath.

Johnson glanced over at Do-rag, then back at Ott.

"Your partner give you pointers and shit?" Johnson asked.

"Yeah," Ott said, tilting his chair back farther, "watch out for assholes in bad T-shirts."

"Good one," Johnson said, swaying. "Mort."

Johnson let loose with a long, guttural burp, like he could do it on demand.

"Ott, right?" Johnson said.

Ott didn't answer.

"Well, I gotta tell ya, Mort Ott . . . that's the lamest fuckin' name I ever heard."

Do-rag beat on his thigh like Johnson was Letterman.

"I got a question for ya, the fuck is an 'Ott' anyway . . . a midget otter or something?"

Ott looked at Crawford and shook his head.

"You done?" Ott asked. "'Cause we're working something here. How 'bout taking your butt boy and getting the fuck outta here."

Ott turned away from Johnson. Crawford watched Johnson out of the corner of his eye. Just in case.

He and Do-Rag shuffled off toward the bar.

Crawford thought about slapping Ott five.

"I had the same question," he said instead.

"About what?" Ott asked.

"What the hell is an Ott anyway?"

"Funny," Ott said, standing up and pointing at his empty beer.

"You ready?"

Crawford nodded.

"Watch out for the knuckle draggers."

Crawford's eyes followed Ott as he headed to the bar, remembering when Rutledge first introduced him to Ott.

✳ ✳ ✳

"CRAWFORD, THIS is Mort Ott," Rutledge had said it fast, like it was one syllable.

Crawford looked Ott over.

"That it?"

"What?" Ott asked.

"Your whole name?"

"Yep, short and strong . . . just like me."

✳ ✳ ✳

JOHNSON AND Do-rag were at the bar, as Ott approached, huddled conspiratorially.

"Two more," Ott said to Jack Scarsiola.

Johnson heard Ott's voice and swung around.

"Hey, lemme ask you a serious question," Johnson slurred. "You ever seen that reality show? Those cops in Memphis?"

Ott didn't answer.

"The dumb fat one," Johnson said, "dead ringer for you."

Ott took the two beers from Scarsiola and rolled his eyes.

"You been working on that all this time?" he said. Then, "Fucking Neanderthal."

He walked away from the bar and back to Crawford.

"Didn't take my advice, did you?" asked Crawford.

Crawford caught a glimpse of Sonny Johnson and Do-rag push off from the bar and start toward them.

A few seconds later they were a couple feet away.

Johnson stared down at Ott.

"What did you say, you fat fuck?"

Crawford looked up at Johnson.

"Go drool on someone else, will ya?" he said.

For a drunk guy, Johnson had a quick right.

Crawford didn't see it coming until Johnson's fist was a foot from his face. He turned and it thudded into the side of his head, almost knocking Crawford out of his chair. Ott exploded out of his seat like he was blasting off a launch pad. He crashed into Johnson, knocked him backward like a blocking dummy, then took him down to the floor.

Crawford got up, unsteady, then Do-rag threw a punch at him. Crawford ducked it and swung back at him. He connected more with the guy's ear than jaw, but it did the trick and Do-rag flipped backward onto a table where three guys were sitting.

Crawford glanced over at Ott. He and Johnson were writhing around on the floor like a pair of mud wrestlers. He saw Ott get off a straight right, his arm like a cobra strike.

Then Do-rag got up. He seemed to have a quick debate with himself about whether to wade back into battle with Crawford. Then, from ten feet away he charged, drawing back his fist. But Crawford's knee was faster. He caught Do-rag square in the three-piece, and when he pitched over, Crawford slammed him with an uppercut. Do-rag staggered and went down hard, done for the night.

Ott climbed off Johnson, and Crawford saw a few drops of blood trickle down onto Joey Ramone's likeness.

"You okay?" Crawford asked Ott.

"Yeah," Ott said, picking up his empty mug from the floor. "Wasted a perfectly good Yuengling, though."

"You got good hands," Crawford said.

"For a fat fuck, you mean?"

"For an *old* fat fuck."

Ott put the mug down on the table and picked up a thick Corona beer coaster.

He frisbeed it over at Johnson and it bounced off his shoulder.

"We gotta go, boys," Ott said, getting up. "Can't get anything done here, with all your distractions."

Crawford and Ott walked up to the bar.

"Sorry about that," Crawford said to Jack Scarsiola. "What do we owe you?"

"I should pay you," Scarsiola said under his breath. "Twelve bucks."

Crawford handed him a twenty.

"Thanks," Crawford said, and put the change down on the bar.

Ott ignored Scarsiola and walked away.

Crawford and Ott went down the sidewalk to their car.

Just before they got in, Ott looked up at Crawford.

"Guys'll never live that down," he said, a big lump coming up on the side of his face, "getting beat up by a couple Palm Beach pussies."

EIGHTEEN

Nick had to fight his first instinct which was to rent a Ryder truck, strip the walls of the Hoppers, Bacons and Freuds, drive up to New York and get Christie's or Sotheby's to give him big guarantees in their spring auctions. But in keeping with his new policy of not doing anything rash, he spent hours on the Internet researching how the art market worked.

He quickly found out about something called *provenance*. It put the kibosh on his get-rich-quick art scheme. The gist of provenance was that you had to prove you owned a painting through a paper trail of documentation. That could come in the form of transaction records or a painting being gifted in a will, but galleries were very strict about it. Possession was definitely *not* nine-tenths of the law when it came to art. Galleries and museums spent a lot of time investigating and verifying in order to confirm that a painting was neither stolen nor fake. And the better known the artist and the more valuable the painting, the more digging around they did.

So Nick decided the answer was to bide his time. He was pretty sure he could sell one or two of the lesser-known pictures in Robertson's house to one of the galleries on Worth Avenue. None of them were going to knock themselves out doing a provenance search on a $20,000 painting by a somewhat obscure artist.

Nick's new life, meanwhile, was hard to beat. A cook cooking him anything he wanted, for starters. Today was eggs Benedict for breakfast, followed by cold salmon and a salad with lots of walnuts and avocado in it for lunch. Tonight, the cook had told him, was going to be a two-inch steak with béarnaise sauce. He spent most of his time reading, novels out by the pool and art books in the library. He wanted to be informed and knowledgeable for the fancy dinner parties he'd soon be attending.

One thing was sure, Nick realized, if he was going to play the role of art connoisseur, he damn well better look the part. He could no longer be a schlub dressed in Haggar slacks. It was time for an extreme makeover, time to overhaul his image, upgrade his lifestyle. The right clothes, he knew, were an investment in the future. Problem was he had maxed out his Sears Discovery card and was now down to the last of his life savings, $1,800 in tip money. He knew he had to bite the bullet and go to Maus & Hoffman, a high-end men's clothing store on Worth. It was known for splashy colored shirts, pants and jackets, with prices way beyond a bartender's salary. He picked out a pair of tan linen pants there that cost $400, then exhaled hard, and bought a long-sleeved pink shirt with a small blue-green flamingo on the breast pocket for just under $300.

Next he found a hand-tailored double-breasted blue blazer marked down from $1,200 to $600 which he felt exuded *GQ*. Fortunately, he didn't have to spring for a tie. He had rummaged through Spencer Robertson's mildewy closet and found a rack of them. He had turned one of them around to examine the label—hoping, praying almost—and yes, there it was, the distinctive label of the fabled Lilly Pulitzer. He was over the moon.

After buying the pants and shirt, Nick walked back to the shoe department. The cheapest pair of loafers cost more than $600. That would come close to wiping him out. He thanked the salesman, then asked for directions to a shoe store he had heard so much about.

It was time to step up—and into—his first pair of Stubbs & Woottons, which he'd heard didn't actually cost an arm and a leg. They were fashionable shoes he had become aware of several months ago, having spotted a pair on a well-heeled Viggo patron. The shoes, actually black needlepoint slippers with martini glasses on the vamp, seemed to immediately proclaim the man a bon vivant, a swell, a player. Nick had seen another pair with crossed golf clubs on another Viggo's patron. They were essentially theme shoes and he just had to own a pair.

He walked across the street into an alley of chic shops, following the directions he had been given. He saw the sign and went inside. There were several pairs in his size. He felt the slightly rough texture of the celebrated slipper shoe. It was a tough choice, between a pair with dice stitched into them—showing a five-two lucky seven, then another with skull and crossbones, and a third, the sun on the left shoe and the moon on the right one. Then he looked up and saw the perfectly coiffed salesgirl come toward him. She had found another pair in his size. They had a caricature of the devil in red with a pitchfork. He nodded, smiled and gave her a thumbs-up.

He wore them proudly to his appointment with a cosmetic surgeon in Boca Raton later that day. He had been told Boca had more cosmetic surgeons than landscapers, pool guys and personal injury lawyers put together.

※ ※ ※

LATER THAT afternoon, when Alcie was off duty, Nick carefully removed a painting by an artist named Seagraves Albaran off of a wall in the powder room of Spencer Robertson's house. He wrapped it in brown paper and took it to a gallery at the corner of Worth and Golfview, which specialized in American realism.

"Oh, my God," said the young blonde working there, "I know a man who collects Albarans. This is one of the best I've seen in a long time."

In less than a half hour, the woman had snapped a shot of the painting with her cell, e-mailed it to her buyer and gotten his approval to buy it.

Nick loved his new line of work even though he had a sneaking suspicion that the woman might not be giving him full market value, and he knew for a fact, that her 50 percent commission was highway robbery. But what did it matter . . . he had gotten a check for $16,000, not to mention her card and cell number.

So in practically no time at all, he had a nice, new bank account—adding three zeroes to his net worth—and had met an elegant Palm Beach beauty to boot. He imagined an intoxicating future ahead of him with the woman. He looked at her card.

Lil Fonseca. Had a nice exotic ring to it.

Besides being suddenly flush with cash and the possibility of a new woman in his life, Nick had become the de facto grandson of a man who had paintings worth millions. So what if the old guy wished him Happy New Year twice a day, wore Depends and called him Oswald?

Nick was seeing Spencer Robertson's life close up—such as it was—and realized, like most people, his was a series of routines. He slept until ten at which time he was served a hard-boiled egg and a piece of toast slathered with Peter Pan chunky peanut butter. Then he turned on the TV and spent the morning watching quiz shows and, in the afternoon, soap operas and the Golf Channel. The *New York Times, Wall Street Journal, Financial Times* and the *Glossy* were delivered daily but, with the exception of the *Times,* were never removed from their plastic bags. The old man opened the *Times* religiously to the cross-word puzzle each morning. He just stared at it, though, knowing he was supposed to do something, just not sure what.

Nick was ecstatic about his new life. He knew he was a much better grandson to Spencer Robertson than Avery Robertson had been, or ever would be. He watched cartoons and inane quiz shows with the old man and listened to his bursts of blather. He even developed a certain fondness for him and even wanted to improve the quality of his life . . . just as long as the old Spencer didn't stretch it out *too* far. All he asked for, in return, were a few dozen paintings. Why not? Spencer couldn't take them with him, so who better to end up with them than an art history minor who actually knew the difference between a Hopper and a Holbein.

※ ※ ※

And, the fact was, he owed it all to one person.

Cynthia Dexter.

She had made it all possible.

But all of a sudden she had become a liability. Particularly after her distressing call to the house earlier that morning.

He had absolutely no idea how she got his number, as she fiercely rebuked him for standing her up. She harangued him about the four messages she had left on his cell, starting with, "do you want to meet me at the movies or pick me up," then, "Nick, please let me know what the plan is," after that, "I hope you're okay, Nick," and finally, "I think it's very rude that I haven't heard from you."

Then, she told him, she'd found out that he lived at the Palm Beach Princess from the nice bartender at Viggo's. So she drove to the Princess and the guy at the desk said no, he hadn't seen Nick for a few days. Last time was when Nick got into a Yellow Cab, which was weird since he had a car.

Next, Cynthia said how she'd phoned Yellow Cab, and convincingly playing Nick's mother, explained where and when her son was picked up by one of their drivers. But she told the dispatcher she had no idea where he went from there, and now he was missing. He hadn't called in days and she was very concerned.

Nick wanted to reach through the phone, grab her and smack her silly. She was so damn smug and pleased with all her little detective work.

Then she continued and told him how the sympathetic dispatcher had checked the records and told her the cab had taken her son to 101 El Vedato.

101 El Vedato, huh?

She said she knew right away that was the address of Spencer Robertson's house. Well, now . . . wasn't that interesting, she thought? How she had told Nick all about how rich Robertson was. Senile, too. Told him how Robertson just had the one elderly butler to protect him from the scam artists of the world.

Guys like you, Nick, she said.

NINETEEN

$\mathbb{N}$ick heard a commotion at the front door as he hung up with Cynthia Dexter.

"Yo, Granpa Spence," a voice boomed out. Nick was in the kitchen getting ice cream out of the freezer.

He hurried toward the front door, wearing the green Poinciana golf hat he had found in Spencer Robertson's hallway closet.

A man in his midtwenties, knapsack on his back, came reeling into the house. Alcie hadn't been able to intercept him because the man had his own key. The man's arm was around a woman whose nipples seemed to be holding up a loose-fitting halter top. They were both inebriated.

"And who might you be?" the man asked, looking Nick over from head to toe.

Nick in his linen pants and Stubbs & Wootton slippers felt he should be doing the asking.

"Avery," he said, "and you are?"

"Jesus, dude . . . it's me, Dickie," the man said throwing a bear hug around Nick.

Nick had to play along until he figured out who Dickie was. According to Cynthia Dexter, Avery was the only living relative of Spencer Robertson. His guess was she had missed one.

"So how's it goin', Dickie?" Nick said, enthusiastically, waiting for an explanation of their relationship. He saw Alcie back out of the room, figuring Nick had things under control.

Dickie released his hug.

"Christ, last time I saw you was at the funeral, you were like twelve," Dickie said, looking him over.

Nick didn't know what to say.

"Even back then, I remember those big ole Mick Jagger lips," Dickie said, giving Nick a punch on the shoulder.

Nick laughed. He hadn't wasted any time making an appointment with the cosmetic surgeon in Boca. But the doctor was a little collagen happy and went pretty heavy on the stuff. For the first twenty-four hours after he got his new lips, Nick had had a problem enunciating his words properly.

"I like 'em," the girl slurred.

It was like Dickie had forgotten about the woman next to him, falling out of her clothes.

"Oh, sorry, this is my girlfriend, Gigi."

Gigi flounced forward and gave an exaggerated curtsy. "Pleased to meet you."

"Same here," Nick said, shaking her hand. "Welcome."

Dickie took off his knapsack and dropped it on the floor.

"So how is the old bastard, anyway?"

"Uh . . . not that great, I mean, you know, he is ninety-six."

"Jesus, really? Time flies when you're havin' fun, huh?"

After his initial panic about getting found out, Nick knew he was now in the clear.

He had a lot of experience dealing with drunks, too.

"Whose funeral was it?" Gigi asked, reaching up to her shoulder and adjusting her black bra strap without any sign of modesty.

Dickie looked over at her gravely. "Avery's parents, my aunt and uncle . . . really bad accident."

Thank you, Gigi, Nick thought.

"Yeah, really bad," Nick said, wondering how they bought it. "How long you down for, Dickie?"

"I'm figuring 'bout a week. Get my shit together . . . see what happened, I got kicked out of Duke."

The guy was like twenty-five and still going to college? And how'd the cretin get into Duke and the best he could do was fucking Hofstra?

"Sorry to hear that, man. You guys stay here as long as you want," Nick said, not meaning a word of it.

"Thanks, man, where you living now anyway?" Dickie asked. "When you're not down here on the gravy train?"

Nick remembered what Cynthia Dexter told him. Avery lived in some place way out there, like Montana or Wyoming.

"Montana. You know, I ski-bum around . . . rest of the time fish and hunt."

Dickie looked envious.

"Sick, what's the name of the place?"

Shit.

"Oh, little town outside of, ah, Helene called . . . Big Elk."

Gigi cocked her head. "Wait, isn't it *Helena*?"

Fuck.

"Yeah, but us locals just call it Helene."

She bought it.

Dickie had a faraway look, like he was fantasizing about life as a ski bum. He was around five ten, had the potbelly of a six-months pregnant woman and was expensively, but badly, dressed. He had dirty blond hair that was combed straight back; a few strands flopped forward on both sides and circled his eyes. His hair had a glossy sheen to it, like he went heavy on the gel.

"All right if we take the yellow bedroom?" Dickie asked.

"Yeah, sure, I'm in the blue one. Want a hand with your stuff?"

"Thanks, dude, I'm good," Dickie said, heading toward the front door, Gigi right behind him.

Nick was glad he sold the Albaran before the two lushes showed up.

A few minutes later they came back in with their stuff, mixed two large vodka and OJs, stumbled upstairs and didn't come back down.

For the rest of the night Nick was kept awake by caterwauling shrieks of passion. The carnal racket started up again around eight o'clock the next morning when Nick was in the kitchen with the old man's nurse. She looked at him, puzzled.

"My cousin, Dickie," he explained.

She rolled her eyes.

Two days later, Dickie and Gigi hadn't left the house. They were heavy maintenance, but gave Nick a chance to study Dickie like a textbook. He couldn't possibly get a better education about the conduct and speech of a spoiled, entitled, debauched young aristo.

Above all else, Dickie Mortimer was a hardcore roué. Nick wondered why it had taken Duke three and a half years to toss his ass out of there. Despite being twenty pounds overweight and having marshmallow skin, Dickie was handsome. But, Nick predicted, he would have a short shelf life. In ten years his features would go soft and mushy.

Dickie's modus operandi was to get out of bed at ten, stumble down to the refrigerator and, in one gulp, drain a half carton of OJ. Then he'd go back up and he and Gigi would come back down two hours later expecting bacon, eggs, the whole nine.

After breakfast, Dickie and Gigi would go for a swim. One time Dickie boasted how he was going to do thirty laps, but petered out after two and a half. Puffing like he had just run three miles, he dropped onto a chaise longue. After slathering on a handful of SPF 30, he flattened out in the chaise, his protuberant stomach the closest body part to the sun. Within minutes he was snoring.

Nick spent as much time as possible in Dickie's orbit, soaking up all he could. One time, Alcie wheeled the old man out to the pool to give him some sun and fresh air. Dickie swung around when he heard the clank of the wheelchair. He looked up at Gigi, mischievously.

"How's it going there, big guy?" he said to the old man.

His bewildered grandfather stared back.

"Happy New Year," Spencer said.

Dickie and Gigi howled.

"So what's happenin', dude? Been down to the club lately? Teeing it up with the boys?"

The old man squinted.

Then Dickie looked over at Nick and smiled his, "aren't I amusing" smile.

Nick felt a rush of protectiveness. He wanted to tell Dickie what a repellent slug he was.

Instead, he flicked his head in Alcie's direction. Alcie got the message and wheeled the old man back inside. He had had enough fresh air, sun and Dickie.

Gigi finally got her fill, too. Nick was wondering how many days in a row a woman—even one with obvious self-esteem issues—could sleep until noon, knock back Bloody Marys at two, blow lines on the backgammon board at four and pass out halfway through dinner.

In Gigi's case, the answer was four days.

She just vanished without a word. No explanation from Dickie. Nothing. And Nick didn't care enough to ask. Gigi was barely out the door when Dickie started clicking away on the Internet. A half hour later, he made a call. He had been on Craigslist trolling for companionship. An hour later, Gigi's perfume still heavy in the air, two skimpily clad white trash bimbos in their early twenties showed up. Facial and body piercings punctuated their emaciated torsos.

Shortly after their arrival, Estelle, the nurse who prided herself on working in an orderly household, informed Nick she had had enough, she was giving her two-week notice.

Nick—delighted to have one less body in the house—told her he was sorry to see her go.

Fifteen minutes later, Dickie and the two women were in the hot tub by the pool quaffing Spencer's vintage Dom Pérignon. An hour later, they were upstairs thrashing around in a pile.

Sometime during the night, the two women snuck out after boosting Nick's new iPod touch in the kitchen.

Nick decided it was time Dickie followed them out the door.

Nick could be very direct when he had to be.

He was waiting when Dickie stumbled down just before twelve the next day.

"Sorry, man, you gotta go."

"What do you mean?" Dickie asked, looking stunned.

"One of your . . . *girlfriends* stole my touch and an Albaran painting from the powder room," he said. "You turned this place into a goddamned crack house."

Embarrassed, Dickie looked down at his scuffed-up Testonis.

"They got my wallet, too," he admitted, the air completely out of him. "Give me another chance, huh Ave?"

But Nick was firm and, without a further whimper or protest, Dickie caved. Like maybe he felt he was on borrowed time anyway. Probably because he had been kicked out of so many places, he figured it was just a matter of time.

Ultimately, Nick felt sorry for the guy and peeled off five crisp hundred-dollar bills from the Albaran sale. Dickie was appreciative.

An hour later he was gone.

So with Dickie out of there, Nick was ready to embark on a bold new phase of his plan. It was an experiment, really. He had decided to see if he could actually pass as the grandson of Spencer Robertson. He didn't see how it would be a problem, since the real Avery hadn't been to Palm Beach in twelve years.

His test run was going to be lunch at the Poinciana Club. It would be his society debut. His coming-out party. A little brazen, but not reckless, because he was absolutely certain he could pull it off.

He had thought a lot about what he would do after he sold his Hoppers, Bacons and Freuds. That was how he thought of the paintings now. As his.

He fantasized about where he would go after he cashed in and sold them. His first thought was the south of France. Where else? That was where his heroes, the Fitzgeralds, the Murphys and their high-minded literary group had spent so much time. Their pitchers of gin and bon mots . . . *sur la plage*. But he wondered—as romantic as it all sounded, stretched out on the same sand as they had done before him—what would he actually do there? He couldn't speak more than a handful of words in French.

Besides, he had really warmed up to Palm Beach. He couldn't wait to spiff up and swagger around like a PB blade. He felt confident he could walk the walk, talk the talk, and do the pink and green shuffle with the best of them.

TWENTY

Crawford and a cop, John Porter, got to the building at the same time. Ott was on his way, be there in five, he told Crawford.

Crawford and Porter rode up the elevator together with the building manager, who was waiting for them. David Ponton, manager of the Poinciana Club, had called the Palm Beach police. Said he was worried about an employee. Explained that in seventeen years Cynthia Dexter had never missed a day of work and she definitely wouldn't miss this morning's budget meeting. Said he called her several times before the meeting. Tried her again after, on both her home and cell phones. Both went straight to voice mail. He repeated his concern and said it was "very un-Cynthia."

Normally, just a cop would go out on a call like this. But the dispatcher had a hunch and told Crawford about it. Crawford decided it was worth the trip.

The building manager pushed the buzzer. He waited. Then knocked. Waited again. Then hit the buzzer once more.

"Better try the key," Crawford said.

The manager put the key in the lock, turned it, then pushed open the door.

"Ms. Dexter," Crawford called.

Crawford walked past him.

"Don't touch anything, John," Crawford said; then to the manager, "Stay right here, please."

The manager nodded.

The place smelled good and looked immaculate.

"Ms. Dexter?" Crawford said.

He went down a narrow hallway, then into the first room he came to. The den. Very cozy and feminine. A nice perfume smell. She obviously spent a lot of time in there.

"*Jes-sus fuck-ing Christ*," Crawford heard Porter say, "in here, Charlie, the bedroom."

Turning, Crawford ran back into the hallway. He practically collided with Ott, who had just come in, and motioned with his head for him to follow.

Porter was crouched down next to a woman's naked body, spread-eagled on a king-sized bed. Her back was propped up against three pillows. Her head, swollen and purple, was tilted up at the ceiling, an alligator belt cinched around her neck, tied to a bedpost.

"Holy Christ," Ott said.

Crawford fought the urge to cut her down. Slice the belt and ease her down on a pillow.

Twenty minutes later, the place was crawling with people. Four uniforms, the ME and the head tech, Mel Carnahan. Five minutes later, Dominica McCarthy entered the room. Crawford hadn't seen her since the Darryl Bill hanging. Rutledge was on his way, too, Ott said, in a tone distinctly lacking in enthusiasm.

The reactions to the dead body were seared into the faces of everyone there. Crawford saw the two young uniforms cast furtive glances at the woman's face. He could see they were virgins. Trying, unconvincingly, to look like it was just another day at the office, no big deal. Even Carnahan, early fifties and twenty years on the job, looked shaken.

Maybe it was the contrast of the cozy apartment, all baby blues and pinks, so clean and neat, with the horrifying, contorted face of the woman.

Ott, having stared down at hundreds of corpses, was on automatic pilot. Hunched down close to the body taking notes, he had walked around and observed the vic from different angles. It was like he was taking snapshots in his head. He stayed out of people's way, while at the same time, staked claim to his territory.

Conversations weren't much more than murmurs. None of the usual tension-breaking wisecracks Crawford was used to. A certain tentativeness, too, a fear of stepping on evidence or other people's toes.

Crawford had just had a brief conversation with the ME and Ott when he noticed Dominica McCarthy, with tweezers and plastic evidence bags, work her way around the bed. He walked up to her.

"How's it going?"

She looked up and pushed her glasses down.

"Hello, Detective," she said, much less cool than last time.

"Charlie Crawford," Crawford said.

"I know." She smiled. "Dominica McCarthy."

"I know," he said. "Anything interesting?"

"Petechiae," she said. "No surprise there."

A petechial hemorrhage. The symptom was burst blood vessels on the eyelids caused by asphyxiation.

Crawford nodded. "Same as the kid who got hung?"

She nodded.

"Anything else?"

She pointed to her sample bags. "Hairs, fibers . . . take your pick."

"A smoking gun would be nice," he said, shifting from one leg to the other.

"Yeah, dream on. I'm pretty sure she had a male caller or callers . . . at some point fairly recently."

"How do you know?"

Dominica reached for one of her bags and held it up to Crawford.

Inside the bag was a big, flat, silver metal button with a Z on it.

Crawford moved his head closer to the button and smelled Dominica's perfume.

"How do you know it's a guy's?" he said, his eyes shifting from the button to her.

"I don't for sure, just . . . it looks too big to be a woman's. Could have been there before she was killed, too. But I doubt it."

"Why?"

"'Cause she kept such a clean house. My guess, she probably vacuumed twice a week."

Crawford flashed to Ward Jaynes. How he'd love to find a missing Z button on a jacket of his. But that wasn't going to happen. Best he could hope for was a missing button on a jacket of someone who did Jaynes's dirty work.

"Found anything that matches up to the Bill scene? Any similarities?"

She looked over her evidence, scratched the back of her head and thought for a second.

"Not really, it was like they took a Shop-Vac to the Bill scene, real pros, knew exactly what they were doing. This one . . . whoever it was, left a lot behind. Either an amateur or someone who got spooked. Took off in a hurry maybe."

Crawford nodded, looked up and saw Norm Rutledge walk in through the bedroom door on the other side of the room.

"Thanks a lot," he said.

"You're welcome," Dominica said.

Rutledge beelined over to Crawford, ignoring Dominica.

"What have we got?"

"Dead woman's name is Cynthia Dexter. Single, age forty-eight, worked at the Poinciana Club."

"We sure as hell don't need this," Rutledge said, his rank breath hitting Crawford like a stiff wind off a landfill.

Rutledge's eyes followed Ott who was walking over to them.

"So it's the same guy?" Rutledge asked.

"They're some obvious similarities," Crawford said, "but I don't know."

"Jesus, Crawford," Rutledge said, shaking his head, "give me something."

"Easy, Norm, I'm just saying I've seen a lot of copycats before."

"What are you talking about? How could it be a copycat? We kept the Bill scene under tight wraps."

Ott stifled a laugh.

"Is that right?" Crawford asked. "Then how come the doorman at my building knew every detail the morning after?"

Rutledge just glared at him.

His eyes finally shifted over to the body. Crossing the room quickly, he almost mowed down a uniform.

Crawford and Ott followed him.

"There's another possibility, you know," Rutledge said, looking down at the body. "Sexual asphyxia ever occur to you?"

Crawford had already talked over that possibility with Ott and the ME.

"ME's prelim says there was no penetration, Norm."

"So? Since when is there always penetration?"

"Since 98 percent of the time," Crawford said.

"Maybe this is the 2 percent."

"So you saying this was an *accident,* Norm?" Ott asked, not disguising his skepticism. "Two consenting adults taking it right up to the edge—"

"And going over," said Rutledge. "I got news for you, Ott, there's a lot of kinky shit in Palm Beach. You got a problem with that?"

"Ah, yeah," Ott said, "actually, I do."

"Anything but another murder, right, Norm?" Crawford asked, giving Rutledge a cold stare.

"Hey, if it's another murder, I can deal with it. All I'm doing is examining all the possibilities, and I'm telling you . . . sexual asphyxia is one."

Ott snuck a skeptical look at Crawford.

"Good news is," Rutledge said with a sneer, "if it's a murder, at least I got Florida's top homicide team on it. Already got one you ain't got shit on . . . think you can handle another?"

"It's been only six days, for Chrissakes," Ott said.

"Yeah, and you got squat. People gonna start sayin', 'guys may have been big homicide cops up north, couldn't catch a fuckin' cold down here.'"

Crawford looked over at Dominica. She had edged away from Rutledge.

"So, we getting it Norm or not?" Crawford asked.

"You already got one."

Crawford knew Rutledge had no other choice. Everyone else in the department was clueless when it came to homicide.

"So . . . is that a 'no'?" Ott asked.

Rutledge's eyes got twitchy, his tics were kicking in.

"You got it for *now*."

"Don't go doin' us any favors, Norm," Crawford said.

"I said, 'you got it *for now*.'"

"Big whoop," Ott said, rolling his eyes.

"Don't give me your sarcastic bullshit, Ott," Rutledge said, saliva in the corners of his mouth. "Hey, by the way, heard about your little brawl at the Hard Case . . . out there making us proud again."

A uniform looked over, like he might have to jump in between them.

"Whoa," Ott said, raising his hands, "we were just sitting there when this asshole sucker punched Charlie."

"Just minding your own business, huh?"

"Talking over the Bill case, as a matter of fact," said Ott. Rutledge just shook his head in disgust and walked off. Crawford shot Ott a glance.

"I know," Ott said, "upper one percentile of world-class assholes."

"No kiddin'. First, the guy's dead sure it's the same perp as Bill," Crawford said, "then he's sure it's asphyxia . . . make up your mind, jackoff."

They watched Rutledge go into a huddle with Carnahan. It lasted about ten minutes and at the end Rutledge slapped Carnahan on the back, gave him a big smile and walked out. Trying to sell his sexual asphyxia theory, Crawford figured.

Crawford and Ott spent the next two hours going over every square inch of Cynthia Dexter's apartment. They watched McCarthy bag eight personal items and tag the alligator belt. Their most interesting discovery was Dexter's address book. As far as names and numbers went, the book was pretty sparse. Pages C through F were blank. Seemed to be more people in it who fixed or sold things than friends or relatives.

They were in her kitchen looking at it, their gloves on.

"Check this out," Ott said, pointing to a wall calendar. On it notes were written: "Mom dinner seven thirty," on one day. "Dr. Martin three," on another. Ott was pointing at one from ten days ago. It read, "Nick G., movies." It had a heart in red ink around it. But, slashed into it was a big black X, etched so deep it cut through the paper.

"This guy, Nick G.," Crawford said, "maybe we should have a little chat with him."

Ott leafed through the address book.

"That guy made her book," he said.

Crawford looked down at the page Ott was holding open.

"Greenleaf, Nick (Viggo's) 855-3033," it said in flowery handwriting.

"I'll call him," Ott said.

He dialed and waited.

"Voice mail."

"Hang up. Ever been to Viggo's?"

"No, what is it?" Ott asked.

"This restaurant in Citiplace. I went there once," Crawford said, like he hadn't relished the experience. "Nouvelle cuisine, meaning three asparagus and a four-ounce piece of meat . . . artfully arranged, of course."

"Of course."

"How about you wrap it up here," Crawford said, looking around for Dominica McCarthy. "I'm gonna get a bite, then head over to Viggo's. Find this Nick guy and ask him what the big, black X is all about."

He detoured over to Dominica. She was standing on the right side of the bed, writing on a pad.

"So, Mac, check you later, okay?"

She looked up and smiled.

"Mac?"

"Yeah, your first name's got too damn many syllables. Let me know what you come up with, that button and stuff?"

"Sure, I'm about ready to get out of here, too. Give me twenty-four hours to get back to you."

He nodded and walked over to Carnahan.

"So?"

Carnahan looked up at him. "Norm was pitching a sexual-hijinx-that-went-bad theory."

"Figured . . . and you weren't buying?"

"Nah, I've heard his theories before. He's right about one in ten. Not this time."

Crawford walked out to the elevator and pressed the button. He waited, but nothing happened. He pressed it again, but it seemed stuck on a floor below.

He heard a door close behind him and looked around. It was Dominica.

"So you done?"

"It's a wrap," she said.

He pushed the elevator button again. Nothing.

"Little problem here, let's take the service elevator."

It came up fast. Crawford looked at his watch as the door opened. It was one fifteen.

"How 'bout I buy you lunch? I was headed over to Green's."

"Sure, but I'm warning you . . . I'm no cheap date. I got a big appetite."

TWENTY-ONE

Nick had just spent two and a half hours at the Poinciana. He had pulled it off. Brilliantly, in fact. That was one of his new, favorite words. *Brilliant.* A Brit thing. He noticed the chic young things said it all the time and he had added it to his daily vocabulary.

Nick had simply walked into the Poinciana, gone to the main desk and said he was Avery Robertson, Spencer Robertson's grandson. The woman at the desk smiled and welcomed him. Then he explained that he hadn't been to the club in a while, and asked her to remind him where the dining room was. She suggested that since it was such a nice day, maybe he'd prefer having "luncheon" outside. Yes, indeed he would, he said, that would be "fabulous." She gave him directions to the terrace, which overlooked the first tee and the putting green.

He had vichyssoise and iced tea, followed by lobster tail and arugula salad. At the end of his lunch, he started to reach for his wallet. But instead of taking his credit card, the waitress asked him for his number. His number? Then he remembered. Oh, yes . . . Cynthia Dexter had told him how every member had their own account number so they could charge anything they wanted. Nothing so crass as credit cards or cash at the Poinciana. He explained to the waitress that he hadn't used the club in a long time and was sorry but had forgotten what his number was. She assured him, with a wink, that was no problem, a lot of members forgot. Then it dawned on him . . . ah, yes, older members forgot a lot at their age.

He watched golfers bustle over to the driving range and foursomes teeing off, then saw three pretty young women sit down a few tables away. He was sure he saw one glance over at him several times. He knew he looked stylish and eligible. Not to mention his sensuous, new lips, and blazing azure blue eyes. He had gotten new contacts. He had always wanted blue eyes.

After lunch he got up from the table and smiled at the woman a few tables away. She returned it, and didn't break eye contact for what seemed like an eternity. He went back inside the club, walking on air. He wandered around, feeling like he belonged. He went into a room where backgammon tables were set up in one corner. Two men were sitting across from each other at one.

He walked over and nodded to one, then looked down at the table.

"How's it going?" one of them said, smiling.

"Gentlemen," Nick said, with a little nod.

The other man, studying his next move, didn't look up. He moved one of his pieces, then finally glanced at Nick. He stared at him for a few seconds, not acknowledging him, then looked back down at his board. Nick knew the type. Damned if they'd say hello if they didn't know you. Or maybe decided if he didn't know you, you probably weren't worth knowing.

"You play?" the friendly one asked.

Yeah, but a fucked-up version, Nick thought.

"Oh, you know, *un peu"* Nick said, thrusting out his hand. "Avery Robertson."

"Related to Spencer?" the man asked, shaking hands.

"Grandson."

"I'm Bill McCullough."

The other one looked at Nick and nodded curtly, his acknowledgment that at least Nick was related to some-one of consequence.

"Ward Jaynes," the man said, no handshake.

Nick remembered that was a name Cynthia Dexter had mentioned. One of the three richest members of the Poinciana.

He went back to watching them play. They played a way different game than the one he, Alcie and Spencer did. They seemed to ponder what they were going to do next instead of just sliding their pieces around. He watched, fascinated, as they took turns and after awhile the game began to make sense. For a few minutes, no one said anything. Then after Bill McCullough hit two of Jaynes's men with a double six, Nick leaned forward and whispered, "double him."

Ward Jaynes heard him, looked up and scowled.

"Hey, you mind," he said, glaring at Nick, "we don't need any goddamn kibitzers here."

Nick had no idea what the word meant.

"It's okay, Ward," Bill McCullough said with a smile, "I was going to do it anyway."

Ward Jaynes was still fuming. A waiter brought the two men drinks.

"Sorry," Nick said, "I'll keep my advice to myself."

"Goddamn right you will," Ward Jaynes muttered into the board.

Bill McCullough smiled to Nick that it was okay.

Nick took silent satisfaction when McCullough won the game after Jaynes accepted his double. The two of them set up their pieces for the next game and Nick looked around the luxuriously appointed but low-key room. It was fine and comfortable and not the slightest bit ostentatious. He could get used to this way of life. The life of a clubman. He felt again that this was where he was meant to be. He had come a long way from the Portuguese section of Mineola.

The thought crossed his mind about needing someone to propose him for membership. Not right away, of course.

Why not Bill McCullough? He could see them becoming fast friends.

He felt triumphant. His first foray into the upper reaches of Palm Beach society had been a resounding success. As for this Jaynes character . . . Nick wouldn't be asking him to write him a letter anytime soon. He was sure there were plenty of other members he would meet who would be happy to do it.

He clapped McCullough on the back.

"Well, old sport," he said, "nice to meet you, I've got a tee time in a half hour. Need to go hit some on the range."

McCullough nodded and smiled pleasantly, then Nick walked toward the door.

Ward Jaynes caught McCullough's eye when Nick was out of earshot.

"'Old sport?'" Jaynes rolled his eyes. "You gotta be *kidding* me."

TWENTY-TWO

Green's, a block from the Palm Beach Princess, was a combination restaurant and general store, with everything from overpriced flip-flops to tasty hamburgers and salads. Located at the corner of Sunrise and County Road, construction guys on lunch break were dumping ketchup onto egg and onion sandwiches, right next to Tory Burch look-alikes picking at green salads lightly sprinkled with balsamic vinaigrette. It was a place where the chic rubbed shoulders with their plumber, and felt better for the experience.

Crawford held Dominica's chair.

"Hey, Charlie," said a waitress, "new girlfriend?"

"Christ," Crawford said under his breath.

"Cute," the waitress said, as if Dominica weren't there, "except the jacket."

"You mean 'cause it's plastic?" Crawford said.

The waitress laughed.

"It's not plastic," Dominica said.

Crawford grabbed a sleeve.

"What is it then?"

"A special material bullets bounce off of," she said, straight-faced.

"Oh, I see," Crawford said, taking a sip of water.

The waitress, pad in hand, came over. "So what are you two gonna have?"

Crawford motioned to Dominica.

"Chicken salad sandwich on wheat toast, please, a bowl of clam chowder and a large coleslaw."

"I see what you mean," Crawford said.

"Told you . . . growing girl," Dominica said. "Wait 'til the banana split for dessert."

"Seriously?"

"Yeah, with a bunch of cherries and a can of Cool Whip."

The waitress snorted a laugh. "And how 'bout you, Charlie?"

"Just a hamburger." Then he added, "I feel like a wimp."

The waitress smiled and walked toward the kitchen.

Crawford saw the two out of the corner of his eye as they walked in the front door.

It was Lil with a younger man in a green golf cap. He had dirty blond hair fluffed out on the sides. He was wearing a pair of funny-looking slipper shoes Crawford had seen around. Little red devils on 'em.

Cute.

Lil sat down with her back to Crawford a few tables away.

The young guy was probably a client. Lil took them out all the time, he knew. Breakfast, lunch and dinner—part of that schmoozing thing people in the art world did.

Crawford ducked down a little and put a hand up to the side of his head.

Dominica leaned forward, and whispered, "Who are you trying not to get spotted by?"

"What do you mean?"

"Come on, Charlie, I'm not just fingerprints and DNA."

He smiled, straightened out and stood up.

He figured it was better to say hello now than have her spot him later.

"Just gonna say hi."

"Sure, go ahead," Dominica said, digging into her coleslaw.

He heard Lil say something about the man's "baby blues" as he walked up to their table.

"Hi, Lil."

"Well, Charlie, how nice to see you," she said, turning up the flirtatious smile. He wondered if she was even conscious she did it.

Crawford turned to the younger guy.

"Hi," he said, "Charlie Crawford."

"Hi," said the guy, "nice to meet you."

The waitress placed menus in front of them.

"So . . . how's everything at the gallery?"

"Oh, you know, okay, but we're still in the middle of this damn depression they insist on calling a recession."

"Yeah, I hear you."

He just nodded and stood there.

"Well," he said after a few awkward seconds, "just thought I'd say 'hi.'"

"Good to see you, Charlie," she said. "Oh, hey, Charlie, my friend here . . . he's got all kinds of time on his hands, and talk about party animals!"

The man looked at her funny. Like where'd that come from? He had no clue what she was talking about.

Lil winked at Crawford.

He returned to his table thinking, chalk one up for Lil.

"Did you miss me?" he said to Dominica, as he sat back down.

She smiled.

"Oh, yes, desperately, I thought you'd *never* come back. Who were your friends?"

"Just some guy," he said. "And a woman I . . . used to know."

TWENTY-THREE

Crawford double-parked at Citiplace, an upscale urban mall that had come in five or ten years back and immediately became the retail and social focal point of West Palm. It had stolen the limelight from Clematis Street, which was always going through boom and bust cycles. The complex's restaurants and sixteen-screen movie theater were magnets that pulled people over the bridge from Palm Beach as well as tourists and locals from miles around.

Crawford walked into Viggo's. It was two thirty in the afternoon and the lunch crowd had come and gone. He went up to the bartender on duty.

"Hi, name's Crawford, Palm Beach police, guy named Nick Greenleaf work here?"

"Used to," said the guy tending bar, "up until about a week ago. Damn good bartender, he was."

Crawford moved closer and put his hands on the brass railing.

"Know where he is now?"

"Sorry, just know he quit."

"You know why?"

The bartender shook his head.

"Any idea where he lives?"

"The Palm Beach Princess, I think," the bartender said, "had a room there, don't know if he still does."

Crawford had been to the hotel once before. Despite its grandiose name, it was a glorified flophouse, a fleabag right smack in the middle of one of the richest towns in America.

"Thanks," Crawford said, peeling a card off the short stack in his wallet. "You see him, ask him to give me a call, will you?"

"Sure."

Crawford figured that was probably the waste of a perfectly good card.

Ten minutes later he was at the the Palm Beach Princess. About all you could say for the place was it had good bones. That maybe fifty years ago it had been nice and cockroach-free. Since then, it had been converted into a bunch of one- and two-room condos. Still had a lot of elaborate architectural flourishes and finishes that would cost a fortune to reproduce today. But now they were covered with a layer of yellow brown film and, in the corners, thick cobwebs. Crawford walked toward the lobby desk and imagined how thirty years ago it was a prosperous, upscale hotel. Whatever it had been, it no longer was.

The guy at the desk looked like Lurch from the Addams family and wore a Salvation Army suit that looked like he might have slept in it.

Crawford flashed his ID and asked to speak to the manager.

The man pointed to an office across the lobby, next to a dimly lit shop that sold T-shirts in neon colors that said, "PB for Me" and had the largest selection of condoms Crawford had ever seen.

He stepped into the office where two identical females in their forties sat in matching faux leather chairs. The walls were bare except for a picture of the two at Disney World.

"Hi, I'm Detective Crawford," he said. "Which of you ladies is the manager?"

"We're comanagers," they said in unison.

One of them pointed to an empty chair, but Crawford, eyeing its moldy patina, chose to stand.

"Thanks, but this'll just take a minute," he said. "Does a man named Nick Greenleaf live here?"

"Formerly known as Todd Tropez," said one in a red top and blue skirt.

The other one in a green top and matching blue skirt laughed.

"Todd Tropez?" Crawford asked.

"As in that place in Spain," red top said.

Crawford didn't correct her geography.

"Ten days late on his rent," green top explained.

"Back up, would you, please?" said Crawford, "What did you mean . . . formerly Todd Tropez?"

"Simple. Nick was Todd," said red top.

"He changed his name," said green top.

"'All perfectly legal'—"

"So he said."

"He signed his second-year lease last month," red top said. "Nicholas P. Greenleaf, to be exact."

"Showed it to us on his license," said green top.

Crawford's eyes were going back and forth between them like he was watching a ping pong game.

"Didn't matter to us—"

"Coulda called himself Santa Claus for all we cared—"

"—long as his check didn't bounce."

"Is he here now?" Crawford asked.

The sisters looked at each other.

"No," red top said.

"We haven't seen him in—" green top shrugged.

"—over a week."

They nodded in unison.

"You think he might have left town?"

"I don't know, maybe—"

"Did Nick have any friends . . . who visited him here?"

They both looked at each other as if to say, "you field this one, sis."

Finally, green top said: "Occasionally . . . he'd have a lady friend over."

Crawford could see it was a sore subject.

"Come on ladies," Crawford said, mustering up his cajoling smile. "A few details, please?"

"We had to tell him to keep it quiet a couple times," said red top.

"Keep what quiet?"

"You know," green top said, her face getting red.

"Having sex," red top blurted, "it disturbed the neighbors."

"Yeah . . . the neighbors three blocks away."

They both howled with laughter.

Crawford decided to get a warrant as quickly as possible, then have a nice, long look at Greenleaf's room.

"His rent's past due," red top said again.

"You mentioned that."

"He used to be one we could count on": green top.

"First of the month": red top.

"Back when he was Todd": green top.

They nodded in unison again.

This guy—whether he went by Todd, Nick or Santa Claus—had piqued Crawford's interest big time. Specifically, why he went from someone with a heart around his name on the vic's calendar to being X'ed out with the violent slash of a pen. And why he had disappeared from the Princess all of a sudden.

"I have a favor to ask you ladies," Crawford said.

They perked up like two schoolgirls.

"Sure, Detective."

"If I get a man over here this afternoon, to do a drawing of Greenleaf, could you describe him?"

The sisters looked at each other.

"You mean . . . a sketch artist?" red top asked.

"Exactly."

"We could describe him to a T," green top said, her head bobbing with excitement.

"Right down to that mole on his left cheek," red top said.

"And that cute little cowlick. Sure, Detective, send him over—"

"—we're very good observers—"

"—and in this place, trust me, there's a lot to observe."

Crawford trusted her.

He thanked them and walked out of the office.

On the sidewalk he took out his cell and called West Palm PD. He asked for a captain there he knew. Whenever he ran into the guy, he always grilled Crawford about his New York collars. Like a Denver Bronco fan getting Peyton Manning to describe his greatest touchdowns. The captain was on duty and said he'd get the sketch guy right over.

Crawford wasn't so lucky about getting the warrant. The judge he called was "indisposed," Crawford was told, which probably meant out playing eighteen. Crawford had heard the guy had a four handicap. The judge's secretary urged Crawford to be patient, saying he'd get back to Crawford as soon as possible.

Patience was not a Crawford virtue.

He tried another judge and struck out with him, too.

He got into his car and just sat there, thinking. Two murders in a week in Palm Beach, after having gone fifteen years homicide-free. Was there a connection between the two or just someone trying to make it look that way?

The Bill killing had to have been at least two guys. One of them was a bull, too, lifting up the 200-pound Darryl Bill a couple feet off the ground. Probably the same guy who worked the kid over until he was out cold. Like Dominica said, that scene had clearly been sanitized, a professional hit, most likely meant to send a message. Two guys almost surely hired by somebody—the leading candidate being

Ward Jaynes—in an attempt to take out a minor-league irritant, maybe.

As far as Cynthia Dexter . . . it could have been two guys. But that was unlikely. His hunch was, thanks in part to Dominica McCarthy's input, that it was just one guy. He had either been spooked and had to get out of there quick or he was an amateur, and wasn't big on cleanup. Not that it couldn't have been the same two guys who did Darryl Bill. Maybe they heard someone coming and beat it out of there. If it was just one, who had nothing to do with the Bill murder, obviously, he was going the copycat route.

Next on Crawford's agenda was to dig in on possible links between Darryl Bill and Nick Greenleaf. Then Cynthia Dexter and Darryl Bill, and also Ward Jaynes and Cynthia Dexter. Last of all, Jaynes and Greenleaf. He and Ott were going to have their hands full.

Crawford felt psyched all of a sudden. A warm, pulsing rush shot through him.

He had never been the fastest guy to clear a case, but he almost always got it done.

He started up his car and called Ott. Told him he was going to Q & A Cynthia Dexter's boss at the Poinciana, David Ponton. Cynthia had worked there for close to twenty years, and he figured Ponton could shed some light on her life. He told Ott the West Palm sketch guy would get the drawing of Greenleaf over to the Palm Beach station as soon as he was done. Ott said he'd make copies of it, then hit the street. See if somebody recognized Nick Greenleaf as more than just a guy who made a mean martini.

TWENTY-FOUR

Having conquered the club world, or at least having gotten off to a very impressive start, Nick knew it was time to add a classy girlfriend to the mix. One who would not just look good on his arm, but might enhance his economic condition as well. Lil Fonseca fit the bill. So far everything had gone fine. They had had a nice lunch at Green's Pharmacy, even though he didn't get her weird comment about him being a party animal.

Next, he wanted to impress her with his adopted grandfather's big house. Find a way to imply that he'd be inheriting it and the vast fortune that went along with it. Having a butler bowing and scraping might help seal the deal, but since Alcie had a tendency to hover, Nick urged him to take the night off.

He called Lil and, to show how in the know he was, chatted her up about the disappointing sales at the latest Christie's auction. He had pulled an all-nighter on ArtAmerica.com and Americanartists.net and now felt almost ready to hold his own with the urbane curators at the Met and the Whitney. He had also gone to Barnes & Noble's and spent a good chunk of his Albaran money on coffee table art books—plus everything he could get his hands on about Hopper, Bacon and Freud.

He knew he had Lil at Edward Hopper, but just for insurance, told her his cook did the most extraordinary duck à l'orange in Palm Beach. Five-star Zagat, he effused.

She accepted almost before he got the invitation out of his mouth and arrived at seven thirty. Nick took her into the living room and asked her what she'd like to drink.

✳ ✳ ✳

"AH . . . VODKA, please," she said, gazing up worshipfully at the Hopper.

Nick had gone to Lil's gallery the day before and had given her a photo of the Hopper. She had immediately called her client, Ward Jaynes, and volunteered to bring the picture over so he could have first look.

"It is just amazing," she said, her eyes locked onto the canvas.

"Pretty incredible, isn't it," he said, watching her hyperventilate.

"Incredible? Are you kidding?" she blurted. "It's a *fucking* Hopper."

She smiled, put her hand over her mouth. "Oops, sorry."

Nick smiled even bigger. He liked women who cursed with such panache.

Her nose was practically pressed up against the Hopper now.

"Want to see my Bacons and Freuds?"

He hadn't mentioned them before.

"Ohmigod, are you kidding?" she said, refraining from F-bombing him again.

"Follow me."

She gazed around the drawing room at the two Bacons and three Freuds.

"Just incredible," she said, her eyelashes batting like windshield wipers in a rainstorm.

"I wanted to surprise you."

She had tuned him out, gliding around the room oohing and aahing. She went up to one of the Bacons.

"This is . . . absolutely fantastic."

"I know," Nick said, going over to the bar and pulling out the Ketel One.

"Soda? Water?"

Lil looked over. "Just lots of vodka."

She had gone from hyperventilating to breathless. Nick imagined her silently calculating the value of each piece or maybe fantasizing about becoming the exclusive representative for the sale of the magnificent "Robertson Collection." Attracting collectors from all over the world. Or maybe she was imagining becoming a rich society wife. Mrs. Avery Robertson had a ring to it.

Nick brought her drink over and motioned for her to sit. But she was too jacked up.

"Lil, I'm glad you like the collection," he said and took a long sip of his Johnny Walker Blue. "I knew you would. I accompanied my grandfather when he bought several of them. He was a great teacher, invaluable at developing my eye, educating me as to value . . . and you know what?"

"What?"

"One day I'm going to own every single one of 'em."

She toasted him, her glass held high.

"Oh, God, please forgive me, that sounded so incredibly tacky," Nick said.

"No, not at all," she said, turning quickly from the Freud she had been studying.

She slugged back what was left of her drink.

"You mind, Avery?" she asked, handing him the empty glass. "I had a brutal day."

"It would be my pleasure," he said, remembering how good his hit rate was with women he plied with stiff drinks.

Suddenly, he heard shuffling.

"Hello, Oswald," Spencer Robertson's voice warbled from across the room.

This was not part of the plan. The old man went to bed at seven every night and stayed put for fourteen straight hours.

"Set up the backgammon board, Oswald," the old man commanded, not seeing Lil.

He was in a pair of white cotton pajamas with blue piping. Nick could see the outline of the Depends.

"Sure thing, Grandpa," Nick said, wishing Alcie was here to intercept the old man. "Grandpa, I'd like to introduce you to a friend of mine—"

Lil, smiling winsomely, took a few steps toward Spencer Robertson.

"Hi, Mr. Robertson, I'm Lil Fonseca."

Spencer's eyes narrowed as he tried to focus in on her. "Hello, Bill, do you play backgammon?"

"Lil, Grandpa."

"A little," she said, holding up her thumb and forefinger an inch apart.

Nick whispered to her. "He's a little . . . you know."

Lil nodded. "Got it."

They played for close to two hours. The old man wouldn't let them stop. Lil had several more vodkas. Nick slipped the cook a hundred-dollar bill and asked her to stay up longer.

The duck ended up dry and Lil soused.

She kissed Nick on the cheek after dessert and a snifter of Courvoisier, then left. Nick was a little disappointed, after all the drinks she had knocked back.

But still, his life was coming together the way he imagined it would back in Mineola ten years before. He was morphing into an F. Scott Fitzgerald character. One of the ones whose life didn't end tragically.

TWENTY-FIVE

The recent article in the *Press* put Crawford in a mood way beyond cranky.

The writer couldn't seem to fathom why Crawford, the detective who had cracked the Taxidermist serial killer case with such dispatch, seemed to be going nowhere in the Bill and Dexter murders. The rest of the local media were piling on, too, and actually seemed happy nobody had been caught. With newspapers dying and circulation at an all-time low, they could go for weeks with headlines like, "Palm Beach Murder Wave. Will There Be More?" Or the one thought to be in particularly bad taste, "Link Sought Between Hanging Boy and Reclining Nude."

It had been years, after all, since Palm Beach had a murder and now, they had two. The *Glossy*, being the somewhat prissy stepsister of the *Press,* was clearly a rank amateur when it came to covering serious crime.

Crawford, and Ott were sitting in Ott's cubicle talking over the *Glossy's* coverage of the case, specifically the fact that the reporter who specialized in writing about architectural review meetings was handling the murders. Not surprisingly, the stories fell short of hard-edged crime reporting.

The *Press* writers, on the other hand, had a lot of practice covering daily drive-bys in Riviera Beach and were no slouches at murder. Word was that they had staffed up, maybe hoping for more. The national press and TV had reporters and trucks camped out all over

Palm Beach. Greta van Susteren, Geraldo Rivera and their aggressive younger associates, had taken over a whole wing of the Best Western in West Palm, turning it into a coed frat house. It turned out, though, that Greta and Geraldo were actually putting their heads down on pillows in Palm Beach—the Breakers and the Brazilian Court respectively.

All of the local and national attention had a predictably bad effect on Norm Rutledge, who had become a huge distraction, always hovering and criticizing.

Ott had run off a hundred copies of the sketch that the West Palm sketch artist had dropped off. He walked out of the station and was on his way to pound the pavement.

※ ※ ※

HE HAD just finished Jungle Road and was now on El Vedato with the stack of sketches. He looked down at the top one. His impression was that Greenleaf didn't look like a man guilty of murder. Soft features and kind of baby-faced. Reminded him of the towel guy at his gym. But Ott had been fooled before. A guy in Cleveland who slaughtered his whole family, then gutted their two cats, looked pretty innocuous in pen and ink.

He and Crawford had done about all they could to track down Greenleaf, including a twenty-four-hour stakeout at the Palm Beach Princess. They thought about scheduling a press conference and declaring him a "person of interest" or posting his name and picture on the Internet but decided it might blow up in their faces. Spook Greenleaf out of town. Might make Palm Beach even more jittery than it already was, too.

This was police work at its most basic, Ott thought: hoofing down the street wearing out shoe leather. It had been a long time since he had gone door to door. The upside was maybe he'd lose a few pounds. He knew the odds were very long that Greenleaf would be answering any doorbells. Or that someone—a mother, a sister, a friend—would go, "Oh, yeah, that's Nick. He's right here, in the kitchen. Let me get him for you." But, maybe, someone might recognize him, provide them with a lead, move their stalled investigation forward.

He had just left a house where nobody had answered the door. Out of habit he looked up to the second floor to see if anyone was peering out from behind a curtain. No such luck. Now he was standing on the porch of a two-story Spanish stucco house with a wide balcony that had views of the Intracoastal.

He pressed the buzzer and a woman in her seventies, with long platinum blonde hair and a string of mega pearls came to the door.

"Yes?" she asked, fluttering her eyelashes and looking at his stack of flyers.

"Hello, ma'am, Detective Ott, Palm Beach police. I'm trying to locate a man, I wondered if maybe you had seen him?"

He handed her a flyer.

The woman reached for the half-moon glasses hanging by a silver chain, then examined the sketch.

A flicker . . . but then it faded and died.

"Sorry, my memory . . . sometimes I forget what I had for breakfast."

She was eyeing him now, like he was Cary Grant.

"Well, thank you m'am, I appreciate it," Ott said, ready to move on.

She studied the sketch, then her eyes got big.

"Can you wait one second, Detective?"

"Sure."

She was back in a few seconds.

"Make you a deal," she said. "I'll keep an eye out for that man, if you keep one out for Scroggins."

"Scroggins?"

She handed him a picture. It was a poodle that looked more like a Fifi, Ott thought. Her neatly hand-printed flyer said that he was lost at the intersection of South County and Banyan, gave the dog's weight, a phone number, then said, reward $25,000.

"$25,000 . . . wow," Ott said, figuring that probably worked out to about five grand a pound.

"He's all I had," she said sadly.

"Give me a bunch of those, I'll get the word out. I'd advise you, though, to put the $25,000 in big red letters at the top."

"That's a good idea, Detective," she said, flipping back her hair and smiling coyly up at him. "You know, Detective, you are a *very* handsome man."

As he walked down the long driveway to the house next door, Ott figured, the last time he got propositioned was back in the nineties. And she was a suspect, trying to get off.

Ott was beginning to wish he had taken his car as he hit the buzzer on the large two-story Mediterranean. A middle-aged black man opened the door. He was dressed in gray flannel pants, a white shirt and dark tie. Ott introduced himself. The man nodded and said his name was Alcie Luvley. He had erect posture and a dignified, yet friendly way about him.

"Mr. Luvley, you ever seen this man?" Ott handed him one of the sketches. "Name's Nick Greenleaf."

Alcie took it, studied it and said softly, "Hmmm."

The he handed the flyer back to Ott. "Sorry, can't say as I have."

"You positive?"

"At first, I thought . . . someone from way back, like twenty years ago."

"This man's only around twenty-five years old."

"Oh, well," Alcie said, "guess not."

"I tell you what," Ott said, handing the flyer back to Alcie, "hang onto it, will you? Just in case."

Alcie nodded.

"Absolutely."

"You never know," Ott said again, handing him his card.

"You never do, do you," said Alcie, his unusually wide smile revealing a sparkling set of uppers and lowers.

TWENTY-SIX

Crawford came back to the station after an hour and a half conversation with David Ponton, manager of the Poinciana. He stopped off to pick up the warrant giving him access to Nick Greenleaf's condo at the Palm Beach Princess.

Ott, who had just returned from handing out sketches, held one up to Crawford.

"This is our boy, Nick, Todd . . . whoever."

Crawford glanced at it, then tore it out of Ott's hand.

"Jesus, Charlie, easy."

"I saw this guy . . . yesterday."

"Where?"

"Tell you later," he was already halfway to the elevator.

※ ※ ※

THERE WERE no open parking spots in front of the Fonseca Gallery, so Crawford went a few doors past it and pulled into a spot behind a black Mercedes stretch limo. Limos—stretch or otherwise—were not an uncommon sight on Worth Avenue, but this one immediately caught his attention. Its engine was idling, barely a whisper, the New York vanity plate read, "Shortem."

Crawford just had a hunch Shortem was related to Rainmkr.

He edged up to the plate glass window of Lil's gallery and looked in. Sure enough. He saw Ward Jaynes through the window, standing near Lil's desk, gesturing to Lil with choppy hand motions.

Lil sat in the chocolate brown leather chair opposite him, chin in hand, listening intently. He watched as Lil handed him a photograph. Another couple was looking at a painting on the far side of the gallery. Crawford turned and headed back to his car. He figured it was better if they didn't know he had seen them together.

✳ ✳ ✳

WHEN HE returned forty-five minutes later, Jaynes and his limo were gone.

As he approached the front door, he saw Lil alone in the gallery, pacing catlike.

He opened the door and walked in.

She swung around and put her hands on her hips.

"So, Charlie . . . traded me in for a woman in a blue, plastic jacket?" Lil asked, wearing a beige skirt that stopped just centimeters short of her crotch.

"We work together, Lil," Crawford said. "And, just for the record, it's not plastic."

"Whatever, she's very cute," Lil said, running her hand through her long, streaked hair.

"I need to talk to you about that guy you had lunch with yesterday," Crawford said, avoiding her assertive cleavage.

"O-kay," she said, like it wasn't okay.

"How do you know him?"

"I sold a painting of his. Why?"

"How much did you pay for it?"

She cocked her head to the side and put her hands on her hips.

"What difference does it make? Is he an ax murderer or something?"

"How much, Lil?"

"Sixteen thousand dollars."

"A check?"

She nodded.

"Made out to Nick Greenleaf?"

Her face tightened and she broke eye contact. Then she looked back at him and her smile returned.

"Yes . . . to Nick Greenleaf."

He heard a whisper of tension in her voice.

"What aren't you telling me, Lil?"

"Jesus, Charlie, I'm not used to the third degree from you."

"Sorry, but once a cop always a cop. I need to know how to find Greenleaf."

He made a note to go around to the banks, find out if Greenleaf was a customer.

The bell tinkled, the door opened and two women walked in.

Lil gave them an enthusiastic wave.

"I need to speak to him, Lil. You have an address?"

"No, I—"

"A number?"

"All right, all right," she said, and walked back to her desk. "You know, I *do* run a business here."

She opened up a red leather book and turned away, so Crawford couldn't see it.

"Here we go . . . . 6-5-5-0-1-2-3."

"Thanks."

Lil put her hand up to her sculpted chin. "What do you want him for?"

"I need to ask him some questions."

"About what?"

"I can't go into it."

She put her hands on her hips, and lowered her voice. "But it's okay you ask me any damn thing you want?"

"Like I said, once a cop—"

"Yeah, yeah . . . bye, Charlie, I got customers to attend to."

TWENTY-SEVEN

After her customers walked out, Lil beelined to the front door and hung up a little sign that said, "Back in fifteen."

She had a lot to absorb.

She sat down at her desk, rested her elbows on it, put her hands up to her head and rubbed her temples.

She flashed back to when she was an eighteen-year-old, five-dollar-an-hour employee of Paul Pools outside of San Francisco. Her job was to scoop out palm fronds and dead chameleons with a long-handled strainer, then add chlorine tablets to maintain a pool's PH balance. Her rounds included rich people's houses in Mill Valley, Tiburon and Ross, where lots of kids her age squinted down their long aquiline noses at her. She was invisible to most of them as she scrubbed green mold off the sides of their pools. She noticed a lot of $300 bikinis on scrawny, flat-chested girls and made sure to thrust out her well-developed breasts when boys were around. She always wore short shorts that showed off her long, perfect legs.

One of the rich boys asked her out one day when she was cleaning his parents' pool. She figured out early on he just wanted to get into her pants, which wasn't about to happen until he spent a lot of money on her. Until she got a taste of what life was like in the big houses behind the high stucco walls.

She had come a long way, for sure. But now . . . Avery Robertson was, in reality, some fraud named Nick Greenleaf. Christ! The goddamn phony even had a phony sounding name. That explained his rough-around-the-edges thing.

So his whole spiel about having tagged along with his grandfather when he bought art was . . . complete bullshit. And the painting she had sold for him was no doubt . . . stolen goods. And the whole divine plan she had cooked up to make her a millionaire was about to come crashing down around her shoulders. She should have figured something was up when his eyes changed overnight from green to blue.

She could always call up Charlie and tell him everything. Admit that she had just told him a white lie—that the $16,000 check was made out to Avery Robertson, not Nick Greenleaf. That she was an innocent victim of this horrible con man, whatever his name was. That he was living at Spencer Robertson's house passing himself off as Robertson's grandson. She could give Charlie his cell number instead of the one at the place where he used to live. Charlie would arrest him and she'd be a hero. Probably make the front page of the *Glossy*. Something like, "Art Gallery Owner Assists in Con Man Takedown."

Whoopee.

And just how did that pay the rent? How did that cover the cost of the Elsa Peretti necklace she'd just sprung for at Tiffany?

And what about the gallery? At the pathetically anemic rate she was selling paintings, the gallery was going to get foreclosed on like every third house in South Florida. So she'd end up the only nonmillionaire in Palm Beach? That was totally unacceptable. She'd already charged up the white sequined Chanel dress, figuring with what she was going to make on the Hopper, she could fill a couple of walk-in closets. So now if the Hopper deal didn't happen . . . what was she supposed to do? And what was she going to wear to the Fall Ball? The three-year-old Ungaro everyone had seen her in?

No way in hell.

Lil got up from her desk, went over to the love seat across from it, sat down, exhaled and did some deep breathing. She did her best thinking when she sank into its deep plush comfort.

She reviewed the plan that had been creeping into her head and taking shape over the last twenty-four hours. No question about it, it was brilliant. Yeah, okay, maybe it was a tad . . . felonious. But it was so damn inventive, plus the jig wouldn't be up until after the old guy, Spencer Robertson, was moldering in his grave. By then she'd be ensconced in a penthouse on Park Avenue, living under the pseudonym she had dreamed up in tribute to her two favorite artists: Stella Hockney.

Then she changed her mind . . . better make it San Francisco. Her triumphant return to her hometown. They had penthouses there, too. Problem with moving to New York was that too many New York people had come to the gallery and knew her. San Francisco would be just fine. Then she remembered one of the reasons why she left . . . but there had to be at least a *few* good men there. *Right?*

She got up from the love seat. She'd made up her mind. She was going to go forward with the plan. All she had to do was keep a close eye on Nick. Make sure he didn't blow it. Get him to stay put at the house on El Vedato, not go out in the open where Charlie or some other cop could spot him. Just keep doing his Avery Robertson routine.

Hell, he really wasn't all that bad at it.

TWENTY-EIGHT

As he headed back to the station, Crawford pondered Lil's reaction when he asked her about Greenleaf. Best he could come up with was a boxing analogy. Like she had taken a punch that stung, shook it off and came back with a series of jolting jabs.

He stopped by CSEU on the first floor. He had finally gotten his warrant from the golfer judge.

Mel Carnahan was at the desk.

"Hey, Mel."

Carnahan nodded back. Crawford caught a reflection of the overhead fluorescent light off Carnahan's chrome dome.

"Any chance I get one of your guys to check out a suspect's condo at the Princess?"

"I'd go, but I'm up to my ass in alligators," Carnahan said.

Crawford never understood where that expression came from.

"Anybody else?"

"Think I can loan you McCarthy."

"Yeah, whoever," said Crawford, trying to act as if his heartbeat hadn't just kicked up a notch.

"I'll have her call you, she's out now."

"Good," said Crawford and gave the counter a rap with his knuckles. "988-6215."

Fifteen minutes later, he got a call.

"Charlie . . . Dominica McCarthy."

"Hey, Mac, can I meet you at the Princess at around eleven?"

"Sure, what are we doing?"

"I need a DNA swab, lift a print or two. Hey, and thanks for the e-mail on that button."

"You're welcome."

"Zegla? Was that the name?"

"No Zegna," she said with a laugh, "Ermenegildo Zegna. High fashion, Charlie, something I wouldn't expect you to know much about."

"That's a diss, huh?"

"See you there, Charlie."

Zegla . . . Zegna . . . whatever it was, it struck Crawford as unlikely to be a button off a hitter's jacket. Somehow he didn't picture them as high-style fashionistas. Also, he wasn't getting any connection between the killers of Darryl Bill and Cynthia Dexter.

Crawford called the number of the twin sisters at the Palm Beach Princess.

"Margaret?"

"Irene."

"Hi, Irene, Detective Crawford," he said, "can you open up Mr. Greenleaf's condo for me at eleven? I have a warrant."

"No prob," she said, like after forty years of waiting, something eventful was finally about to occur in her life.

"Oh, also, can I ask you a big favor?"

"Sure, Detective."

"You gotta cell phone?"

"'Course."

"Would you mind going up to Mr. Greenleaf's condo, dialing 655-0123, see if you hear a ring inside?"

Crawford had a hunch that the number Lily gave him was not Greenleaf's cell number.

"Sure. I'm on it."

Five minutes later, Crawford got a call back.

"It rang in there," Irene said.

"You're the best. You get an honorary detective badge for that."

"Cool."

Crawford walked out to Ott's cubicle. Splayed out on his desk was a Checkerburger and ketchup-soaked fries.

"Looks like a goddamn battlefield," Crawford said.

Ott wiped his lips with a napkin and looked up.

"I hear envy in your voice. What's up?"

"I forgot to ask you how it went on the street?"

"Zilch." Ott offered him a limp, greasy fry.

Crawford frowned. "No, thanks."

Ott popped it in his mouth.

"Total strikeout with the flyers. Nobody'd seen the guy. Stopped by CSEU when I got back. Nada on prints at the Dexter scene. So far no connection between the two scenes, and we don't get DNA results for two weeks."

"Battin' a thousand, huh," Crawford said, finally grabbing a fry.

"Oh, also, I made a bunch of calls to phone numbers in Dexter's book to see if any of them knew Greenleaf. Tried the name Todd Tropez, too."

Crawford looked up, hopeful. "And?"

"Nothin'."

Crawford shook his head.

"So . . . all in all, had yourself a real productive day, huh Mort?"

Ott looked up and chuckled.

"An old broad propositioned me."

"I don't want to hear about it."

"Smokin' hot," Ott said, shoveling six of the ketchup-spattered fries into his mouth. "This guy Greenleaf . . . slippery as a fuckin' eel."

"Yeah, no kidding," Crawford said, pointing to a ketchup stain above Ott's upper lip. "Tell ya, man, I've never had two cases with so few suspects . . . ever."

Ott wiped the ketchup off his lip.

❋ ❋ ❋

CRAWFORD GOT to the Palm Beach Princess fifteen minutes late. There were eight people in the lobby, clustered, at a respectful distance, around Dominica in her blue vinyl jacket.

He walked up to her. She was holding a kit in her right hand.

"Hey," he said.

"You're late." Her piercing green eyes flashed.

"I apologize, I'm going to get one of the managers to let us in."

He went toward the sisters' office and brushed past a few older residents, who were whispering and pointing.

"Hello, Detective," said one of the sisters, in an orange top, with a wink.

He noticed she was wearing makeup and had coiffed her hair, like she expected to be on the six o'clock news.

"You're Irene, right?"

"That's me."

"Could we get into Mr. Greenleaf's condo now?"

She held up the key and stood up.

"That your partner in the jacket?" she whispered.

"She's from our crime scene unit."

"Like the TV show?"

"Yeah."

"Awesome."

Crawford walked past the group of whispering women, who had been joined by a man with a walker.

"Irene," Crawford said, "this is CS Tech McCarthy."

"Hello . . ." Irene said.

"Hello, Irene."

"Just follow me," Irene said.

They got in the elevator. Irene hit the button for the eleventh floor. Crawford and McCarthy followed her down the hallway to 11J, where she opened the burgundy metal door with a key.

"Be careful what you touch," Dominica said, handing Crawford a pair of vinyl gloves.

Crawford patted his jacket pocket.

"Got my own, thanks."

Irene smiled. "Okay, I'll leave you two alone to get on with your forensics."

"Thanks," Crawford said.

Crawford followed Dominica in.

Dominica walked toward a brown sofa that was shiny in two spots. She leaned over it and examined it closely. Using a tweezer-like tool, she picked up a few small samples and put them in a plastic bag.

Crawford watched.

"I'll just look around a little," he said, not big on spectating. "I want to check out that desk over there."

She was hunkered down on the living room carpet now with her tweezers.

"Do me a favor," she said, not looking up. "Not 'til I'm done. You might contaminate something."

He was going to say something about this not being his first rodeo.

"Okay," he said instead.

Before he sat down, he looked at the painting over the sofa. It was a symphony of browns and oranges—abstract and ugly. He studied the painting. Looked like something a guy would do on the side of a subway car. Not like something you'd actually pay money for. But then again, that dead shark in formaldehyde he saw in a Time magazine article hardly looked like it would fetch twenty bucks, let alone $20 million.

"You got a problem if I take a few pictures of this?" he said, pointing at the painting.

"Snap away." She looked up and saw the painting, "Jesus, is that ugly."

After he took the pictures, he kept quiet and let Dominica do her thing. He observed her from a few different angles as she crawled around on the floor lifting samples. She had thick dark hair that bounced nicely, and a lean, athletic body. Her green eyes flicked around constantly, alert to everything.

"So," he said, making conversation, "I heard about that guy you popped last year, got DNA off his toothbrush."

"Yeah," she said, examining something Crawford couldn't even see.

"Doing a nice long bit up at Starke, I heard," he said.

"Yeah."

"Nice goin'."

"Thanks," she said, down on all fours, "still creeps me out, perp using the girl's toothbrush."

Crawford remembered using the toothbrush that belonged to his old girlfriend, Gwen Hyde, a few hundred times.

"Yeah, I agree," he said.

Dominica looked up, and shook her head, "A guy would use someone else's toothbrush. A woman? Never."

After awhile she stood up and went into the kitchen. She started dusting for prints on the kitchen cabinets and refrigerator. Crawford checked out her CSEU pants. They had about seven pockets and were made of something in the rayon family. Whatever they were, they fell short of Worth Avenue haute couture.

"Where you get a pair of pants like those, Mac?"

She looked up and rolled her eyes.

"Saks," she said, straight-faced. "How 'bout letting me work, huh?"

After a while she reached into a pocket of her jacket and pulled out a pair of glasses with thick Coke-bottle lenses. He had seen them before and knew they were some kind of super vision-enhancing things.

He was impressed with her speed and precision at dusting. Totally focused.

"Anybody ever tell you, you look good in glasses?"

She groaned. "Anybody ever tell you, you talk too much?"

He smiled.

"Hey, okay if I check out that desk now?"

"A couple more minutes."

Finally, a few minutes later, Dominica picked up her case.

"I'm gonna go through the bathroom, go ahead and check out the desk."

She shot him a quick smile.

Crawford got up from the sofa and started going through the drawers of the old wooden desk. He was looking for a picture of Greenleaf or an address where he might be. Nothing. All he found were five yellow pads with a few pages ripped off of one. He looked closely to see if there was a pen imprint on the top page. But there was nothing.

"Any luck?" Dominica said, coming out of the bathroom.

"Nah, you get the guy's toothbrush?"

"There wasn't one," she said, then held up a blue plastic disposable razor blade in a plastic bag. "Got this instead."

Crawford nodded and followed her as she walked out the door. He closed it, then walked behind her to the elevator. She had a smooth, confident walk. Long legs, a nice roll and sway.

When they got down to the lobby, there were even more people there, talking in little knots of three and four. One of them turned and clicked a picture of Dominica in her blue jacket.

"I'm a big CSI fan," a woman said to her.

Dominica kept walking. "New York or Miami?"

"New York, definitely."

Dominica gave her a thumbs-up.

The man in the walker thrust a pad and pen at her.

"How 'bout an autograph, honey?" he said, with a wink.

She smiled and signed it.

Crawford went over to Irene. It was like she had mass e-mailed the tenants announcing a surprise celebrity visit.

"Remember," Crawford said to Irene, "if Greenleaf shows up, call me right away, okay?"

"You got it."

He gave her a smile, went over to Dominica and they walked outside.

"A little tip . . . if you're going to be signing autographs, do a really fast scrawl."

Crawford scribbled in the air.

She looked up at him. "That from personal experience?"

"Personal observation."

He wasn't about to tell her it was from watching Gwen Hyde.

TWENTY-NINE

Alcie had to hand it to Nick, the man was slick. "Slick Nick" he mumbled to himself, then shook his head and chuckled. Just what kind of scam was the kid working? Obviously, something to do with the old man's big, ugly paintings. Big and ugly, yes, but worth big money, he knew.

There was one he really liked, though. By a guy named Francis Bacon. Dude had a fucked-up way of painting people's heads. But he could definitely see it on a wall of his, though.

Then he thought about the old man. Shit, guy didn't even know his name, called him Zapruder, for Chrissakes, which made it highly unlikely that he would be provided for when the old man bought it. Unlike one of those beloved, loyal retainers who becomes part of the family and ends up getting more than the black sheep son.

Alcie realized this was the only opportunity he'd ever get.

Grab it or end up being some homeless guy living under a bridge. Instead of returning to his mother in North Carolina as the conquering hero, the way he always dreamed it.

He went back to the library where Nick was reading an art book.

Nick looked up from the white wingback chair. It was beginning to develop an avocado-shaped dark stain from the back of his head—spending all his time reading all those books.

"Hi, Alcie," Nick said.

Alcie noticed the book was called, *Lucien Freud. His Life and Art.*

Artist? Alcie always thought the guy was a shrink.

"Hi . . . Avery," he said, then looking down at the sketch he got from the cop, "or should I say . . . Nick?"

"What?" Nick said, putting his book down quickly.

"Thought you might want to take a look at this." Alcie handed him the sketch.

Alcie sat down in the chair opposite Nick.

Nick glanced at the picture and looked up.

"What in God's name—"

"From day one, I had a feeling. You were good, man, don't get me wrong," Alcie said, pointing a finger, "but after a coupla paintings walked out the door—"

"Alcie, you better stop right there, before I—"

"Come on, man, give it up, that's you. Even though your lips grew a little. Want me to call Paul Broberg, tell him good ole Avery's back in town?"

Nick put a hand up.

"Okay, okay, let's talk about this," his face the color of sushi.

"Yes, let's," said Alcie. "Hey, I'm not lookin' to queer your action, just want a piece of it. Those paintings . . . I know they're worth a shitload of cash . . . why you lookin' at me that way, bro? Hey, somebody's gotta read that god-damn *New York Times*. Why the cops after you anyway?"

Nick shook his head. "I don't know . . . some misunderstanding."

Alcie gave him his two-foot-wide grin. "That's good enough for me, man."

Nick suddenly looked like he had shrunk a size.

Then he took a glance at his watch.

Alcie smiled.

"You gotta get somewhere, Nick?"

"Yeah, matter of fact, a guest . . . is coming for dinner."

"A guest?" said Alcie, with a knowing smile. "Wouldn't happen to be the owner of a certain gallery on Worth Avenue, by any chance?"

Nick realized just how badly he had underestimated Alcie.

"Yeah, actually it would."

"Wonderful," Alcie said, walking out of the room, "I'm dying to meet our partner."

✖ ✖ ✖

NICK TRIED to get back into the Freud book, but it was impossible. He was a complete mess after the one-two punch of having just seen himself in a remarkably accurate police sketch and having been found out by Alcie. He realized with profound sadness that, even though he had made a smashing debut at the Poinciana, his days in Palm Beach might be numbered.

He thought about Alcie some more. He wanted to cold cock the impudent bastard for the crack about his lips.

He was on the same page of the Freud book he'd been on fifteen minutes before. Lil was late. She had called him that morning. Said she was psyched up, just had a $10 million brainstorm. Wanted to come talk to him about it. He told her to come on over, he'd love to hear all about it.

He wasn't thrilled about having to tell her about their new partner.

✖ ✖ ✖

A HALF an hour later, Nick was pouring Lil a hefty vodka when Alcie walked in. Nick noticed that the former butler had wasted no time trading in his knife-creased gray flannel pants, crisp white shirt and gray tie for khakis, a blue sports shirt with the Poinciana logo and a pink cable knit sweater tied at the waist. Then he looked down and saw Alcie's shiny shoes. Belgian loafers, he knew they were called. But the real shocker was Alcie wasn't wearing socks. Nick had recently experimented with the no-sock look himself and—though in no way racist—didn't regard it as a look that befitted an elderly black man.

After dropping his bomb earlier, Alcie had come back and said to Nick that if he had any regrets about the new partnership arrangement or contemplated any form of violence toward him, that that would be extremely ill-advised. For if anything happened to him, Alcie warned Nick, it would automatically trigger the mailing of letters to the authorities saying that Nick should not only be regarded as a blatant perpetrator of fraud and art theft, but should be taken into custody as the primary suspect in whatever foul play befell Alcie.

Lil was staring up at the Hopper again, mesmerized, when she heard footsteps and swung around.

"Hi," Alcie said, putting out his hand, "I'm Alcie Luvley. Avery's, ah, distant cousin."

Lil realized immediately it was a team scam. This guy was in on it, too. She had to play along with his nonsense.

"Nice to meet you, Alcie, I'm Lil Fonseca."

Alcie smiled broadly and shook her hand enthusiastically.

"I know what you're thinking, 'Avery's cousin?'" he said, like he was dishing with her. "Well, it's one of those things we don't talk about much *en famille*—ole Spencer's little Thomas Jefferson indiscretion—if you know what I mean?"

He gave her a wink.

"I think I do," she said, looking over at Nick.

Nick forced a smile.

"Alcie, we're expecting someone, if you don't mind—"

"I don't mind at all, I'll just go hang with Uncle Spence," he said, turning to leave. "Very nice to meet you, Lil."

"Nice to meet you, too."

As Alcie walked out of the room, the doorbell rang.

"Let me handle this," she told Nick.

He nodded and smiled. "Absolutely . . . this is your department. I'll just get the door."

Nick opened it. He couldn't believe it. It was the arrogant dick who had been playing backgammon with his friend, Bill McCullough, at the Poinciana.

"The kibitzer," the man said.

"The name's Avery Robertson," Nick said, returning Jaynes's haughtiness.

"Ward Jaynes."

"Yes, I remember."

They shook hands as if the other had warts.

"Hello, Ward," Lil said, coming up behind them.

"Hello, Liliana," Jaynes said, "turns out me and your sidekick here have met before."

Lil looked at Nick.

"The Poinciana," he said.

She nodded.

Ward Jaynes stepped from the foyer into the hallway.

"Can I see it now?" Jaynes asked.

"That's what I love about you, Ward . . . cut right to the chase. Follow me."

She led the way into the living room, stopped in front of the fireplace and looked up at the Hopper.

"Beautiful, isn't it?"

Jaynes's steely eyes surveyed the picture. He studied it for close to thirty seconds without saying a word.

Then, finally. "Not as good as my 'House on a Hill, Monhegan.'"

Lil turned to him. "What a surprise, Ward, I do believe you're trying to negotiate."

"It's a good picture, Liliana," Jaynes said, stepping closer. "Not one of his best, though."

"It's a very good one, Ward."

"I'll give you . . . $8 million for it," Jaynes said, "but I need to see something that proves you and . . . junior here are authorized to sell it."

The sack on this guy, Nick thought, insulting him in his own house. He felt like booting him out onto the street, but knew he was their meal ticket.

"Wait a minute, Ward," Lil said, unblinking. "I guess I didn't make it clear, we're not selling it."

"What are you talking about?" Jaynes threw his arms up.

"What we're offering you is an option. You said $8 million, which means you think it's worth twelve. Avery won't officially own the piece until his grandfather dies and he inherits it, so we're prepared to give you an option."

Jaynes took a threatening step closer to her. "Fuck an option. I came here to buy a painting."

"Our proposition is simple, you pay us 10 percent now—$800,000—which buys you an option to get it for $8 million. You doing the math, Ward . . . that's a one-third discount off what it's worth and what you would have paid if you walked out the door with it tonight."

Jaynes looked like he was crunching numbers.

"How old is Spen—"

"Ninety-six and fading fast," Lil said, smiling, "Want your doctor to check his vitals?"

Alcie Luvley, listening intently from the hallway nearby, was impressed. He shook his head and chuckled. He couldn't believe the balls on this white chick.

THIRTY

Ott saw Crawford come off the elevator and followed him into his office.

"The guy in the sketch," Ott asked, "where'd you see him?"

Crawford hung up his jacket and sat down in his chair. "With Lil Fonseca. She sold a painting of his."

Ott scratched his cheek. "Your friend, Lil . . . she gets around pretty good."

Crawford agreed. "Yeah . . . I got Greenleaf's number from her."

Ott leaned forward. "And?"

"No help, it was his number at the Princess."

"You think that's all she had?"

"I don't know." He had a pretty good hunch she might be holding back. "You gotta hear what I got from the manager at the Poinciana."

"Good?"

"Yeah," Crawford said, nodding. "So I go to the guy's office and his secretary sits me down. He wasn't there and I saw this little book. I took a look at it and it's got all the Poinciana's members' names in it. Phone numbers, addresses, these committees they're on. I see Jaynes's name on a bunch of 'em. Finance, Golf, Club Operations . . . anyway, the manager comes in and I ask him a bunch of questions about Cynthia Dexter. Halfway into it, I steer it around to Jaynes. Guy's loosened up a little by then and tells me Jaynes is a big time muck-a-muck there—"

"Yeah . . . but any connection to Dexter?"

"Hold on, I'll get to that," Crawford said. "I'm working the guy pretty hard, but, you know, his job's all about discretion, keeping his mouth shut. Anyway, we go back to talking about Dexter and he tells me how she was like a mother hen to some of the younger female employees. They got a lot of young girls from like Mexico and South America working there."

"Illegals?"

"You kidding? It's the goddamn Poinciana," Crawford said. "At one point the guy mentions something about 'the incident' and I go, 'What incident?' And I can see he thinks he screwed up. Told me something he shouldn't have. So I press him and he gets nervous. Then he says it was in all the papers, he's not 'speaking out of school.' Besides, he figured, I knew all about it. I go, refresh my memory. Anyway . . . the 'incident' turns out to be some affair Jaynes had with a seventeen-year-old girl who works there. Brazilian, I think she was."

Ott smirked. "So an affair . . . you mean, like candlelight, soft music?"

"Yeah, right," Crawford laughed, "more like nailing her in the broom closet kind of affair."

"That's what I figured."

"I keep pushing the guy, finally told me the whole thing got messy 'cause some ambulance chaser lawyer heard about it. Gets his hooks into the girl, becomes her lawyer and ends up threatening to sue not just Jaynes, but the Poinciana, the Board of Governors, everybody he can think of. Going after 'em for $200 mill."

"So how's Dexter fit in?"

"Supposedly she knows all about what happened, she's helping out the girl," Crawford said. "Lawyer puts pressure on Dexter to testify against Jaynes. Says he's gonna subpoena her if she doesn't do it voluntarily."

"So she's between a rock—"

"You got it," Crawford said. "Lawyer figures she's the key to taking down Jaynes—"

"—*shaking down,* is more like it."

Crawford nodded.

"So Jaynes's play is to discredit the girl," Ott said, "or get her on the first plane back to Rio."

Crawford nodded slowly. "So guess what happens?"

"What?" Ott leaned closer.

"Absolutely nothing. Not a goddamn thing. It all just goes away."

"Payoff, huh?"

"What else? The lawyer and the girl get nice fat checks."

"How long ago was this?"

"I asked the manager . . . about a year and a half. Then he tells me—guess he and Dexter were pretty tight—the lawyer called her again just a couple weeks ago."

Ott nodded. "So the lawyer got greedy or pissed through the money . . . decided to come back for another bite?"

"I guess," Crawford said. "One thing for damn sure, Jaynes's life is way less complicated without Dexter around."

THIRTY-ONE

Crawford drove down Jaynes's driveway and pressed the buzzer at his house. A strawberry blonde with a tempting smile and a skimpy thong opened the front door.

"Well, *hello*," she said, jiggling her stuff.

"Hi, I'm Detective Crawford . . . Mr. Jaynes here?"

"Sorry, you just missed him. I'm Hannah, we're having a pool party. Want to . . . join us?"

She pulled the door open and Crawford looked through the foyer down a long, wide hallway, then into a massive room with a coffered ceiling and out through a set of open french doors.

A football field and a half away—was Jaynes's pool. The same one he had seen two weeks before. The perspective was totally different this time. He saw the same woman who was with Jaynes back then talking to a younger woman. They both had drinks in their hands. Then he saw another group of three women—talking, gesturing. There were probably ten women altogether. Half were topless.

"Come on in, take a swim, cool off," Hannah said.

"Thanks, but I'm not allowed to swim on duty. Unless, of course, someone's drowning."

"I could pretend."

Crawford laughed, looked over her shoulder, then his eyes came back to her.

"Do you know where Mr. Jaynes went, Hannah?"

"He's at his gym . . . down the driveway, turn left, just before you get to South Ocean."

"Thanks," he said.

Crawford followed the woman's directions to the gym.

He pulled in next to a golf cart and got out of his car. The entrance to the building was through two columns supporting a flat roof with a railing on three sides. Crawford grabbed the knob of the door, opened it and went inside.

Two big, burly guys were on him in a second.

"Who are you?" one asked.

"Crawford, Palm Beach police."

He saw Ward Jaynes on an elliptical machine twenty feet away. Sweat was flying off his face, his arms and legs pumping like pistons.

He saw Jaynes look over and give a nod to the two men. They backed away. Crawford walked over to him.

"Your usual M.O., Detective." Jaynes wasn't even breathing hard. "Show up uninvited."

Crawford got closer. Five fit-looking young people— three men and two women—dressed in identical white sweatpants, sneakers, and tight white T-shirts stood in Jaynes's orbit, like they were awaiting commands.

"Know why I just show up?" Crawford asked, a foot away from Jaynes now.

Jaynes slowed down. "I'm dying to know."

"'Cause one time when I just showed up, I found a suspect burying a body in his backyard."

A beautiful Asian girl handed Jaynes a bottle of water. Jaynes took a swig, then shot a scowl at Crawford.

"Sounds like a bullshit story to me."

"I don't do bullshit stories," Crawford said, looking around. "This place puts any gym I've ever seen to shame. 'Course I go to places with medicine balls and fat, sweaty guys who grunt a lot."

He looked around some more. Jaynes had to have a couple million into the place. A glass-walled squash court. A long, narrow pool with two lap lanes. No barbells or free weights, just sleek, silver machines, so glossy they looked wet. Every piece, he figured, was either brand new or cleaned and polished daily.

"So . . . I just came by to talk," Crawford said, "get to know you a little better."

"Aww, that's sweet," said Jaynes, putting on a burst of speed with his legs, like he was slashing through a defensive line.

The Asian girl handed him a towel. He mopped his face and forehead, then looked up at Crawford.

"So . . . All-America in lacrosse, three years on the Dartmouth football team, course . . . it *was* the Ivy League."

"You do your homework," Crawford said. "I'll give you that."

Jaynes had researched him just like some company he was about to short.

"I like to be informed," Jaynes said, taking his hands off the elliptical and sitting up straighter. "It's what I do."

"I heard what you do is . . . hatchet jobs. Companies, people . . . you name it."

Jaynes put his hands back on the elliptical and smiled.

"Only when they deserve it."

"Not the way I heard it."

"Well, then, someone's got their facts screwed up. I do my homework, find out what I need to find out, then . . . act accordingly."

"Is that what you did with Darryl Bill, acted accordingly?"

Jaynes ignored him and pedaled harder. Crawford couldn't believe he wasn't at least breathing heavily.

"A word of advice," Jaynes said, finally. "I've been very tolerant of you, but I wouldn't show up a third time thinking you can throw around accusations."

"The third time I show up is usually when I make my arrest."

Jaynes slowed down again, sweat dripping off his face now. He climbed off the elliptical machine and walked over to Crawford. He got almost nose to nose with him. Crawford smelled something stronger than sweat. He wondered if endorphins or testosterone had a scent.

"You ever box, Detective?"

"Couple times in college, why?"

"I got a ring over there," Jaynes said, flicking his head, "how 'bout a little exercise, go a few rounds?"

"Are you serious?"

"Why not," Jaynes said. "You're probably ten years younger than me, plus being the big jock and all."

"I got a much better offer from Hannah up at your house."

"Come on, Detective, just a round or two. Fifteen-ounce gloves, nobody gets hurt."

Crawford shook his head.

"They frown on me taking swings at taxpayers," Crawford said. "Know a guy named Nick Greenleaf, Mr. Jaynes?"

"No."

Crawford eyed him for a tell.

"Why were you at Lil Fonseca's gallery the other day?"

"'Cause I like art . . . I like Lil, too."

Crawford ignored that. "Talk to me about Cynthia Dexter."

Nothing moved on Jaynes's face.

"Can't help you there," he said.

"I think you can," Crawford said. "We can talk in a room down at my station, if you prefer. You know, drink shitty coffee together?"

Jaynes turned and, on cue, the Asian woman thrust another bottle of water into his hand, like a nurse handing a surgeon a scalpel.

"How 'bout a little mano a mano target shooting?" Jaynes asked.

"What?" Crawford said, cocking his head.

"I got a shooting range, room on the other side of the pool."

Crawford shook his head and smiled.

"You're not too competitive are you, Mr. Jaynes?"

"Nah, just like to see who I'm up against. I'm gonna take a quick shower and get a massage. We can talk in my massage room . . . I'm not a big fan of shitty coffee down at your station."

Jaynes walked away.

The Asian woman handed Crawford a bottle of water.

"Thanks, so tell me," he said to her, "what do you all do here?"

"Well, John's Mr. Jaynes's trainer," she said pointing to a husky guy with a shaved head. "Over there's Mira, Tai Chi, and Terry . . . Pilates, Gual's the masseur."

She pointed to a huge man who looked like a Samoan Mr. T.

"And how 'bout you?"

"Water and towels."

Crawford wondered if that was all. He walked around the gym, checking everything out.

Five minutes later Jaynes padded out in a thick white terry cloth bathrobe and sandals.

Gual, a square man with spiky hair and a barrel chest, came up to Jaynes's side. His beefy hands dwarfed the tiny, gold Tank watch on his wrist. Jaynes didn't introduce them.

Jaynes gestured toward a door.

"Follow me," he said, "into Gual's house of pain."

Gual smiled. He had little Chiclets teeth.

Crawford followed Jaynes. Gual motioned for Crawford to go in before him. The room had thick, dark-tinted glass on two sides.

"Soundproof," Jaynes said.

So Gual could jump him and start working him over with his gigantic hands, Crawford thought.

The room was surprisingly spartan, lit only by a circular overhead, hi-tech-looking fluorescent light. Crawford had never seen a bigger massage table. Figured it probably cost more than a midsized Kia.

Jaynes took off his bathrobe and flung it over a chair. He had a towel around his waist and turned toward Crawford, his posture military and square shouldered. Crawford noticed again how chiseled he was. He had slabs for biceps, more rectangular than round, but they were show muscles, not the kind you got from working in a field.

Jaynes climbed onto the table and lay facedown.

"The detective here," Jaynes said to Gual, "thinks I did some horrible, unspeakable acts."

Gual chuckled with something other than mirth.

"So go ahead . . . Detective, fire away," Jaynes said.

Crawford suspected Jaynes saw this as an opportunity to show off his dazzling mind to one of his employees.

"Same question I asked before . . . what was your relationship with Cynthia Dexter?"

"Relationship? She was the goddamn bookkeeper at my club."

"Assistant manager and social secretary."

"Whatever . . . woman was a nosy bitch who played queen bee with the girls who worked there. Closet dyke is my theory."

"That's a little harsh, seeing how she just got murdered."

Gual's big fingers were digging in to Jaynes's shoulders.

"Did I say I was happy she was dead, Detective?"

"I heard you had a thing with one of the girls at the Poinciana."

Jaynes groaned.

"I got a thing for females, in general . . . so shoot me."

Gual looked up at Crawford and smiled.

"What about that assault charge?"

Jaynes's head turned slowly to Crawford, his eyes dark with menace.

"One hundred percent bullshit."

"You know, that seems to be your mantra about things you don't want to talk about. I heard you broke her collarbone."

Gual shot Crawford a nasty look.

"One thousand percent bullshit," Jaynes sighed theatrically, his eyes looking pitch-black in the dim light.

"What about Misty? The sixteen-year-old?"

"We already had this conversation."

Then Jaynes pushed himself up, swung around and sat on the edge of the table facing Crawford. His muscles were taut, his forehead red and pulsing.

Then he smiled, retrieved his calm, serene look and turned slowly to Gual. "I want to be alone with the detective."

Gual left quickly.

"Let's talk the facts of life," Jaynes said, after the door closed.

"Okay."

"You're the new guy in town. That's obvious 'cause anybody who's been around knows it's a bad idea to fuck with me. Picture the following scenario . . . you take a nice all-expenses-paid trip down to the Cayman Islands for the weekend. You take along your little friend, Lil Fonseca, or maybe your buddy, Mort the fat cop. Then on Monday, all rested and relaxed, you go and meet with Mr. Alonzo at the Bank of the Caymans. He gives you a key . . . to a safety-deposit box."

Crawford put his hand on his chin and nodded.

"Then what? I forget you even exist?"

"Or maybe, we become fast friends," Jaynes said. "You know, fellow bachelors. You come over, use my gym, we box a little, go chase women afterward."

"One big problem . . . I like 'em over sixteen."

Jaynes sighed and shook his head.

"And two, I'm not really a big fan of Bangkok," Crawford said.

Jaynes smiled and put his hand on Crawford's shoulder.

"Charlie, Charlie, Charlie . . . what am I gonna do with you? You really like living in that dump of yours on Evernia Street, driving that Toyota beater to Dunkin' Donuts every morning?"

Crawford took a sip from his water bottle and screwed the cap back on.

"You know, you remind me of some jock who just signed a $100 million contract. All bulletproof and invincible—"

"Come on, spare me, will you." Jaynes eyes hardened, his patience run out. "You're so far out of your league, you just have no clue. To go with a sports analogy, it's like a Triple-A farm team from Sheboygan up against the Yankees. So what I'm going to do for you is even it up, level the playing field a little—"

Jaynes took a step closer.

"And what I'm going to do is give you what every cop dreams of. I'm going to give you a full confession, Charlie, so listen carefully," Jaynes said, and a demonic look spread across his face.

"I killed that kid. I strangled the little redneck at Mellor Park. He thought he was meeting me to get a nice, big, fat check. He had absolutely no idea who he was dealing with. It was so easy. And you know what I really liked about it? Watching the expression change in his eyes. And the sounds he made. You know what, Charlie . . . I liked it so much, I could even see doing it again."

THIRTY-TWO

"No, Mort," Crawford said into his cell, a few minutes after leaving Jaynes's gym, "I think I can say with certainty, that in all my years in law enforcement, that's the first time that's ever happened."

"So what happened after he strangled the kid?" Ott asked, tapping his foot on the floor and a pencil on his desk at the same time.

"He had everything all set up. After he strangled him, he called a guy, who called another guy, who called two guys, who went and hung him up on the banyan."

"Ho-ly shit."

Crawford pulled over on the side of South Ocean Road. He was having trouble driving and concentrating on what he was saying.

Ott just kept tapping his pencil.

"He said he liked it, he wouldn't mind doing it again," Crawford said, getting out of his car and looking out at the green, murky ocean.

Ott tapped harder. The lead on his pencil snapped and, without a pause, he picked up another one.

"So what do we do, Charlie?"

"Well, I been thinking about that," Crawford said, looking at an older woman pick up a seashell a hundred feet away. "I could go to Rutledge and say, 'Guess what Norm, Jaynes confessed. Told me he did the kid, strangled him.' And he'd say something like, 'That's great, Charlie, congratulations, you got him locked up?' Then I'd go, 'No, Norm, problem was he wouldn't put it in writing.' And he'd go, 'Well, then, Charlie, it's kind of worthless, isn't it . . . you sure he told you?' And I'd say, 'I'm sure.' And then he'd say, 'So Charlie, why don't you just trot him down to the station and put him in a room with Jeanie the stenographer. Think you could get him to do that, Charlie'? And then I'd go, 'Ummm, probably not, Norm.' And he'd go, 'Well, then, maybe you better just forget this ever happened—if it did, that is—you know, keep this little story to yourself.'"

Nothing from Ott.

"You know, Mort, there's only one way to play this," Crawford said, looking out at a tanker a few miles from shore. "We don't say anything about it to anybody. Especially Rutledge."

"Yeah, I guess you're right."

"You understand why, right?"

"Yeah, I get it," Ott said, "'Cause Rutledge'll use it against us. Chumps couldn't catch Jaynes even after he confessed. Or maybe spin it like you just made the whole thing up."

"Yeah, exactly."

Ott drummed his desk a few more times.

"This is really fucked up you know, Charlie," Ott said. "Hey, let me ask you, did Jaynes say anything about—"

"Cynthia Dexter? Yes. That he had nothing to do with it."

"You believe him?"

"I think so . . . but I'm not sure. I'm not sure about anything he says."

Crawford watched the woman toss a shell back down on the beach.

"You know, Charlie . . . this guy's a major-league freak."

Crawford watched the woman put a towel down, sit down on it and stare out at the green, murky ocean.

"Fine line maybe . . . between a freak and a genius, huh Mort?"

"That's profound, Charlie, very profound."

THIRTY-THREE

Fulbright and Donnie were in a redneck dive on Dixie Highway, just south of Lake Worth. Or Lake Worthless, as Fulbright called Donnie's hometown, just to piss him off.

Fulbright raised a shot of tequila and downed it.

It was three in the afternoon and Donnie was glued to a soap opera on the wall behind the bar.

"Look around this dump," Fulbright said, his contemptuous slit eyes cruising the dark, dirty bar. "Guarantee you, half the scumbags in this place are laid off, the other half on food stamps. Guy over there's been working the same beer for an hour."

"Country's in a world of hurt," Donnie said, "when people are sipping instead of chugging."

"You know, Donnie," Fulbright said, hefting his empty shot glass, "you have a simple man's way of capturing the basic essence of things."

He tried to slap Donnie five, but Donnie kept his slapping hand to himself. Donnie watched the guy Fulbright pointed to take a quarter-ounce sip of beer.

"You're going to rot your brain watching that shit," Fulbright said.

"Got a problem with *The Young and the Restless*?"

Fulbright didn't acknowledge it being a legitimate question.

"I should be doin' your Za-dukey puzzles instead, is that it?" Donnie asked.

"Sudoku, numbnuts."

Donnie kept his eyes on the tube. He had a major jones for the actress who was playing the tarty receptionist.

"Think I'll stick to the *New York Times* crossword puzzle," Donnie said.

Fulbright laughed. "Like you gotta fuckin' clue what it is."

Despite having forty IQ points on Donnie, it was usually a draw between the two when it came to banter.

"I'm thinking about getting a really nice car instead of a house," Fulbright mumbled, after awhile.

Donnie turned to him. "What? Like a Mini? Or one of them . . . Smart cars?"

Donnie sprung a lot of short jokes on Fulbright.

"Funny, I'm thinking Escalade or a Navigator, maybe a Hummer. Big old gas hog . . . fuck the environment."

"Your feet gonna reach the pedals?"

That was how it went. Fulbright gave Donnie shit about his brain. Donnie gave it right back about Fulbright being five two, one twenty.

A moment later Fulbright's cell phone rang.

"Rozzetti," Fulbright answered, going by his real name.

For a full thirty seconds he just listened.

Donnie took his eyes off the tarty receptionist for just an instant to get a read from Fulbright's face.

It was definitely another job, Donnie could tell. Fulbright was taking it all in . . . name, address, method of payment, not writing anything down.

Fulbright hung up. A lot of his business calls were one-word conversations just like this one. He'd say his name, memorize the information, then . . . click.

THIRTY-FOUR

Crawford slept an hour. Maybe less. He could never sleep on his back, but he could think on it just fine. So after six hours of staring up at his moonlit popcorn ceiling, he had a plan. Well, actually more like a concept, but one that could easily make the leap to plan with the proper tweaking, refining and adjusting.

He had never had so little at this stage of two simultaneous murder investigations. On the other hand, he never had so much either. A confession. Now that was a first. But, of course, it was totally meaningless. All Jaynes's confession really was was a taunt. Jaynes saying, "Okay, I'm going to tie one hand behind my back, and still beat the shit out of you."

The reality of it hit him like a stiff fist to the jaw.

There was no way they were going to catch Jaynes with what they had. Because basically, they had nothing. No DNA. No prints. Nada. Nothing at all from the Bill crime scene. And one lousy button with a Z on it from Dexter.

Even if somehow they caught the guys Jaynes hired to hang Darryl Bill, where would that end up? What was the charge going to be? Murder? Hardly. The kid was already dead. Can't kill someone twice.

So what was left?

Creative detective work was all he had. That was Crawford's name for it. Some other guys up in New York might have had a different name for it. Anything from "going rogue" to "operating recklessly outside of the law," though the latter was a little strong.

The way he had finally caught Artiste Willow was hardly by the book, after all.

The chief of detectives up at the Deuce had called it "outside-the-box crime solving" right before he pinned the Medal of Valor on Crawford's chest for Willow's takedown. But the same guy might have called it grounds for dismissal if it had all blown up.

Like most everything, it was all about results.

Like most everything, the end justified the means.

Another case of his, which the press dubbed the Skinny Texas Girl Murders—even though victims number two, three and four were from Iowa, New Jersey and Florida respectively—was way outside-the-box crime solving. And, in fact, a defense attorney for the killer tried to make an evidence-tampering charge stick.

But he couldn't, because it wasn't.

So—once again—as Crawford saw it, his only alternative was to get creative. Or else, there was a good chance Jaynes was going to get away with it.

The main thing Crawford's just-hatched work-in-progress was going to rely on was convincing a certain person—female in this case—that she was the only one who could play the starring role he had created for her. He planned to ask her to dinner, casually broach it, then try to reel her in.

His alarm clock pounded unmercifully on his head at six o'clock.

At the station by seven, he got back-to-back telephone calls from Norm Rutledge and the mayor an hour later. They both used the same phrase; they needed to have a "little talk" with him. Crawford had met the mayor just once, right after he started work. His name was Malcolm Chace and he seemed like an okay guy. They set up a time to meet the next day. Crawford was about to hang up when the mayor said pointedly, "Season's right around the corner you know, Charlie."

It was straight out of *Jaws*. Crawford in the Roy Scheider role, the beleaguered police chief who was reminded every five minutes that the big shark was not just attacking people in the waters off Amity, but killing tourist business as well.

Chace had stopped short of the obvious, that dead people weren't good for Palm Beach's already depressed economy. That it was time to wrap up this messy murder business before it put an even bigger crimp in the all-important season. In fact, the mayor's breezy tone made it sound as if he was saying this ought to be no big deal for Crawford, compared to all the other famous cases he had solved.

Maybe Crawford was reading too much into it.

He was pretty sure that he was going to hear it from the mayor about harassing Ward Jaynes in the confines of his $1 million gym. He decided to head Rutledge off at the pass before he went into full-scale rant.

He was keeping an eye out for him to come off the elevator as he sat in Ott's cubicle.

At 8:05. Crawford saw him come in. He got up and walked toward him.

"Hey, Norm," Crawford said, "how 'bout I buy you a cup of coffee? Make peace. Get back to being buddies again."

Ott chuckled loudly.

"Sure, Charlie," Rutledge said, "what'd you have in mind?"

"My private table, Dunkin' Donuts on South Dixie."

It was about four blocks from his condo, always his first stop of the day.

"You drink that shit?" Rutledge asked with a frown.

As if Rutledge hadn't seen his hand glued to a Dunkin' Donuts cup a few hundred times.

"On a daily basis."

Five seconds after the olive branch had been extended, they were going at it.

"How 'bout we keep it local, Charlie?"

"Starbucks?" Crawford asked, trying not to grimace.

"Yeah, got a problem with that?"

Crawford was going to take the high road. Shrug and say something like, "Sure, man, coffee's coffee."

But he couldn't.

"I fuckin' hate that Kenny G shit they play there."

"Yeah, but they don't play anything at Dunkin' Donuts."

"Who the hell needs music to eat donuts by?"

Rutledge thought for a second.

"Plus Starbucks has wall-to-wall yummy mummies . . . and sweet young things that work in the shops."

Another thing about Rutledge, guy was a lech.

They went in separate cars to the Starbucks on Worth.

Crawford got a "tall" coffee, which he knew in Starbuckese meant small, and Rutledge got a "venti"—the biggest, of course, since Crawford was paying.

They sat down at an outside table. Rutledge had a blueberry muffin with four pats of butter.

"I'll buy next time," Rutledge said.

Crawford had already decided there would be no next time.

Rutledge took a long, noisy slurp and looked up. There was coffee in his pubic-hair mustache, scorn in the slant of his mouth. He leaned back in his chair and sucked on his teeth. Crawford wondered if there was just one tacky habit the man didn't have.

"Ward Jaynes's house is off-limits from now on."

Crawford wasn't exactly blindsided. "So you're *saying* my number-one suspect is off-limits?"

Rutledge gave him a look like it was the most stupid thing he had ever heard any human being say.

"No, just you don't show up at his house unless you got ironclad proof."

Unfortunately, Crawford knew, a confession—unless it was in writing, signed and notarized—was a long way from ironclad.

"I got stuff on him—"

"That doesn't work for me, Charlie. Hey, I don't love that asshole any more than you do, but the guy above me keeps telling me how much Jaynes does for the town. Like he gives a shitload to the Patrolmen's Benevolent Fund and Fire Rescue. Paid for a bunch of new equipment. Guy's a big supporter."

"Yeah, sure, you would be, too," Crawford said, "if you wanted to keep your ass out of Gun Club jail."

Rutledge leaned in close to Crawford.

"Bottom line. You got nothing solid on the guy or you woulda told me. So go fucking get something."

Rutledge had ratcheted it up a few decibels. A couple of customers looked over.

"It kills me," he said, shaking his head, "you come down here with your Charlie-the-hero-cop bullshit and want everything done your way. Maybe that flies up in New York, but we got a quiet little town here, lots of prominent citizens whose feathers I ain't about to ruffle."

"Jesus, where the hell'd that come from?" Crawford asked, shaking his head. "We're talking about Jaynes and out of nowhere you jump on my ass . . . get all personal."

"I just don't see what you bring to the party, Charlie. I mean, s'posed to be homicide Wonder Boy, and what are you doing? Out harassing citizens and duking it out at a fuckin' lowlife bar."

Crawford let that swish around.

"What is your *real* problem with me? What is it really, Norm?"

He stared at Rutledge, but Rutledge just scowled and looked away. A woman in a peach halter top suddenly had his undivided attention.

Crawford wondered why he had bothered. Out eight bucks and a total waste of time.

"It's just this simple," Rutledge said, his eyes undressing the woman, "you and your boyfriend ain't got shit. Simple as that. Let's get out of here, I gotta talk to you and Ott back at the station."

Crawford stood up. Whatever it was Rutledge wanted to talk about, Crawford wanted to get it over with quick. He dialed Ott as he got into his car. Maybe Ott would be lucky enough to be out of the station.

※ ※ ※

UNFORTUNATELY FOR Ott, he was at his desk, and fifteen minutes later the three were sitting in Rutledge's office. The office had too many cute family pictures for Crawford. There was a picture of Rutledge with his wife, Eileen, both in matching burgundy, smiling like no one smiled in real life. Then one of Rutledge, Eileen and their son, little Timmy, in a pathetic pyramid. Rutledge and Eileen were on their hands and knees on the bottom and six-year-old little Timmy on top, looking like he was already painfully aware that he had two complete a-holes for parents. Guys with family pictures all over the place, Crawford figured, were always the ones who screwed around.

Rutledge leaned back and put his hands behind his head.

"I wanted to give you guys the courtesy of telling you I got two other teams on the murders now. Shoulda done it in the first place. This is no two-man op any more."

"So you're goin' to give it the old Philadelphia rat fuck," Ott groaned.

"Call it what you want," Rutledge said, glaring at Ott. "Way it was, wasn't workin' for me."

Crawford was focusing on a black speck on the wall midway between Ott and Rutledge.

"I'm not hearin' your two cents' worth, Crawford?" Rutledge asked.

Crawford kept his eyes on his spot.

"Nah, you made up your mind already, plus . . . I agree with you."

"Thank you, Charlie, love it when you got my back. So three teams, each working different angles and suspects."

"I'm telling you, it's gonna be a fuckin' rat fuck," Ott said again, looking at Crawford for backup. None came.

"Tough shit," Rutledge said. "That's the way it's gonna be."

Crawford stood up and headed to the door. Ott followed him back to his office.

Crawford closed his door and glared at Ott.

"You dumb bastard," Crawford said.

"What," Ott threw his hands up in the air, "the hell'd I do?"

Crawford shook his head.

"Think about it, for Chrissakes. If Rutledge gets involved, running his little teams, he'll have less time to get on our asses."

Ott thought for a second.

"I don't know, Charlie."

"Just think about it, we got our suspects, Jaynes and Greenleaf. They're ours. Nobody else works 'em, we tell Rutledge's 'teams' not to go within fifty miles of them."

"What if the perps are someone totally different?"

"First of all, they're not." Crawford smiled. "Second of all, if they were, you don't think we'll figure it out before those dipshits do?"

Ott grunted in agreement.

"I want to tell you about something I been working on," Crawford said.

Ott put his hands on the side of Crawford's desk and leaned closer. "Okay . . . let's hear."

"It's not all completely worked out yet."

"So give me the basics."

"Has to do with Jaynes."

"I figured."

"Not that Greenleaf hasn't got my attention, too."

"Yeah, I hear ya," Ott said. "So tell me."

"Okay, the key is our little Lolita . . . Misty Bill."

"Keep goin'."

"And her big sister."

"What big sister is that?" Ott asked.

"The one I made up."

THIRTY-FIVE

Crawford was uncomfortable with any restaurant that had valet parking and it wasn't just because he'd have to shell out five bucks to some guy. But the place was Dominica McCarthy's choice, so what was he going to say? Besides, before he sprung his plan on her, he had to get her to warm up to him a little.

Crawford got the stub from the valet, went in, and found her waiting just inside the door.

"Only ten minutes this time. You're getting better," she said, smiling.

He looked at his watch. "Sorry."

They went in, sat down and ordered drinks. Crawford leaned back and put his hands on the back of his head.

"So, tell me, Mac, just how'd you get into this line of work?"

"My father was a detective," she said, pushing a dark strand of hair over her ear.

"Around here?"

"Miami."

The waitress showed up with a Bud for Crawford and a glass of red wine for Dominica. Crawford took a swig.

"So you were what . . . a tomboy who wanted to be just like the old man?"

"Yeah, you know, beat up guys, drive like a bat out of hell, put the little flasher on top of my car."

"So how'd you get into hair and prints?"

She took a sip of wine. "I don't know . . . just did."

"You're pretty damn good at it."

She laughed. "Putting stuff into little bags, you mean?"

Crawford took another sip.

"I think there's a little bit more to it than that."

"Yeah, but I been thinking about a career change. Becoming a cop. Maybe detective even."

"Really, why?"

"'Cause, I don't know, I like a little more action. CSEU's kind of the same old, same old."

He raised his bottle.

"So here's to you . . . the girl out to steal my job."

She clinked it with her wine glass.

"I think it's safe, Charlie . . . so what about you, what's your story?"

"It's kind of a long, not particularly interesting one."

Dominica moved closer and put her elbows on the table.

"You must have stuck out like a sore thumb up in New York. Big old slice of white bread—no tats, scars, facial hair—right smack in the middle of that melting pot of brothers, goombahs, micks and spics—"

"—Whoa, Offi-cer Mc-Carthy . . . you gotta read your manual. Can't talk like that," Crawford said, in mock shock.

"I can when half of 'em are my people."

"By the way, check this out," he pointed to the tiny scar above his right eye.

Dominica leaned forward and examined it.

"You trying to call that a scar? Probably got it in some duke-out at your frat house."

"Lacrosse."

She nodded.

"Figures . . . quaint little Indian game played by rich white boys."

He toasted her again.

"So what made you choose this noble profession?" she asked.

His first instinct was to give her his usual twenty-five-words-or-less answer. But she actually seemed interested.

He decided to tell her the story as dinner showed up. It actually served his purpose, since he wasn't quite ready to launch into the main reason why he had asked her out. It took a second for him to figure out where to start. This was the first time he had told anyone the story since Gwen Hyde.

At Dartmouth he had become best friends with another freshman on the football team named Owen Mars. Fast forward to the end of senior year. Crawford, Mars and another guy were going to youth-hostel their way across Europe before Crawford started his job in the training program at J.P. Morgan. He wasn't sold on being a Wall Street guy, but figured it was something his father would have wanted him to do. Follow the Crawford family tradition. He toyed with the idea of taking a year off, but could just hear his old man on the subject. ("Christ, Charlie? You have to find yourself? How 'bout just finding yourself a nice apartment and getting your ass in gear.")

On graduation day he got a call early in the morning. Owen had been in a car accident. Bobby Wister, another guy on the team, called from the hospital and said it was serious. Crawford told Bobby he'd be there in fifteen minutes. When he got there, he saw Bobby outside the emergency room. Choked up and bleary-eyed, Bobby gave him the news: Owen was dead. Crawford couldn't even begin to comprehend it. There was no way. He had been drinking and celebrating with Owen just a few hours before at a bar in White River Junction.

Impossible. There had to be some mistake. Goddamn Owen was indestructible.

Bobby explained what happened after Crawford left them at the bar. Some local had gotten pissed off at Owen for dancing with his girlfriend. Owen had no clue the girl was with anyone. But the guy had come flailing up to him and said, "Get your fuckin' nigger hands off her." Owen took a step toward him, stopped and just shrugged it off. He had heard it all before. Awhile later Bobby and Owen left. Owen went to get the car while Bobby stopped off at the men's room. From inside Bobby heard tires screeching, like someone had gunned it hard. Then he heard Owen yell, then a loud thump. He found Owen face down in an oily puddle, his belt snapped and his pants bloody and shredded. He had been broadsided by a car that kept on going.

Crawford's best friend was dead. A pile of broken bones in a parking lot.

It was four in the morning. Crawford knew he had to pull himself together and take charge. He wished there was a manual for this. He told the cop at the hospital he'd call Owen's parents, since he knew them. He borrowed the hospital's phone and called them in Bridgeport. There was no answer.

Then he drove back to his dorm, took a long shower and got dressed. He went up to Owen's room, which was never locked. He made Owen's bed and cleaned up his room. For the next hour he sat at Owen's desk thinking: about football, about Dartmouth, about times with Owen and about what he was going to say to Mr. and Mrs. Mars.

At nine o'clock there was a rap on the door. It was awful because it sounded so eager. Crawford opened the door. The Mars's smiles went from confused to sensing something was very wrong. Mr. Mars asked his daughter, Darletta, to go outside. Then Crawford told them what had happened. It was the worst moment of his life.

They were devastated, but held it together. The classiest people Crawford had ever met. Crawford's family and the Mars's went to graduation together. Mr. Mars wanted Crawford to go up and accept Owen's diploma, but Crawford suggested Darletta go instead. And somehow that little twelve-year-old girl was able to compose herself and make the short, sad walk to get Owen's diploma—just hours after her beloved brother's tragic death. She got a standing ovation because everyone knew. Eight years later she got her own diploma from Dartmouth. Crawford took a day off and drove up from New York for her graduation.

A month after graduating, Crawford was still in Hanover, New Hampshire, preoccupied with nailing Owen's killer. The cop in charge of the investigation, who knew Crawford from security at football games, let him tag along, like some kind of kid deputy.

The case had a bad ending. No ending, really. The police did all they could to pressure the guy and his girlfriend. Crawford watched a couple of sessions through the two-way mirror. Neither one of them broke, though. They didn't even bend. Crawford had a few strong urges to attempt to wring a confession out of the guy.

Two months later, Crawford left New Hampshire, frustrated, outraged and sad that probably nothing was ever going to happen to his friend's killer. But, for once, he knew for sure what he was going to do with his life.

Dominica looked a little choked up.

"And they never got him?"

Crawford shook his head.

"That is so incredibly sad," she said.

Crawford got the check and a few minutes later they left. Crawford had decided to hold off on springing his plan on Dominica. It needed some work, more tweaking. The timing wasn't quite right. He had to think it through some more, get the whole setup perfect.

They walked outside and the valet came up and took their tickets.

"Well," she said, resting her hands on her hips, "I had fun, Charlie."

"Yeah, let's do it again; sorry I bored you with all the autobiographical stuff."

"I liked it," she said, her green eyes sparkling.

"Well, in that case . . . I got plenty more . . . not all of it's sad either."

The valet drove up Dominica's car. Crawford tried to slip him a five. She stopped him.

"Thanks, Charlie, I pay my own way."

He shrugged. She got in her car.

"Goodnight," she said rolling down the window.

"Goodnight," he said.

That was another thing he hated about valet parking. The guys always got in the way of a goodnight kiss.

THIRTY-SIX

Crawford wasn't looking forward to his meeting with the mayor. Something about it had the déjà vu of bad boy Charlie reporting to the principal's office.

He was in the reception room outside the mayor's imposing-looking office a few minutes before two. Maybe it was Crawford's big-city bias, but he couldn't see how being mayor of Palm Beach could be stressful or require more than twenty minutes of work a day. He compared the office and its mayor to its New York City counterparts. And there was no comparison. Being mayor of New York was obviously heavy lifting, even if you were a billionaire and got paid a dollar a year. Crawford had been on the job for most of Giuliani's tenure as well as Bloomberg's first term and had seen it close up. How they had to be on call twenty-four/seven to bang heads with union leaders, fight budget battles, go to the cops' funerals, and—oh, yeah—deal with little things like 9/11.

Malcolm Chace was a man who had inherited a considerable amount of money but, word was, hadn't increased the principal much. Intellectually capable of being chief executive of a town that essentially ran itself—and probably not much else. So he'd heard anyway. The one thing everybody seemed to agree on was that Chace had few equals when it came to likability, and definitely looked the part.

Crawford dialed his cell phone while he waited for the mayor.

Misty Bill answered.

"Hello, Detective," she said, eagerness in her voice.

"I don't have anything yet, Misty, but I want to give you a heads-up. I might be needing you to help me. How would you feel about that?"

No hesitation. "In a heartbeat."

"It could be dangerous."

"I'm in."

"I'll be in touch."

He hung up and a few minutes later the mayor came out and introduced himself.

"Hello, Detective. Welcome," Chace said, giving Crawford a mayoral smile and a firm double-handed shake.

"Thank you . . . Mr. Mayor."

"Make you a deal. I won't call you 'detective' if you don't call me 'Mr. Mayor.' It's Mal."

"Okay, Mal."

Crawford followed Chace back to his office. It was high-public-servant generic—leather chairs, mahogany desk, pictures of Palm Beach's better-known landmarks. The Flagler Museum. The Breakers. Mar-a-Lago. A diorama of Worth Avenue from the fifties.

Chace sat down, put his elbows on his desk and laced his fingers together.

"You got your hands full, huh Charlie?"

"Sure do."

"I want to talk to you about two things."

Crawford nodded.

"First is Ward Jaynes. Jaynes is probably the most . . . powerful man in this town."

Crawford noticed that Chace chose his words very carefully. Not "richest"—even though he was—or "most important," which he might well have been.

"What that means in plain English, Charlie, is . . . it's a bad idea to piss him off."

Crawford just waited.

"Which is exactly what you did."

"Hold on—"

"Charlie, please," Chace said, holding up his hands, "hear me out, I'll give you your say. First of all, basic economics . . . you know how they compute real estate taxes in Palm Beach?"

Crawford shook his head, no idea.

"Just go with me here," Chace said. "What happens is an appraiser calculates what your house is worth, then you pay about 2 percent of that amount in real estate taxes. So if Jaynes's house is worth $80 mill which I'd say is about right—then he pays close to $1.6 million in taxes. *Every year.*"

Chace stopped to let it sink in.

Crawford did some quick math in his head. He hadn't made $1.6 million in his whole lifetime.

"One mill-ion six hun-dred thou-sand dol-lars . . . a year, Charlie," Chace said, dragging it out. "Some of that money goes to cleaning the streets, some fire rescue, some into pensions, some your salary. Without big taxpayers like Jaynes, we'd probably have smaller paychecks . . . follow me? Our public services would suffer, too."

It sounded like a variation on Rutledge's don't-rock-the-rich-guy's-boat spiel.

"I got the concept," Crawford said.

Chace pushed up his horn rims.

"I'm not sure you do quite yet, and please, don't think I'm being patronizing—"

Crawford waited.

"It's important to get a handle on this. We're in the middle of the worst economy you and I have ever seen. Goddamn media says as bad as the Depression. So now add to that, Palm Beach's got two unsolved murders. Gets people thinking . . . that our little town's not such a safe place anymore."

Jaws again, thought Crawford. Chace complaining to his Roy Scheider character about the economic damage being wrought by something with the same effect as the big marauding fish made out of nuts and bolts.

Crawford maintained his silence, knowing the economic tutorial had a few more chapters.

"We got people canceling their reservations at the Breakers, the Chesterfield's at 70 percent occupancy, businesses are way down."

Crawford nodded. He had heard the grumbling.

"And, as of this morning, Ward Jaynes threatened to sue the town for $100 million."

Crawford felt like he just took a Louisville Slugger to the gut.

"He's claiming he's been the target of repeated harassment. Charlie, we don't have the time or the money to fight something like that."

Crawford leaned forward.

"Okay, Mal, my turn, I gotta tell you . . . this is bullshit. This is how Jaynes operates. Intimidates people, a whole damn town in this case. I've done a lot of homework on this guy. Spoke to a guy I went to school with, an investment banker. I don't know much about this stuff—all these big businesses and car companies going bankrupt or getting bailed out—but Jaynes made a fortune shorting them, spreading rumors, bringin' 'em to their knees."

Chace started to say something but Crawford plowed on.

"Hang on, I got some notes." Crawford pulled a pad from his breast pocket. "For one thing, Jaynes got the word out that one firm that went under a few months ago, Lehman Brothers, had $30 billion of subprime mortgages. I was an econ major, but I wouldn't know a subprime mortgage if it bit me in the ass . . . but bottom line, every nickel Lehman stock went down, Jaynes's net worth went up."

Chace nodded impatiently.

"Where I'm goin' with all this, Mal, is that Jaynes is a professional trasher. Companies, people, most of all women . . . especially very young ones. And there's no two ways about it, Jaynes killed the brother of one of 'em. The kid was Darryl Bill."

Three deep creases cut into Chace's forehead.

"You're saying, had him killed, not actually—"

"Doesn't make any difference."

"But you don't actually have—"

"Trust me on this, he's the guy."

"But, obviously, you can't prove it yet."

"We're getting there," Crawford said, stretching it.

"Charlie," Chace said, lowering his voice, "I hardly even know Jaynes, but I do know he's a bad guy to have as an enemy. You have to be real careful with him. He was the governor's biggest campaign contributor, owns a majority interest in the *Press*. Guy's very adept at—"

"Buying people?"

Chace leaned back in his chair and didn't answer.

"My question is this, how'd you manage to jump to the top of his enemies list?"

Crawford scratched the back of his head and thought for a second.

"Last thing I do is go out of my way to make enemies, but his fingerprints are all over everything. That sixteen-year-old girl and her dead brother. That incident with the Brazilian girl at the Poinciana Club last year. Guy's a sleazy creep. Like I said, man's got a sick thing for underage females. Let me ask you this . . . forget about murder, what does it do to the image of Palm Beach if word gets around we got a pedophile and sexual predator running loose?"

Chace thought for a few seconds, then stood up and paced around his desk.

"You really think he had something to do with the homicides?"

"The Bill kid, absolutely. One hundred percent. Cynthia Dexter, I don't know. But is it so hard to believe that a rich, powerful white guy could be behind a couple murders? Or, what, Mal . . . is that just a black and Hispanic thing?"

Chace was mulling.

"I mean, come on," Crawford went on, "here's a guy, a habitual sex offender who gets away with it every time. A kid tries to blackmail him for having sex with his sister and Jaynes takes him out. Really, what's with you and Rutledge . . . you think rich guys never kill people?"

Crawford stood up to go.

"And one last thing, the guy tried to bribe me. Offered me a pile of money in a safety-deposit box in the Caymans to leave him alone."

"You're kidding," Chace said. He looked out his window and didn't say anything for a few moments. "Okay, Charlie," he said, finally, "I hear you loud and clear. You made your case. Do whatever you can to nail Jaynes's ass."

Crawford smiled.

"Thank you, Mal, I intend to."

"'Nother thing you should know. When you applied for the job here, I wanted you as chief of police. I liked your résumé. Liked the idea of having a guy like you on the job."

Crawford just waited.

"That's a compliment, Charlie, for Chrissakes. First, I thought hiring a guy who busted serial killers might be overkill. But I liked how everyone said you spoke your mind. Didn't play politics. And, clearly, I see that's the case. So here we are, we got two murders—a serial killer maybe—least I know I got the right guy on it."

"Thanks," Crawford said, with a little nod. "Funny how Rutledge sees it just the opposite."

"Well, isn't it obvious why."

"Why?"

"He found out I was thinking about you for chief when I got your résumé," Chace said, leaning forward in his chair. "That would have been a demotion for him."

"So now it all makes sense. Thanks for clueing me in, Mal. I was in the damn doghouse with Rutledge before I even got here."

"Yeah, I know, sorry about that."

Crawford got up.

"That's all right, I can deal with Rutledge. And, fact is . . . I never woulda accepted it. Woulda made a shitty chief. I totally suck at delegating."

THIRTY-SEVEN

Crawford and Ott were at the Hard Case and didn't really care whether it got back to Rutledge. Crawford wanted to talk more about his plan, but not at the office where Rutledge could pop in on them at any moment.

Ott was telling a story he just heard about one of Rutledge's "teams."

"Fucking Roper gets this anonymous tip some guy's sleeping in a car at the Poinciana and goes and rousts the guy. Guy's sound asleep in the back of this old BMW at three in the morning. Somehow Roper's gotten it into his head this guy's got something to do with the murders—"

The team was Roper and Vendazzo. Ott described them as eager as a pair of Cub Scouts with half the brains.

Crawford had his feet up on a chair at the table, knowing no way this had a good ending.

"So they get this guy out of his car," Ott said, "take him in, figure he's guilty of something."

"Based on what?"

"Beats me, based on he's sacked out in the back of his car, I dunno. Meantime, the guy's telling 'em he's a member of the Poinciana, what the hell are they doing to him—"

"So he had a few too many at the bar?" Crawford asked. "Better to pass out there than drive home drunk?"

"No, you're not gonna believe this shit. Vendazzo doesn't buy the guy's a member, says he's gonna call up the manager. Guy pleads with him not to call, it's three in the morning. But Vendazzo calls anyway and, turns out, the guy is a member."

"So what happened?"

"So Vendazzo wears the guy down and gets him to talk."

"About what?"

"He tells him he's living there."

"Where?"

"In his car . . . in the Poinciana parking lot. Tells 'em he used to work on Wall Street before the shit hit the fan. Lost his job, all his money."

Crawford shook his head.

"You're kidding?"

"No, worked for that place, Bear whatever—"

"Stearns," Crawford said. "Christ, I had a college buddy there. Worth $10 million one day, fourteen cents the next."

"Wait, so listen . . . this poor bastard's house got foreclosed on and he's desperate. Camps out in his car, wakes up every morning, goes to the men's locker room where he takes a shower, shaves, the whole deal—"

Crawford took a pull on his beer.

"—he gave the security guy at the Poinciana a few bucks to, you know, look the other way."

Ott shook his head. "Hold on, how long's this been going on?" Crawford asked.

"Couple of months, living on cheese and crackers from the men's bar, washes his car where they wash the golf carts—"

"You're shittin' me."

"Swear to God, fucking Roper told me the whole thing. So awhile back apparently, some of the members catch on—but everyone likes the guy and figures, hell, they could have worked at that shithole Bear Stearns—"

"So they let him keep doing it?"

"Yeah, everybody just looks the other way, 'til the guy hopefully gets back on his feet."

"Tell you what, Mort," Crawford said, shaking his head, "I got a whole new respect for Poinciana guys now."

"I hear you . . . those guys take care of their own," Ott said, big smile lighting up his face. "So enough of that . . . how'd your 'businesss' dinner go . . . with your friend, McCarthy?"

"I didn't spring it on her yet. Think we might be able to get her on board, though. I gotta have dinner with her again tonight."

Ott leaned forward and slapped him on the arm.

"Oh, you poor bastard, the sacrifices you make."

"Yeah, well, someone's got to."

Ott drained his Yuengling. "Hey, ever see that show, *To Catch a Pedophile?*"

"You mean where some freak shows up looking for a thirteen-year-old he met in a chat room?"

"Exactly, then gets a camera and mike shoved in his face."

Crawford nodded. "What about it?"

"I was just thinking, that fucking Jaynes, a rich version of those scumbags. A pedo with eleven zeroes after his name."

Crawford nodded and held up his empty mug.

"Your turn to fetch, fat boy."

A few minutes later Ott was back.

"I been doing some refining . . . of my plan," Crawford said, taking the beer from Ott. "Imagine you're Jaynes and an envelope shows up on your doorstep."

Ott nodded. "You mean, from Misty's *sister?*"

"Exactly."

"You don't think Jaynes'll find out there is no sister? He's pretty good at doing his homework, as you'll recall."

"I know, but if we play it right, he's not gonna have time. She gives him a quick deadline."

Ott chewed on that.

"Okay . . . but what if Misty doesn't want in?"

"She's in. I talked to her. Wants to nail him worse than we do."

"All right, assume she's in and assume Jaynes doesn't do his homework—"

"No, I'm saying he won't have time to. Gets the envelope with a note saying he's got twenty-four hours to come up with $10 million, or else a bunch of nasty photos gets plastered all over the *Enquirer*. You really think he'll take the time to check whether Misty's got a sister or not?"

"Yeah, I hear ya."

"He'll be hearing the clock ticking."

Ott took a swig.

"So big sis puts the squeeze on him?"

"Yeah, and know what . . . I don't think $10 mill is enough, now that I think about it. Big sis has been around . . . she knows Jaynes is way up there on the Forbes list."

Ott grinned. "How 'bout $20 million then?"

"Now you're talking," Crawford said. "So when Jaynes's guys find out Misty's in the wind, he can either pay her—"

"Or snuff her . . . and based on Darryl Bill and Cynthia Dexter, I'd say Jaynes prefers taking the latter route."

Crawford started to take a sip, then put his bottle down.

"Yeah, assuming he did Cynthia Dexter."

"Which I am, I don't care what Jaynes said. He had motive," Ott said. "Why? You thinking the bartender?"

"I don't know."

"Jaynes did 'em both, trust me," Ott said.

"Maybe, but the bartender's putting out some pretty nasty vibes."

Crawford took a long sip.

"So Jaynes got the goons to string up Darryl Bill," he said, "but him doing the sisters himself is way out of his

- 206 -

scope of expertise. Darryl Bill he could handle, because he caught him by surprise. No surprise element with the sisters, plus there're two of them."

"Yeah, I agree," Ott said. "This is a job where he calls in the pros."

"And all we need to do is feed them a few crumbs."

A smile spread across Ott's face.

"Then we catch 'em in the act . . . when they're just about to take out Misty and Dominica."

"So then they make the only deal they can, give up the big fish to save their asses."

Crawford flashed to an image of Jaynes and the hitters in handcuffs. It warmed his heart.

"You are aware, Charlie, your plan is not exactly . . . by the book?"

"Which part?"

Ott scratched his head.

"Well, there's the entrapment part . . . then there's the blackmailing-a-suspect part. And if I thought harder, I'd probably come up with a few more."

"Technicalities."

Ott slapped him five and raised his glass.

"One more?"

"My turn," Crawford said, getting up and going to the bar.

While he was up there, he dodged Scarsiola's twenty questions about the second murder.

He walked back to the table, set a beer in front of Ott, then sat back down.

"The hell's that?" Ott asked, eyeing Crawford's clear drink. "You graduate to vodka?"

"Club soda. Gotta be clear-eyed and sober for my business dinner," Crawford said, taking a long pull.

Crawford had called Dominica and asked her what kind of restaurant she wanted to go to. She said a seafood place, she was big on grouper.

Crawford looked at his watch and finished off the club soda.

"So you ditching me?" Ott asked.

Crawford smiled, pushed his chair back and stood up.

"In a Cleveland second."

THIRTY-EIGHT

Crawford got to the restaurant a few minutes early so Dominica wouldn't be able to bust him again for being late. On the ride over, a few major doubts about the plan had crept into his head and wouldn't go away. Like how seriously dangerous it was, for starters. What if something happened to Misty or Dominica? Sure, he and Ott would be right there, but they couldn't anticipate everything. The whole thing could blow up fast. One of them could get hurt. Worse . . . killed.

Crawford could just see the gleeful look on Rutledge's face as he fired him and told him about all the charges being filed against him. He'd be sporting a grin twice the size of the Sunshine State.

Crawford decided to either scrap the whole plan or at least change it drastically. Take Misty and Dominica out of the mix. An alternative was that he and Ott could play crooked cops. That they had dreamed up a blackmail scheme after seeing the Misty pictures. Crawford figured it wouldn't be hard for Jaynes to believe a cop would go dirty for $20 million.

Crawford watched two attractive women and a much older man walk into the restaurant and wondered what the arrangement was. Figured the man's bank account probably had a lot to do with it.

A few minutes later, in came Dominica, wearing a beige skirt and a white top that suggested cleavage but didn't push it. He noticed the bounce in her walk again and the sparkle in her eyes . . . and what amazing emerald green eyes they were.

"You look really . . . nice," Crawford said, thinking "hot."

He stood up and held her chair.

She looked at him funny. "You sure you're a cop?"

"Sorry, I don't know what got into me."

He pushed in her chair and sat down opposite her.

He looked around for the waitress, spotted her, and raised his hand. She came over.

"Pinot Grigio, please," Dominica said.

"Thought you liked red."

"I switch around," Dominica said, taking a look at the menu.

"You realize that's the preferred drink of the Palm Beach ladies-who-lunch bunch?"

"Yeah, but they have like five or six."

He smiled and picked up the menu. He could feel her staring at him.

"So . . . how come you got nobody yet, Charlie?"

"Jesus, what are you, Rutledge's echo?" he asked, and took a sip of his club soda and lime. "This place is famous for their grouper, by the way."

She gave him the thumbs-up.

"Why do I get the feeling, Charlie," she said, looking around the restaurant, "you asked me here to talk shop?"

He shrugged and gave her a quizzical look. "You got me."

She was observing him as closely as she would a hair follicle at a crime scene.

"Somehow I got the sense you had something very specific you wanted to talk about."

"Like what?"

She shrugged and glanced down at her nails.

"Not that I wouldn't think you'd ask me out to dinner, just to be with me."

"But?"

"But us girls down in CSEU talk. A lot, actually—"

"Yeah, and . . . ?"

"And, for whatever reason . . . the subject of Charlie Crawford comes up a lot."

"Is that a good thing?"

"Yeah. But word is, according to the girls anyway," she said, "you're maybe more into criminals than women."

Crawford frowned. "What's that supposed to mean?"

She just shrugged and smiled.

"Okay, McCarthy, I'm going to come clean with you."

"I like Mac better."

"Okay, Mac, here goes . . . I was going to give you a chance to be a hero, but nixed it, decided it was too dangerous. You are, after all . . . a girl."

"Jesus, who writes your stuff?" She looked both amused and like she could slap him.

"Ott and I had this idea. Well, actually it was my idea, maybe not one of my all-time great ones—"

He told her about transforming her into Misty Bill's fictitious older sister.

Dominica listened closely as Crawford explained how he and Ott planned to step in at the last moment and save Misty and Dominica, then nail the hitters.

"Wait a minute, '*save us*?' What in God's name makes you think you'd need to save us?"

"Christ, don't get all macho on me. Thing is, I already killed it."

She looked at him suspiciously.

"I'm serious, I don't want you to play the bait. As tough as you may think you are, something could happen. And I can just hear Rutledge now. 'Nice goin', Crawford, screwed the whole thing up and got the cute CSEU killed.'"

"The 'cute' CSEU?"

Crawford looked sheepish.

"Yeah . . . that's what cops call you."

Dominica turned matador red.

The waitress showed up with her grouper.

"Thank you . . . but what if, Option Two, Jaynes just pays the blackmail money?"

"That works . . . proves he did it, plus it doesn't put anyone in harm's way. But it's never gonna happen."

"Why not?" Dominica asked, taking a bite of her grouper.

"'Cause he's gonna figure a blackmailer can always come back for another bite of the apple. That happened to him a year or so ago. This sleazeball lawyer came back and hit him up again. I think that was a policy changer. Why he took out Darryl Bill. Killing Bill was his 'don't screw with me' statement. Guy just might like killing people, too. Got a little bored with stocks and bonds."

Dominica was processing. She took the last bite of her grouper, finishing off her plate before Crawford was half done with his pompano.

"Jesus, for a skinny broad, you sure got a hell of an appetite."

She cocked her head and smiled.

"Is that a bad thing?"

※ ※ ※

Fifteen minutes later, sipping an espresso, Crawford asked for the check.

A few minutes later they were outside.

Crawford looked up at the sky. It was one of those amazing Florida nights where the clouds formed a kind of ghost-like Grand Canyon formation. They had a majestic architectural mass to them and appeared to be dead still, not moving an inch.

"Want to take a walk?" he asked.

"Sure."

They went east a half block, then down a street. They were in the heart of what West Palm city officials called "the new West Palm Beach," and what residents called "the ghost town." There were four or five high-rise condominium buildings that had all been built at the same time—the wrong time. A time, five or six years ago, when demographers and developers were giddy over the 20 percent increase in prices that had been going on for years.

"Bet you could get a good buy in that building," Crawford said, looking up at a brand new twenty-story building that looked eerily abandoned.

Dominica pointed to the three huge retail spaces on the ground floor that were meant to be occupied by upscale home furnishing shops or restaurants.

"Been vacant for close to three years," she said.

"See that building over there," Crawford said, pointing to a new office building.

She nodded.

"That's where Jaynes's offices are. He owns the building and his office is on the penthouse floor. Gets to look down on his four-hundred-foot yacht on the Intracoastal."

Dominica looked up to the top of the building. "Is that the one that rotates?"

"Yup, the Lazy Susan building, they call it, does a slow 360 every day. At some point in the day everyone gets killer ocean views."

They walked east over to Flagler, then south along the Intracoastal.

After a while Dominica asked, "Want to sit down?"

There was a bench a few feet in front of them.

"Sure."

They both sat and looked across the Intracoastal at Palm Beach.

Then Dominica turned to him.

"I been thinking; I want to do it."

"What?"

"Be your decoy, play the big sister. I don't care whether you were trying to con me or not. It's time you put somebody in jail. It's not good having killers running loose on the streets of Palm Beach."

Crawford turned toward her and they locked eyes.

"But there's more to it than that, isn't there?"

"What do you mean?"

"Just a gut feeling I got, like Jaynes represents something to you maybe."

She exhaled slowly.

"Don't overanalyze it, Charlie, but yeah, I've run across men like him before," she said staring over his shoulder. "And they're not my favorite types."

"Go on."

She looked him straight in the eyes. "That's it . . . that's all you're getting out of me."

It was against his nature not to poke and probe.

"Okay," he said.

"So let's go, we gottta solve this sucker. The rate you're going you'll be a grandfather by the time you wrap it up."

"Don't know if being a grandfather is in the cards."

She laughed and—out of the blue—seeing no one in sight, he put his arm around her.

She looked up at him.

"What's this, Charlie?"

"Just . . . figured you might be . . . cold."

"It's eighty degrees out."

"Yeah, but the breeze—"

He leaned toward her and kissed her, violating his cardinal rule about public displays of affection. He found it so tacky when other people did it, but couldn't help it.

He kissed her again, this time putting a lot more behind it. She suddenly responded as if he had touched a secret button. She put both her arms around him, one hand going first to the back of his neck, then up into his hair.

Still kissing her, he put his hand on her back, moved it under her blouse. What the hell was he thinking? In a public place. He moved his hand down her back. She was breathing in short gasps.

She pulled away. Her eyes looked unfocused.

"Where's your place again?" she asked.

"Down Flagler, about a mile."

"Mine's closer."

"So what are we waiting for?"

✳ ✳ ✳

DOMINICA'S LONG brown, naked body had no tan line.

"What . . . you go to France to get a tan?" Crawford asked, running his fingers lightly across her shoulders.

"Nobody can see me on my balcony," she said, leaning toward him and kissing him. "You know, Charlie, I been thinking . . ."

"Yeah?

"The girls down at CSEU . . . they really don't know what they're talking about."

THIRTY-NINE

Nick Greenleaf was antsy. He had been holed up in the house on El Vedato for days. But he was afraid about going out, having someone point at him and say, "hey, you're the guy on the flyer."

Lil was preoccupied, going full speed ahead lining up option buyers. If she wasn't so busy, he was certain, she'd be spending all her time with him, doing the deed by now. He called her late in the afternoon and she assured him that she had buyers committed for at least five more paintings. According to her, that would translate into more than $6 million in cash.

Nick needed a change of scenery bad. He also wanted to execute a side plan, which he had no intention of telling his new partners about. There had been some hard bargaining between them about the partnership structure. Specifically, Lil said she deserved 50 percent for coming up with the whole thing and having the buyers. Nick saying no way, none of it would have been possible if he hadn't become a fixture in the Robertson household. And Alcie, the little weasel, had said, "Look here, you dudes already broke the law. I ain't. You don't cut me in for a third, an anonymous letter gonna find its way to the po-leese."

It ended up being a third, a third, a third.

Nick's side plan involved one Lucien Freud and two Francis Bacons that he had found in the front coat closet, behind a big leather golf club bag and two walking canes. He had stumbled across them one day when he was looking for an umbrella and was positive he was the only one who knew they were there. His guess was that Spencer had absent-mindedly set them down there, probably just before his brain went permanently AWOL.

Nick set his alarm for two in the morning, when Alcie would be dead to the world. He got up, took one of the Freuds and one of the Bacons from the closet into the library and locked the door. The other Bacon was huge, probably four-by-six feet, so he left it for another day. Then he bubble-wrapped the two paintings and taped them together. His plan was to take them over to his condo at the Princess for safekeeping, knowing his partners would never be the wiser.

He picked up the paintings and walked to the garage. Nick got a chuckle every time he walked in and saw the juxtaposition of Spencer Robertson's vintage Rolls-Royce Cloud Three and classic Ferrari Testarossa bookending Alcie's dented gray Corolla. That was another thing he had recently spent time studying online. His next car. He had it narrowed down to a Lamborghini Gallardo or a Tesla Roadster. But for the moment, Alcie's Corolla, with the keys on the floor, would do just fine. It had a good-sized trunk and was unlikely to attract attention.

He pulled onto El Vedato, keeping an eye out for police cars, and five minutes later was in front of the Palm Beach Princess. As he expected, the area was dead. No one on the sidewalks or in the Princess's lobby. He could see from his car that Albert, the night manager, had assumed his usual position at the front desk: splayed out, his head resting on his folded arms, dead to the world. Nick had observed the sleeping position before and wondered how it could possibly be comfortable.

He popped the trunk button, got out of the car and lifted out the paintings. Then he walked into the lobby and took the elevator to the eleventh floor.

He went into the apartment and looked around for a place to hide the paintings in his cramped closet. He put them behind an old headboard that was standing vertical against the rear wall. Then he smelled something. Perfume. Very faint.

Those weird twin sisters, he figured, snooping around again on the pretext of coming to get his rent check.

He wasn't ready to go back to El Vedato right away. He wanted to enjoy the change of scenery for a while, even though he had become acutely aware of the tawdry seediness of his condo. It was funny how, a couple of months ago, it seemed just fine. But now that he was under the roof of Spencer Robertson's stately Mediterranean, as well as having had a peek at the exalted world of the Poinciana, it was time to leave the grubby condo behind. Just as he had done with his childhood split-level ranch in Mineola, Long Island.

He got a beer from the refrigerator and sat down on the couch. He looked around at the minimal furnishings and decided never to return to the depressing hovel except to retrieve the paintings. He leaned back on the couch and smiled . . . life was good, he thought. Even though so far all he had sold were two Seagrave Albarans and the Hopper option, netting him just over $400,000, he knew big pay-days loomed ahead. The days of English suits, Italian sports cars and vintage French champagne were right around the corner.

He was sorely disappointed about one thing, though. The fact that he might never enjoy membership in his beloved Poinciana, for it seemed inevitable he'd have to leave Palm Beach behind. He did take some solace, however, in the fact that he'd leave it in style. Flying off in a shimmering G-4, he pictured it.

Nick finished his beer, walked out of the condo and got on the elevator. Albert was still flopped over on the front desk, but it seemed that he might have woken up at one point because Nick heard Lucy and Ricky Ricardo squabbling on the small TV inside the desk's console, which wasn't on before. He went outside and immediately spotted a man across the street in a white Ford Crown Victoria. Nick knew right away he was a cop. Sound asleep, his mouth was open like a vast cave, eyes shut tight. The man was obviously on a stakeout. Looking for him. Nick flashed to the paintings upstairs. The stolen goods. His golden future.

He crept back to the elevator, went upstairs, got the paintings out from behind the headboard. He decided he'd take them to his twenty-four-hour storage unit on Okeechobee instead. He'd get the big Bacon out of the front closet, too, and take it over. But not tonight.

Then he came down the elevator, and careful not to wake up Albert, set them down against a wall in the lobby.

He snuck outside to make sure the cop was still asleep. He could have jammed his whole foot in the cop's gaping mouth. He went back into the building, picked up the paintings and slipped outside. He carefully placed them in the back seat of the car. He didn't want to put them in the Corolla's trunk for fear that closing it might wake the cop. He was ready to drive away from the Princess for the last time. He looked back at the building. It was such a dive.

He put the key in the ignition and started to turn it. Then he had an idea. It might be a little risky. Foolhardy, even. But then he thought . . . *What the hell, Why not?*

FORTY

The envelope was taped to Ward Jaynes's Sunday *New York Times*, which lay next to the *Financial Times*, under the columned portico of his front entrance. Next to it was a heap of other newspapers, which included *Barrons,* the *Wall Street Journal*, the *Palm Beach Press* and the *Glossy*. Jaynes liked the ritual of going out and getting his papers himself and didn't let anyone else do it. First, he'd gut the papers, tossing the advertising circulars and the sections he had no interest in—like book review and arts and leisure—into a pile. Then he'd scour the financial pages for companies in trouble. Rarely, however, did he find anything he hadn't known about for weeks.

He went into his library, tore open the envelope and saw the four pictures inside a single piece of folded white bond paper. He took the pictures out and looked at them one by one.

The first one was of him and Misty walking into his kitchen. The second was of him handing a can of Diet Coke to Misty, his eyes unmistakably trained on her ample cleavage. The third was of him and the girl going toward a back stairway. The fourth was . . . the one that would ruin him.

Furious, Jaynes flipped it across the room. It ended up face up, leaning against the elaborate molding on the other side of the room. He could see the girl's naked body under his, her face grimacing into the camera. The five-inch scar on his left shoulder was irrefutable evidence.

He calmed down almost immediately, realizing it was just another situation that needed to be dealt with. In terms of severity, it didn't even register in his top ten of the year. He read the handwritten note.

"I'll call at ten A.M. We'll talk about how much the originals are going to cost."

Whoever had written it had absolutely no idea who they were dealing with, Jaynes thought. A pathetic attempt by some lightweight to establish himself as a take-charge, we're-gonna-play-by-my-rules guy. That would go up in smoke in five minutes.

It was just seven thirty which left Jaynes plenty of time to think things through and get set up to deal with the situation in his usual straight-ahead manner. Make sure the blackmailer sorely regretted he had ever heard the name Ward Jaynes.

He took his Blackberry out of his shirt pocket and thumbed seven numbers.

Then he changed his mind and hit the *off* button. He wanted to play out the scenario to its logical conclusion, every detail, every nuance, before he took action.

He thought about the girl's lowlife brother, Darryl. How he had taken the money shot of Jaynes and his white-trash, teen-dream sister. Climbed up on the roof somehow and used his cell phone camera, Jaynes thought at first. But then he realized that wasn't it at all. From the angle of the picture, all the kid had done was walk in the open door of the house, go up the back stairs and open the bedroom door a crack. Misty must have told him beforehand where the bedroom was. Left the door open, too.

Jaynes walked across the room and looked at the picture again, then he smiled. He reveled in stuff like this. People trying to hold him up, extort and blackmail him. Getting them back was almost as much fun as shorting stocks.

He knew exactly what the deal was. The girl had probably hooked up with some bottom-feeding attorney, a guy whose ad she had seen on the back of a bus stop. Similar to what happened a year ago with the Brazilian girl at the Poinciana. Probably some lowlife with just enough of a brain to get himself in way over his head. Jaynes looked forward to the guy's call.

Jaynes let his mind wander to what would happen if the press got their hands on the photo. Then he imagined a trial, on the charge of sex with a minor. He pictured the lurid testimony of the girl, her cleavage splashed all over the *New York Post* and every other tabloid. Not to mention all the other soft porn purveyors like *Nancy Grace* and *E!*

Jaynes didn't relish being the subject of the sex scandal of the week. Because his story would be way bigger than the others. It would be a lot more than a flash in the pan like John Edwards, the straying ex-vice presidential candidate on whom Jaynes wasted a hefty campaign contribution on. He'd be the next O.J., and have a long shelf life, since his story was not just about sex, but murder, too.

Then Jaynes thought about what the blackmailer would try to hit him up for. A lot more than Darryl Bill had. Millions. Probably at least ten. Maybe he should just pay it? Because, fact was, it was nothing to him. But then he played it out. Having spent some time with Misty, he knew all he needed to know about her. She'd start power driving through designer clothes, drugs, hi-def TVs, boats and cars, like a basketball player after his signing bonus. And her blackmailing partner? He'd probably do the same. Jaynes imagined getting the call . . . within a year, two max. "Hello, Ward, remember us . . . we're tapped out, need more cash."

He'd been there, done that, was not about to do it again.

So, bottom line, killing Misty and getting the pictures was the only way to go. He'd need to terminate whoever showed up to do the negotiating, too. Otherwise, they, too, would be coming back to the well whenever they needed grocery money.

He punched seven numbers on his Blackberry. He spoke to his guy, who said he'd call the subcontractor right after they hung up. Jaynes always made sure to put plenty of layers between him and a victim. The subcontractor got back to his guy and said he'd get the two "mechanics" on it right away.

Then Jaynes flashed to the detective, Crawford, and a particularly nasty smile crept across his face. He had come up with something wonderfully, creatively cruel to take the cocky swagger out of him.

He stood up, stretched, and walked out of his den into the living room. The big Kandinsky caught his eye. Lately he had begun to think that it was not quite in the same league with his other paintings. It did nothing to enhance his reputation as one of America's foremost collectors. Plus, it would be totally outclassed on the wall across from the Hopper, after the old man checked out.

He called Lil Fonseca and told her he had a few more spaces that needed Robertson canvases. She assured him that would be no problem. She had always been so good about accommodating his every desire.

FORTY-ONE

Crawford was on his way to Dunkin' Donuts from his apartment at seven thirty in the morning.

He was wondering why Jaynes, the "most powerful" man in town according to Mal Chace, hadn't come at him with more firepower than the few wrist slaps from Rutledge and Chace. And as far as Jaynes's lawsuit went . . . it hadn't really seemed to have gone anywhere. Crawford got the sense that it might go away altogether if he didn't go near Jaynes for a few days. He guessed Jaynes probably had bigger fish to fry. Or maybe he was just all talk . . . though history certainly didn't seem to indicate that.

His mind drifted to Dominica, just as the sun popped out from behind a cloud. The symbolism was not lost on him and he felt a flush. He was happy, a word he considered slightly unmanly. But screw it, it was how he felt.

He had thought a lot about her. How they could have something good together.

In the last twenty-four hours he had probably second-guessed himself at least ten times about getting her involved in his high-risk scheme to take down Jaynes. At one point he started walking down to CSEU to tell her again that he was permanently pulling the plug on the whole thing. Explain that he was killing the plan because it could . . . kill her. But he knew she'd push him hard to do it, because of how Jaynes represented some unrighted wrong in her past, and also, he could tell, the idea of an action role had a lot of appeal to her. Like maybe hair follicles and DNA just weren't doing it for her anymore.

Meantime, Ott had spent a lot of time with Dominica coaching her in the role of blackmailer and extortionist. He told Crawford she was a natural, she had the perfect combination of toughness and gut instincts.

Crawford didn't volunteer that she had a soft side, too.

He put two quarters in the blue metal box outside of Dunkin' Donuts and pulled out the *Palm Beach Press*. He saw the headline, then the byline. It was written by the same *Press* reporter, Barrett Seabrook, who had interviewed him right after he came down to Florida. Crawford didn't want to do the interview, but the Community Relations guy at Palm Beach PD told him it was typical when a new guy came onboard. Reluctantly, he agreed to it.

The reporter had written an embarrassingly sycophantic puff piece about him back then. The headline of the article, he remembered, had read: LAUDED NY DETECTIVE TO SERVE PALM BEACH.

Today's was far different: PALM BEACH DETECTIVE A NEW YORK THUG?

Crawford knew he was in big trouble at the question mark. Whenever he had seen that dubious journalistic technique employed before it always meant that a reporter, battling a deadline, didn't have all his facts checked, but had gotten the green light from his editor anyway.

Then he flashed to what Mal Chace had told him. About Ward Jaynes's majority ownership in the *Palm Beach Press*. This sure wouldn't be the first time a media owner twisted the truth—or invented it—for his own purposes.

He didn't need to read past the first paragraph to know this was way more than just a twist of the truth.

The substance of the three-column story was that although Crawford had been a very effective, dogged detective who had cracked many high-profile cases in New York, a trail of violently obtained confessions or sleazy informers, even lower on the food chain than the perp, had always been in the mix. There were a lot of references to "unnamed police sources" and "retired law enforcement officers." There was one very specific mention of a case where Crawford, "in a blind rage repeatedly administered kicks to the head of suspect Rafael Guittierez, who ended up face-down on the sidewalk."

Rafael Guittierez had been a habitual wife-beater who had come at Crawford with a broken bottle of cheap tequila ten years ago. Crawford would have been justified to drop him on the spot. That would probably have been the smart thing to do. Instead Guittierez lunged at him and Crawford took him out at the knees with his left foot. That was all. But the guy screamed police brutality and there were always ten lawyers on hand, defenders of the oppressed and downtrodden, looking to knock down high-profile guys like Crawford.

A routine investigation followed the Guittierez incident that didn't amount to much more than a quick conversation with Crawford's partner at the time.

Crawford was seething now. He had read plenty of articles about his cases where the reporter didn't quite get it right—a detail here, a name or date there—but this was all dubious inference and flat-out fabrication.

He finished the first page and stopped. He slammed the paper down on the table.

He dialed his cell phone, got the number for the *Palm Beach Press* and hit the seven numbers.

He asked for Barrett Seabrook.

"Sorry, Barry's not in yet," the voice said. "Would you like his voice mail?"

"Yes, give it to me."

"Hi," the recording said, "this is Barry . . . talk to me . . . later." *Beep.*

Seabrook was apparently playing a hip, hard-boiled reporter he had seen in some forties film noir.

"Barry, you lying sack of shit," he said at the beep. "It's Charlie Crawford. Call me. I want to know how much Jaynes paid you."

Crawford took a sip of his extra dark and a bite of his blueberry donut, his concession to eating healthy. Then he picked up the *Press* and read the rest of the article. It got worse. It recounted another completely fictitious incident of police brutality he reportedly committed. Then he got to the last paragraph.

He read it over three times.

"According to a longtime partner of Detective Crawford's, his father, a managing director of the prestigious Wall Street investment banking firm, Morgan Guaranty, was found dead inside his car in his New Canaan, Connecticut, garage. According to the partner, Crawford's father, a highly respected and successful banker, 'snapped' after the public humiliation and disgrace he felt over his son's conduct. The intense and vocal backlash over the repeated allegations was apparently too much for the father, Charles V. Crawford, to bear."

FORTY-TWO

Crawford looked up, and in slow motion put the paper down on the bright orange tabletop. His head slumped forward, then he put his hands up to cover his eyes. He stayed that way until an older woman came over from another table. She put her hand on his shoulder, asked him if he was okay and handed him a few napkins.

※ ※ ※

CRAWFORD WAITED for Barrett Seabrook for over an hour at the *Palm Beach Press* building. He was glad he had time to cool down. He wanted to kill the guy . . . slowly . . . with his bare hands. He sat in a lobby which Seabrook would have to pass through, and made calls on his cell, trying to take his mind off his father. But he couldn't. The whole gut-wrenching incident had been ripped wide open again, bringing back the most searing pain of his life.

His father *had* committed suicide. He was a managing director, but at J.P. Morgan not Morgan Guaranty. His father was a manic-depressive—the "Crawford family curse," as one shrink called it—and back when he killed himself, antidepressant medications weren't what they are today. Crawford was the one who found him. He was just sixteen, back home on vacation from boarding school. He had gone to get his lacrosse stick in the garage and pushed the garage door opener. As the door came up, a thick cloud of car exhaust poured out.

His grandfather had killed himself, too. Depression, as well. They had a quaint name for it back then. Melancholia. There was nothing quaint, though, about the .45 service revolver he stuck in his mouth.

Crawford called Rutledge and got his voice mail: "Norm, you either already read or heard about the *Press* article. It's all bullshit."

Then he got the mayor's answering machine: "Mal, it's Charlie Crawford. There's an article in today's *Palm Beach Press* about me. It's a complete fabrication. I'm going to force them to print a retraction."

He realized the damage was done, though. Ward Jaynes was a pro. He'd done to Crawford what Crawford had done to Rafael Guittierez: taken him out at the knees. Tomorrow, or the next day, there might be some microscopic retraction at the bottom of the editorial page, apologizing for an inaccuracy or two.

Eleven people would read it.

Ott picked up on the second ring.

"You see that thing?" Crawford asked.

"Yeah."

"Guy didn't even get the place where my old man worked right."

"I knew it was a crock of shit, I'm sorry, man. Anything I can do, give me the word. Why would that shitbag reporter come up with that?"

"Jaynes owns the paper. For all I know he wrote the damn thing."

"Jesus, you're kidding, where are you now?"

"At the *Press,* waiting for the guy," said Crawford. "I just spoke to some NYPD guys. They're calling the publisher to tell him that, 'cept for the spelling of my name, it's all bullshit. I talked to a lawyer, too. He called the paper, told them they're defendants in a defamation of character lawsuit."

"Beautiful, how much you going after 'em for?"

"A hundred million."

If Jaynes could, why couldn't he?

Ott laughed. "That's a nice round number."

Crawford saw Barrett Seabrook walk through the front door.

"Gotta go, my buddy's here."

"Who?"

"The reporter."

"Give him a kick in the nuts for me."

Seabrook saw Crawford coming toward him and almost started to run.

"Whoa there, Barry." He would have tackled him if he had to.

Seabrook stopped, his eyes got huge, like he was scared Crawford might pull his gun.

"What do you want?" Seabrook said, his voice up an octave.

"Well, let's see," he said, using every bit of self-restraint he could conjure up not to go postal, "your job . . . a retraction . . . an apology . . . but I'll settle for just one thing. You telling me Ward Jaynes put you up to this."

"Who?" asked Seabrook, lamely.

Crawford had a strong urge to throw him through a wall.

"Cut the shit, asshole. You want to end up in Yeehaw Junction doing obits and girls softball?"

Seabrook sighed and looked around. "Can we go some-where?"

They walked out of the building. Crawford pointed to a bench, like Seabrook was a dog he was ordering to sit. Seabrook sat down, Crawford stayed on his feet facing him.

Seabrook's eyes were fixed on an areca palm twenty feet away.

"Talk to me," Crawford said.

Seabrook cleared his throat.

"He said he'd—" Seabrook's voice trailed off.

Crawford leaned forward and got within six inches of Seabrook's face.

"He said he'd what?"

Seabrook's eyes were jumping all over the place.

"Get me fired."

"Jaynes did?"

"No, a lawyer. Said he represented 'one of the owners.'"

"Didn't say Jaynes?"

"No."

Crawford's face stayed in Seabrook's.

"What's your home address, Barry?"

"Why?"

"What is it?»

"243 Gregory Road, West Palm."

Crawford wrote it down on a pad, then looked back down at Seabrook.

"Thank you, Barry, a process server will be waiting for you when you get off. He'll drop by your office, too."

"What for?"

"Serve you personally with a libel and defamation of character lawsuit. The *Palm Beach Press,* too. A hundred million."

"But you said—"

"I said I'd settle for you telling me Ward Jaynes put you up to it. You didn't. Said some lawyer did."

"Yeah, but—"

"Give Ward a call. Maybe he'll float you a loan, it's only a hundred mill," said Crawford, walking away. "If not, place around the corner sells lotto tickets."

FORTY-THREE

Crawford was in his car, headed to the station. His cell rang.

"How you doing, Charlie?" It was Dominica.

"I'm okay."

"You sure?"

"Yeah, not a word of that was true."

"I knew that."

He wished she was right there, so he could wrap his arms around her.

"Thanks for calling."

"You're welcome; sure you're all right?"

"Yeah. I'm fine."

"Well, you take it easy, 'kay Charlie?"

"I will."

"I'll see you soon."

"You will," Crawford said, stopping at the bridge to Palm Beach.

He watched a massive yacht go through the drawbridge between Palm Beach and West Palm. There wasn't much room to spare on either side. He saw a tanned, white-haired man standing erect on the rear deck, like he wanted to be seen and envied.

✳ ✳ ✳

HE FLASHED back to his roommate's 330-foot Feadship. Tim Hall had asked Crawford and twelve other Dartmouth classmates to go on a cruise out of Newport. The second night, when they were having dinner at a Nantucket restaurant, Crawford felt completely out of place. All his old buddies were talking a strange language. He understood every third word. Most of them were Wall Street guys, or guys who were pretty high up at big companies. Their conversations seemed to be mostly about money. Money, fancy trips to Saint Bart's, NetJets shares, Berlinettas—he thought that was a car but it could have been a boat.

Crawford didn't have much to contribute. The next morning he told Hall that he had gotten a call and had to get back down to Palm Beach. Something big had just happened.

Hall, of course, had offered to fly him down on his private jet.

* * *

HIS PHONE rang again.

"Hey, just wanted to tell you something, cheer you up maybe, take your mind off that shit," Ott said. "Turns out our guy, Nick Greenleaf, has a sense of humor."

"Why? What happened?" Crawford asked, crossing the middle bridge.

"I saw Mayo at the station, asked him how his stakeout at the Princess was going."

"Yeah?"

"Yeah, and the guy started hemming and hawing."

"And?"

"Finally tells me . . . he fell asleep last night, wakes up and sees this note on his windshield. It says, 'Sorry I missed you. Nick G.' "

"That was pretty ballsy," Crawford said, with a laugh. "Hey, Jaynes got his envelope a little while ago."

"I know. I talked to McCarthy; she's real excited about her new starring role. Chick's way into it."

"Yeah, Jaynes's guys will be all over her after she meets with him, you know."

"Tailing her, you mean?"

"Yeah, but they're gonna know they can't do it for long without getting made. So they'll plant a bug, I figure."

"So she'll lead 'em up to Misty's doorstep?"

"Exactly," said Crawford, going up the station's elevator.

"Probably bug her car while she's meeting with Jaynes, right?"

"Yeah, that's their best shot," Crawford said, getting off the elevator.

He saw Ott in his cubicle thirty feet away.

Ott switched the phone from one ear to the other. Crawford saw a grin spread across his partner's face.

"You got this all scripted out, don't ya, Charlie? Just like Steven fucking Spielberg. Like you're inside of Jaynes's fucked-up head."

Crawford watched Ott put his feet up on his desk as he approached him.

Ott looked up and saw Crawford.

He clicked off his cell. "Oh, hey, Charlie."

Crawford sat down in the chair next to Ott.

"So then the pros show up to take out the sisters—"

"And we'll be the welcoming committee," Crawford said, grabbing a pen and tapping it on a coffee mug.

Ott looked away and didn't say anything.

"Okay, Mort, what's going on in that big, lopsided head of yours? It's almost smoking."

"Sure you don't need to run this by Rutledge?"

"Don't go soft on me now, Mort," Crawford said, shaking his head slowly.

"I just—"

"You just what?"

"It's just . . . we got ourselves a real high-stakes game goin' here."

Crawford put the pen down and smiled up at Ott.

"Yeah, no kiddin' . . . just the kind of game a gnarly, old fuck like you was made for."

FORTY-FOUR

When the blackmailer called, Jaynes was shocked to hear a woman's voice.

"I'm the one who sent the pictures," the voice said. "Meet you at your house at twelve."

Jaynes knew it was time to grab the wheel.

"No, my office. 12 Philips Point."

"Fine," the woman said.

"Tell the guy at the parking garage you got an appointment with me. Save you a couple bucks."

"That's very kind of you, Mr. Jaynes."

✳ ✳ ✳

"Charlie," Dominica said on her cell phone, "meet's set for twelve."

"His place?"

"His office, told me to park in his parking garage."

"He's gonna bug your car there."

"Oh, Christ."

"No, that's a good thing."

"Why?"

"Just trust me. I'll tell you later. I want you to leave your cell phone in the passenger seat, too."

"Why?"

"So they can bug that, too."

✳ ✳ ✳

Jaynes got the call from the gate attendant a few minutes before twelve.

"Mr. Jaynes, your visitor's in a dark gray Camry, license plate 1Z55431."

"Thank you."

Jaynes dialed a number. "Dark gray Camry, plate number 1Z55431."

He hung up.

Jaynes looked at his watch. Five minutes later his secretary buzzed him. It was not unusual for her to work on Sunday. He paid her a big salary and she had no life. She told him his visitor had arrived.

A minute later she knocked on his office door. Jaynes was writing something. He didn't look up until after his secretary had left the room and closed the door. A beautiful woman was standing there. She had a dark complexion, a body that looked hard and tight and an expression of focused enmity.

"You're not exactly what I expected," he said.

Her eyes drilled into his.

If she was nervous, Jaynes couldn't see it.

"I was expecting someone with a shiny suit and thin black tie."

He was trying to charm her. It didn't take.

"My name is Jennifer Montell, I'm Misty Bill's sister."

Jaynes didn't let his face show anything. Her sister? The girl and this woman didn't seem to have anything in common except very dissimilar good looks.

"Not the same father," the woman said, like she was in his head. "Mine had an IQ."

Jaynes laughed and pointed to a chair.

She shook her head. "Let's take a walk outside."

"What? You think I have a listening device in that pen or something?" Jaynes asked.

"You probably do."

He shrugged and they walked through the reception area and out into the corridor.

"This okay?" Jaynes asked, stopping. "We could always go onto my roof garden. Or are you afraid I might have something planted in a potted palm?"

She was close to him now.

"No, that you'd throw me off."

Jaynes laughed.

"If I was that kind of guy, I'd have some goon do it for me."

"You saw the pictures?"

"Of course," he said, and without warning he stepped into her space. "Open your blouse."

She smacked him in the mouth.

"Meeting's over," she said, starting to walk away. "Photos go out after I call my sister."

"Whoa, whoa," he said, touching his mouth, looking for blood, "just wanted to make sure you weren't wearing a wire."

Her hands went to her top button. She undid it, then the other three. She pulled open her collared top.

"Okay?"

"More than okay," Jaynes leered.

"Asshole."

He laughed. "You're a feisty one."

"You're gonna pay for taking my brother's life."

Jaynes took out his wallet, pulled out a twenty-dollar bill, and dangled it.

"Price just went up $5 million," she said. "I want $25 million now."

Jaynes chuckled. "Who doesn't?"

"In unmarked hundreds."

Jaynes smiled and held up his hands. "Let's just say I play along. Agree to give you something—"

"Not 'something' . . . $25 million."

"First of all, where would you suggest I get that kind of money? It's Sunday. Think I got it under my mattress?"

"Not my problem. Just get it to me by eight tomorrow night. Last time I checked, banks are open on Monday. I did some math. If you're worth $4 billion dollars, like I read, $25 million is around half a percent of your net worth . . . so just look at it as a tip."

"You're a piece of work. Sure you're related to that girl?"

"That girl? You mean the sixteen-year-old kid who you—"

"Please, spare me," Jaynes said, raising his hands. "Best thing that ever happened to you and her."

Dominica's face quickly morphed from a frown to a smile.

"You know, you might have something there."

"You're good, very good. Somebody I'd actually hire."

"Thanks," she said, heading for the elevator, "but I'll be retiring soon."

❋ ❋ ❋

FULBRIGHT WAS reading the *Palm Beach Press*. About the hot-shot New York homicide detective who liked to kick Spanish guys when they were down. Right after getting the call, they had driven west on Okeechobee, past the tree farms and evangelical churches, and located the house where the girl lived. They weren't surprised to find nobody there and the girl's closet half-empty. They tossed the place anyway, looking for phone numbers or any sign of where she went. All they found were a couple of pictures of the girl.

The subcontractor told them the guy who ordered the job wanted them to go to a parking garage in an office building in West Palm at quarter past twelve. They'd have fifteen minutes to break into a car, plant bugs.

"A no-brainer," Fulbright said, as Donnie drove them into the garage, "so we know the whereabouts of our intended . . . at all times."

Donnie thought it was classy how Fulbright used words like "whereabouts" and referred to someone who would soon be dead as "our intended."

"What kinda car again?" Donnie asked, as he drove up the ramp.

"Dark gray Camry, tag 1Z55431."

It still impressed Donnie the way Fulbright would hear something just once, then memorize it for life. Ten-digit phone numbers, anything. Donnie was only good up to three numbers for about two minutes.

Fulbright pointed to a car, "There."

Donnie parked right next to the Camry and popped the lock in under two minutes. This was another specialty of his, along with driving fast and shooting straight.

He saw the cell phone on the front passenger seat.

"It's like they're trying to make our job easy," Donnie said, pointing to the cell phone.

"Awesome," Fulbright said, "I got the perfect size bug for that."

Fulbright opened the cell phone and put a fingernail-size chip in it, then found a spot under the dashboard and taped a bug there.

At 12:21 they were done and had wiped the Camry clean.

Donnie got behind the wheel of Fulbright's new Navigator and calmly drove down the ramp of the parking garage, putting his Aviators back on and pulling down the bill on his Seattle Mariners baseball cap. Fulbright slumped down in his seat and held the paper up over his face. Donnie paid the attendant on the ground floor, nodded and drove out.

❋ ❋ ❋

OTT WAS handy with a camera and even better at making sure he never got spotted. He and his telephoto lens were fifty yards away when the two drove up. He watched them from behind a dark-tinted rear window. He got twelve good shots of the two. They reminded him of Mutt and Jeff on a bad day.

※ ※ ※

DOMINICA, STANDING next to Jaynes, pressed the elevator button. Within seconds the high-speed elevator hummed to a stop. Dominica got in and pressed the button, but the doors didn't close. She looked out at Jaynes. He had his hand on one of the doors to prevent it from closing.

"You sure you know what you're doing, Jennifer, or whatever your name is? That you're not in over your head?"

The predatory look on his face chilled her, but she forced out a smile.

"It would be terrible for something to happen to that beautiful face."

"Just worry about getting my $25 million," she said, then leaned back casually against the rear of the elevator.

"Give me your cell number."

Without moving a muscle, she recited it as he wrote it down.

"Tell you what, I'll give you ten million. You bitch about it not being enough, I drop it a million for every word you say."

She didn't hesitate.

"Twenty-five million."

"That makes it $7 million. Take it or leave it."

"Leave it," she said, pushing the elevator button.

He just stared at her and kept his hand on the door.

She pushed the button again.

He let go of the door.

"I look forward to spending your money, Mr. Jaynes."

FORTY-FIVE

Nick high-fived Lil just inside the front door at El Vedato. "You were brilliant. Absolutely brilliant."

Ward Jaynes had come to the Robertson house right after meeting with Dominica.

He was just about to stroke a check for $2.7 million—for a painting which Lil referred to as an "important" Bacon, and an option on two Freuds—when Lil asked him if he would wire transfer the funds instead. Nick was certain he detected a barely suppressed smirk on Jaynes's face as he left, like he felt he'd gotten one over on Lil.

Somehow, Nick doubted it.

So far—including the $800,000 for the Hopper—Jaynes had committed to a total of $3.5 million. That was after having Lil and Nick sign a twelve-page contract he had his lawyers draw up, ensuring that he got the paintings just as soon as Spencer Robertson went cold. Nick had volunteered—not too eagerly, he hoped—a copy of a bogus will he'd paid a lowlife lawyer 500 bucks for. The guy was a Viggo's regular who owed him a favor. Jaynes looked over the will carefully, then looked up and said menacingly to Lil, "Hey, if there's any problem, I know where to find you."

Before finalizing the sale, though, Jaynes demanded to see Spencer Robertson.

Nick wouldn't have been surprised if he had shown up with a team of doctors. Jaynes told them the last time he saw Robertson was at the Poinciana five years before. Said the old guy was starting to babble even back then. Giving people weird nicknames, too.

Robertson was asleep when they went in to the dark room. Jaynes clicked on the bedside lights on either side of the bed, but Robertson didn't wake up. Jaynes pressed in close to the old man, studied his crazy quilt of liver spots and pried open one of his egg yolk eyes with thumb and forefinger.

"Six . . . eight months max," Jaynes declared.

Then he turned away and, not bothering to turn out the lights, walked out of the room.

Nick slid a pillow under the old man's head and turned off the bedside lights.

After Jaynes left, Lil asked Nick whether he had any champagne. It was time to celebrate, she said.

Nick said he'd check. He didn't think there was any left, remembering how Dickie had powered through copious amounts of it, until he wised up and started hiding it.

Nick went to the wine cooler in the kitchen. There was one bottle left, but it was chardonnay, not champagne.

Lil seemed disappointed, but forced it down anyway. The whole bottle, in fact.

❊ ❊ ❊

Lɪʟ ᴡᴀѕ going around the library, wine glass in her left hand, pad in her right, a pen between her teeth. Going from painting to painting, she was taking inventory of those she hadn't yet optioned. She'd get to one, stop, put down the glass, write the name of the artist, the year it was painted and—if there was one—the name of the painting.

Nick watched her closely. He got the sense that what she was really seeing were giant dollar signs.

He watched her go into Spencer's bedroom like Jaynes had done before, and seemingly oblivious to the smell of rot, flatulence and VapoRub, inventory the four paintings on the walls there. Nick waited for her in the living room. He went and turned on the TV and caught the tail end of *The Real Housewives of New York City.*

The bitchy one, Ramona, was going off on the ditzy one, Robin, when Alcie walked in. He had been in his room, apparently fully confident of his partners' abilities to conduct their flourishing new business.

"Where's Lil?" Alcie asked.

"Looking at paintings."

"Think she'd get sick of all that shit."

The phone rang. A rare sound at 101 El Vedato. Nick looked at Alcie.

"Hey, I'm retired, don't do phones no mo'."

Nick noticed how Alcie had gone from speaking the King's English before to talking street now . . . with a little Ebonics thrown in.

"Hello," Nick answered the phone.

"This is Avery," said the voice, "who's this?"

Ho-ly shit. Nick felt like someone had bitch-slapped him across the room.

"Ah, this is Nick," he sputtered.

Alcie inched closer, knowing something was wrong.

"Hi, Nick," the voice said, "I'm Spencer's grandson, you work there?"

Nick felt a surge of panic; the whole gig was about to crash and burn.

"Yes, I do," he said, wobbly.

"Do me a favor, I know my grandfather's not doing so hot, just tell him I'm coming down to see him."

"Yes, sir, I'll tell him."

"Make sure you do."

The guy sounded just like his cousin, Dickie.

"When, will you, ah, be arriving, Mr. Avery?"

Alcie flinched when he heard Nick say the name.

"I'll be there in ten days."

Thank, God. At least they had a little time.

"Very good, sir. I'll tell your grandfather. I'm sure he'll be thrilled. I look forward to the pleasure of meeting you."

Avery had already hung up.

Nick's legs felt shaky.

"Avery Robertson," Nick said, "gonna be here in ten days."

"The real deal," Alcie said, a frown appearing on his shiny face. "Shit."

Quaking, Nick went and sat down.

"We're gonna be okay," Nick said, struggling to focus. "Just need our partner to pick up the pace."

Lil walked into the living room. She looked a little unsteady from the chardonnay.

"What's wrong?" she said, seeing their faces.

"Oh, nothing. How long do you figure it'll take you to option off everything in the house?"

"All of it?" Lil asked, then a pause. "Bet I could get it done in two weeks."

Nick didn't hesitate.

"You got a week."

FORTY-SIX

Jaynes went back to his office, sat down at his desk, put his hands together as if in prayer, and thought about his next move. Number one—the obvious—was to stall Jennifer Montell on the money. Number two, he decided, was to call the "lawyer" and get him to dial up the subcontractor right away, add a bonus to get the job done fast.

Then he relaxed a little. In a little more than twenty-four hours it would all be history. He could go back to busting the kneecaps of Fortune 500 corporations and buying art on the cheap.

✳ ✳ ✳

The subcontractor called Fulbright right after he heard from Jaynes's "lawyer," a man who he called Mr. Williams, even though he had dug around and found out his real name and identity. The subcontractor told Fulbright that the man who ordered the hit now wanted a double. The girl, Misty, and her older sister, Jennifer. Said the client was a very impatient man and wanted it done yesterday. He had upped the fee to $500K—*if* they got it done in the next twenty-four hours. But he had thrown in a penalty clause, only two fifty if it took longer than that. Fulbright grumbled, but what could he do? He was already on the case. Psychologically committed. That was how he got. Besides . . . $500K. That was serious money, just for offing a couple of low-rent bitches. Just as important, it would catapult Donnie and him to the top of hitter hierarchy. No other guys got that kind of cash.

Fulbright was totally confident that they could do the job on time. He did well when he was under the gun. He didn't worry about rushing it, or getting sloppy because of the deadline. And Donnie? Goddamn rock solid, fucking champ under pressure.

✳ ✳ ✳

THE SWEAT poured down Dominica's face as she got into her car in the parking garage of Jaynes's building. Her heart was pumping like she'd just done a hundred yard dash. She wondered if she could have gone five more minutes playing tough broad with Jaynes.

To make sure no one was tailing her, she went home taking a long, circuitous route. Then she took a quick shower and did a double application of deodorant before going to meet up with Crawford and Ott. She drove into the parking lot of a church and called Crawford.

Crawford had given her another cell phone, a red one, to call them on. Just to be sure, he had put a piece of white tape on it, which said "Craw/Ott."

He answered.

"Hi," she said.

"Call you right back."

A few seconds later the red phone rang.

"Hi."

"You called me on the red one, right?" Crawford asked.

"Yes. What's going on, Charlie?"

"I'm with Ott. Gonna put you on speaker."

"Okay."

She heard the click and Crawford's voice like he was in a cave.

"Jaynes's guys are on the street," he said, "got your car bugged. Cell phone, too."

Dominica tensed.

"How do you know?"

"'Cause I followed you into the garage," Ott said. "Set up a telephoto, got some nice pics of two guys breaking into your car when you met with Jaynes."

"You're kidding?"

"No," Crawford said, "turns out I've seen these guys before . . . looking at houses."

Crawford had called Rose Clarke twice to find out the identity of the two men but hadn't heard back from her yet.

"Must be a good economy for hitters," Ott said.

"So how'd it go with Jaynes?" Crawford asked Dominica.

"Guy's one scary creep. Something I don't get . . . why would he bother to negotiate with me, if he planned to kill me?"

"Yeah," Ott looked at Crawford, "why not just say yes to the twenty mill, then dial up his guys?"

"Except I jacked it up to $25 million," Dominica said.

"Atta girl," Ott said, "Don't go selling yourself cheap."

"To answer your question, why's he bother to negotiate," Crawford said, "'cause that's what he does. Got a reputation for negotiating the price of a candy bar. If he didn't, you might think something was up. This way he makes you think he's gonna pay, puts you at ease."

"Makes sense," Dominica said.

"Where you now?" Crawford asked.

"Parking lot of a church . . . off Flagler."

"Here's what you do," Crawford said. "Check and make sure they're not on you. Then drive to the parking lot of your building, go into the lobby and wait. We'll pick you up in five."

"What about the phones?"

"Bring 'em both. I'm taking you off speaker now—" he clicked the button—"oh, I almost forgot, where do you live?"

"Come on, Charlie, you know," she said and laughed.

"505 North Flagler, thanks, see you in a few."

Five minutes later Crawford and Ott pulled up to Dominica's building. Crawford got out of the car and swept the area with his eyes, then went inside and got Dominica.

"You okay?"

"Fine . . . like you didn't know where I lived."

"Ott didn't need to know that."

He asked her for her cell, opened it, saw the microchip bug, then snapped it shut.

They walked out to the car and got in. Dominica smiled at Ott. He smiled back.

"So where are we going, boys?"

"Econo Lodge on Palm Beach Lakes. We're gonna leave your car here 'til this thing's over. Your cell phone's all they care about."

Dominica cocked her head.

"So . . . okay, tell me again why it's good they got it bugged?"

Crawford thought for a second as Ott turned left on Palm Beach Lakes Boulevard.

"'Cause . . . now you can spoon-feed 'em information we want 'em to have. Frustrate them for a while, then once we're ready, you lead 'em to Misty—"

Dominica nodded.

"So, you got her at that cheesy Econo Lodge? Nothing but the best for my sister, huh?"

"Yeah," said Crawford, "low-budget operation we got here."

FORTY-SEVEN

"So tell me again, why are we taking her somewhere else?" Dominica asked as they pulled up to the Econo Lodge.

"'Cause there are way too many exit points here," Crawford said. "I want a place where we can watch her like a hawk. I got the perfect spot."

"Where's that?" Ott asked.

"Know that boat that got impounded on that drug bust—a twenty-six foot Mako down at the north dock?"

Ott nodded.

"Anyone goes near it, we can see 'em from a million vantage points."

They pulled up to the Econo Lodge parking lot. Crawford led the way to the room where Misty was staying. He knocked.

"Who is it?"

"Your sister," Dominica said.

Misty opened the door. She was wearing a low-cut yellow top and cutoffs.

She shaded her eyes and looked up at Dominica.

"Hey," she said to Dominica, cocking her head, trying to get a read.

"Hey, I'm Dominica, but call me Jennifer."

Dominica eyed Misty like she thought the kid was showing off too much skin. Like she needed to talk to her about it, get her in line.

"I like your shoes," Misty said.

"Thanks," Dominica said, checking out the messy room. "You never learned how to make a bed?"

"Okay, girls, feel the love," Crawford said. "For the next couple of hours we're going through the plan. Dress rehearsal. You don't like your role, you can drop out. We'll understand."

※ ※ ※

THEY SPENT two hours in the fourteen-by-sixteen-foot motel room. They went over different scenarios and crafted a rough script. Dominica seemed to get into it and, after awhile, she and Misty began to hit it off. At five in the afternoon, all four of them got into the Vic, headed for Misty's new digs. Misty asked if the new place had hi-def and a pool. Dominica rolled her eyes.

Even though he was way out on a limb, Crawford wanted to cover his ass as much as possible by bringing Norm Rutledge into the loop. He called him from the car and ran the plan by him.

Sort of.

He omitted a detail or two. Like their intended use of Dominica, Misty and the impounded drug boat. In fact, all Crawford actually told Rutledge was that he was going to fake a blackmail sting with a suspect. He also neglected to tell him the suspect was Ward Jaynes. When Rutledge started up with a barrage of questions, Crawford cut him off, saying he had an incoming call from an informer. Said he'd get back to him. He figured he could duck Rutledge's calls until he either had Jaynes in jail or the whole plan blew up in his face.

When they got to the docks, Crawford took Misty aside and explained to her again the risk she'd be taking. It was the least he could do, he figured. She nodded and said she understood. Said she'd sign whatever papers were necessary to keep him out of trouble if something happened to her. He explained there were no such papers. Just stick to the plan, he said, and she'd be fine.

One thing he had to give the kid, she was long on guts.

On the way to the boat, Ott went over a basic code with Misty that she and Dominica would use in phone conversations. At first, Misty looked at him funny—like the old guy was giving her some Dick Tracy secret decoder mumbo jumbo. But Dominica, riding shotgun, turned and gave her a look. That was all it took. Ott, Dominica and Misty went over it a couple of times, just to make sure it had sunk in.

Misty wasn't thrilled with her new quarters. It was a bare bones boat and had a distinct smell of marijuana and motor oil. Ott told her she'd be there a day and a half max. She groaned. Dominica told her to suck it up.

Then Crawford showed Dominica where he and Ott were going to set up. It was a small, enclosed area close to the drug boat. All they needed now was a vantage point for Dominica, where she could watch Misty and monitor the hitters' arrival.

There were some nearby roofs which could work, but they ruled them out because tree branches partially obstructed their view. A hotel roof had a clear shot, but they were concerned that employees might spot Dominica and unknowingly tip the hitters. Finally, Ott pointed across the Intracoastal at the ghost-like 1515 Building on South Flagler Drive in West Palm. It was a skinny, twelve-story modern building that had apparently been built with substandard materials, by an incompetent builder, or both. In any case, it had been seriously compromised by Hurricane Wilma, three years ago, back in '05. It had been condemned, but not yet torn down. Its tenants had all moved out back in '06. The 1515 Building was empty except for some gulls that had gotten through the boarded-up windows.

"The front entrance is nothing but plywood held on by a bunch of two-by-fours," Ott said to Crawford. "We sneak in, nobody'll be the wiser."

"Let me get this straight . . . so now you're suggesting we add B & E to entrapment and blackmailing a prominent citizen?" Crawford asked.

Ott smiled back. "In for a penny . . . in for twenty mill."

"Twenty-five," Dominica said.

※ ※ ※

At EIGHT P.M., Crawford, Ott and Dominica were on the balcony of an abandoned twelfth-floor apartment of the 1515 Building looking down at the boats in the marina. They had walked up using flashlights and carrying high-powered optical equipment and tripods. Ott said he was a little winded, Dominica said he was a wuss.

On top of the building, Crawford took in the view of the Intracoastal, then Palm Beach and the ocean beyond. The view beat the hell out of the parking lot his condo looked down onto. They set up the equipment and tested it. Then they reviewed the plan.

Afterward, Crawford looked through a pair of binoculars, then motioned to Dominica.

"That's the place I showed you," he said, pointing, "where me and Mort are gonna hang out.

He handed her the binoculars.

"You can fit in there?"

"*I* can."

She looked at Ott. He smiled.

"Gonna be a little tight," he said.

Crawford and Ott had checked it out earlier. It was about fifty yards from the impounded boat.

Ott handed Dominica the photos he had taken of the suspected hitters.

"Coupla real dreamboats," she said. "Short, scrawny mutt and a tall, creepy-looking guy."

"Yeah," Crawford said, "but don't go underestimating them."

"I won't. They look like a pretty nasty duo."

"Yeah, and when they hear where Misty is, they're gonna swing into action fast, guarantee you."

"First thing they're gonna do, once we tip 'em to where she is, is come here, check out all the boats," Ott said.

Dominica nodded.

"Probably go around, try to figure out how to bust through one of those gates. But it ain't gonna happen, it's like getting into Fort Knox," Ott said.

All the docks had locked metal gates and around them sharp rods that pointed out. They were as welcoming as razor wire on the walls of a penitentiary.

"So then they'll be figuring where to take their shot from," Ott said.

Dominica nodded.

"You okay?" Crawford asked her, fighting an urge to put a comforting hand on her shoulder.

She nodded again.

"We're going to run these guys around a little," Crawford said. "Make it too easy for them, they'll smell something."

"So, their plan's gonna be to first take out Misty," she said, "then . . . they come after me?"

Crawford nodded, then looked over at Ott, who was taking in the view. He gave Dominica a soft pat on the shoulder. It bordered on the unprofessional, but he could tell she liked it. Ott turned and looked over at them.

"You ready?" Crawford said to Ott.

"To go back down?" Ott groaned.

"Yeah," Crawford said, "it's downhill, for Chrissakes."

When they got to the bottom, Ott wheezed out something about going up and down Everest and gimped toward the car.

✳ ✳ ✳

So far Fulbright had listened to a couple of conversations between the two sisters. They didn't sound much alike. Different accents even. He hadn't gotten anything useful yet. No location. Nothing.

At one point he got frustrated and lashed out at Donnie, the way he always did if things didn't go quite right. But Donnie was one of those guys who just stared back at you, then slowly shook his head. He never lost it or got crazy. Unless, of course, he was paid to.

Finally, at eleven o'clock that night, Fulbright listened in on the call he'd been waiting for.

"So what's happening?" Misty said. "Heard from Jaynes yet?"

"I'll let you know when I do," Dominica said. "Meantime, stay right there. *Don't* go outside."

Misty sighed.

"You said it was gonna be a 'slam dunk.'"

"Just let me take care of it, how's the boat?"

"Sucks, stinks like old reefer."

"Just one more night."

"Better be."

"Talk to you soon."

Fulbright heard the click, turned to Donnie and gave him a thumbs-up.

"A boat," Fulbright said, "awesome . . . she's a sitting duck."

He looked at his watch. Close to twenty hours left. Talk about slam dunks.

Problem was, since then, the sisters had only had two conversations and, though they made several references to "the boat," hadn't given any clue where the boat was. The older one, Jennifer, seemed to be holed up in her apartment off Flagler, based on the fact that the LoJack they put in her car indicated she hadn't gone anywhere. The clock was ticking and Fulbright was edgy, ready to rip into Donnie again. They drove up a long stretch of Flagler Drive on the Intracoastal, stopping at five marinas along the way, with the picture of Misty taped to the dashboard. Donnie said something about a "needle in a haystack," and Fulbright just glared at him. There were a lot of marinas, and besides, who said the boat was at a marina? Or in West Palm, for that matter? Could be down in Lake Worth, or up in Riviera Beach. Could be anywhere. There were a million boats in South Florida.

Finally they pulled into a parking lot and slept for a few hours.

It was seven thirty in the morning and they had decided to head over to Clematis and get a cup of coffee, when they heard Misty's voice:

"Hey, a Palm Beach police boat just went by," Misty said, "like they were looking for something."

"Don't worry, it's not you," the older one said.

"Heard anything?"

"Nah, not yet. Told you, I'll let you know."

Fulbright smiled, reached across the seat, cuffed Donnie lightly on the cheek.

"Bingo, let's go, man. She's at the Palm Beach docks."

Right after going over the middle bridge, Fulbright signaled Donnie to take a hard right. A minute later they saw the Palm Beach police boat tied up at the dock, nobody in sight. They cruised the extra couple of blocks to the south end of the docks, getting a closer look at some of the most expensive yachts this side of Monte Carlo.

"Believe the size of these suckers," Donnie said, shaking his head in awe.

"We're gonna have one of our own before too long," Fulbright said.

Donnie looked over at him. "When we start doin' a guy a day, you mean?"

Fulbright snorted a laugh and nodded.

For the next hour and a half the two of them just observed.

Then Donnie left. They had decided on their choice of weapon . . . well, Fulbright chose it and Donnie would do the aiming and trigger pulling. Donnie was going over to their storage unit on Congress where they had an arsenal that included every conceivable size, shape and caliber of firepower. Fulbright thought this particular job called for the RPG, a rocket-propelled grenade launcher. Why screw around? he figured. They had it, why not use it?

Baseball cap pulled low, Fulbright gazed out from a bench and took in the billions of dollars worth of yachts bobbing on the Intracoastal. Unless you owned one, were a guest, or scrubbed one of their decks, this was as close as you got.

Fulbright was focused on just the small boats and there weren't many of them. That was where the girl had to be. No way the sisters had a friend loan them a 200-foot yacht.

Forty-five minutes later, Donnie showed up in Fulbright's new Navigator. Fulbright had it narrowed down to four boats and had a hunch it was one all by itself at the end of a dock.

Donnie walked over and sat down next to him.

"So?"

"It's one of those," Fulbright said, pointing them out. Then he smiled broadly. "Got the big sucker?"

"'Course . . . bet I could take out the whole fleet here with it."

After a few minutes, Donnie got up from the bench and looked around. His eyes did a slow 180, checking out the cars and buildings behind him. Then he turned and looked back out at the boats. There wasn't going to be anything particularly subtle about this job.

A surgical strike? *Not.*

As soon as Fulbright figured out which boat it was, Donnie was going to blow the fucker to smithereens— toothpick-sized slivers raining down in a 300-foot radius. Light up the sky like the Fourth of July. Treat Palm Beach to a pyrotechnical show the likes of which they'd never seen. Then pass go, collect $500 Gs and start going around looking for their own pleasure boat.

FORTY-EIGHT

"I got our guys," Dominica said, looking through the infrared binoculars, high up on the 1515 Building, and talking on her cell. "Short one's wearing a baseball hat, sitting on a bench trying to dope out where Misty is. Tall, skinny guy's in a blue jean jacket, just drove up a few minutes ago."

"How far from us?" Crawford asked.

"Um, 'bout seventy-five yards. Skinny one keeps getting up and pacing around, like he's ready to get the show on the road."

Crawford looked at Ott.

Ott nodded.

"Well, okay, then," Crawford said, "let's get the show on the road."

And Dominica dialed her phone.

"Hey, sweetie, it's me," Dominica said, a few seconds later, "how you doing?"

Fulbright heard the voice in his earpiece.

"Feelin' really cooped up," Misty said.

"Just stay there, a little bit longer."

"I'm just going out for a cig."

"No, goddamn it, Misty."

That wasn't part of the plan.

"Hey, check it out," Donnie said, pointing.

Fulbright whipped the binoculars up to his eyes.

Misty was on the rear deck of the Mako. A cigarette dangled from her mouth. She kept moving, at least, something Crawford had told her to do.

Dominica dialed Crawford on the red phone. He picked up.

"Shit, Charlie," Dominica said, her heart pounding, "see her, outside on the deck."

Crawford tightened his grip on the Sig.

"Well, well," Fulbright said, spotting Misty, "our little friend."

Donnie was psyched, his prey in sight.

"Let's do it," Fulbright said.

They both got up.

"They're moving," Crawford heard Dominica say in his earpiece. "Heading toward the street . . . going across it now . . . into a building. Ah, 325, the sign says, Casa de Lago."

"Mac, quick," Crawford said, "call the girl, give her the code. Right now."

A few seconds later, Crawford heard Dominica make the call.

"Hey," Dominica said, tamping down her adrenaline, "looks like Jaynes stiffed us, I'm pickin' you up in two hours."

Misty didn't hesitate. "Good, I like dry land way better."

Fulbright didn't give a damn whether the older sister picked up the younger one in two hours or next July, because in ten minutes there wasn't going to be anything left to pick up.

Donnie had a big aluminum golf case slung over his shoulder that he had taken out of the back seat of the Navigator.

Fulbright hadn't noticed any lights on in the four-story building where Donnie was going to take the shot from and figured all they'd have to do was pick a lock or two. Worst case, knock a door off its hinges. Both things Donnie was an expert at. Fulbright's only concern was that the big banyans between the building and the dock might block Donnie's shot. But over on the left side of the top balcony there was a good-sized gap between the trees that Donnie had scoped out.

Turned out the only lock Donnie had to pick was the outside one. The stairs went straight to the top floor. From there it was just eight steps up to the door, which opened out to the balcony. Worst security Donnie had even seen.

Donnie walked over to the south end of the balcony—pure focus now—put down the heavy golf case and exhaled. Fulbright knew Donnie had popped a Valium fifteen minutes before. He was hardly the high-anxiety type, that was just part of his routine, his way of cutting down on the adrenaline.

Donnie opened the case and broke out the RPG.

Fulbright loved to watch Donnie get into it. He was total concentration and economy of motion. Fulbright knew it was the army training. How doing something every day for a couple of years made it automatic. Eighteen years back, Donnie had almost gone to the Olympics for the army, part of the Fort Benning shooting team that did nothing but aim and fire all day long. But for this job he didn't even need to be all that accurate. Wasn't like he needed his sniper rifle. Just aim at the boat and blow the sucker to hell and gone.

Donnie had the RPG pointed in the direction of the boat now, resting it on the balcony rail. He wore the same soft, thin kidskin gloves he always used and had his earplugs in. Slowly, he adjusted a sight, then moved the big barrel to his right.

He looked at Fulbright and nodded. Fulbright put his hands over his ears.

Donnie closed his right eye and squeezed the trigger. Even with earplugs, the explosion was deafening. A chunk of loose stucco tumbled off the wall behind them.

Fulbright was mesmerized by the sight below. The color of the explosion was yellow and blue and reminded him of the hissing flare, then the flame, when you struck a wooden match—but times a thousand. Pieces of metal and wood came raining down, as if in slow-motion. It was a frozen moment of brilliant chaos.

Donnie grabbed Fulbright roughly by his shirtsleeve.

"Come on, man," he said, strapping the RPG over his shoulder. He had wiped down the aluminum golf case and was going to leave it behind. "Time to get the sister."

Fulbright got to his feet, followed him to the door and went down the steps.

They were on the street now. Donnie had just clicked the door opener for the Navigator when he saw two men running toward them from the dock. One of them shouted something, then a few seconds later Donnie heard a bullet thunk into the Navigator's side. Donnie started the engine and accelerated, but immediately saw a police car with flashing lights blocking their way to the middle bridge. He hit the brakes hard, executing a skidding U-turn, and the Navigator started speeding south, its big engine whining like a stock car out at Moroso speedway.

FORTY-NINE

At least the real Avery wasn't going to just show up unannounced the way Dickie had. Nick had ten days to get things done and Avery did Nick a huge favor by giving him advance warning. Ten more days gave him a lot of time to fatten up his bank account.

In that time he could make enough to live very comfortably in the south of France. He still wanted to stay in Palm Beach, but that possibility was a long shot now. Living where Scott, Zelda and the Murphys had spent their golden youths was a good second choice. As for learning French . . . screw that, everyone spoke English there, even if they hated Americans. Word was there were some very exclusive clubs like the Poinciana on the Côte d'Azur, too. All he needed was to meet some people who'd write letters for him, say what a swell guy he was.

Still, it was hard, the idea of uprooting himself from here. He had actually been toying with another idea. One that would allow him to live happily ever after in Palm Beach. It would require him to do something he wasn't absolutely sure was worth the risk, but he was giving it serious thought. He still had that detective and the Palm Beach Police Department looking for him, describing him as a "person of interest."

※ ※ ※

First and foremost, Nick wanted to keep Lil focused on selling options until every painting on the swirled stucco walls of the palatial Robertson mansion had been sold. Nick couldn't tell Lil the real reason they only had ten days, so he told her he had booked a flight a long time back to leave town next week. Big party on a friend's yacht in Cap d'Antibes, he told her.

Nick was disappointed she hadn't begged him to stay in Palm Beach or insisted on going along with him to Cap d'Antibes, but figured she knew her biggest priority was to get out her Rolodex and dial. Spencer Robertson's house at 101 El Vedato turned into a Madison Avenue gallery, as Lil shepherded in eager buyers with the irresistible offer of being able to buy world-class paintings for one-third off. On Wednesday alone she brought in seven prospective optionees and ended up with sales of $500,000, $1.5 million, and $800,000. On Thursday she got another commitment for just over $2 million for two Bacons, plus $100,000 for the Hepplewhite chest in the living room that they weren't even trying to sell. Friday was a slow day but by the end of Sunday, they had a total take of $9.2 million. Not bad for a week's worth of work.

The only problem was that Nick had set a goal of $5 million for himself alone. Or in his new country's currency: 3.5 million Euros.

So in order to make his quota, he had called up a real estate broker whose name he had seen in *Glossy* ads and invited him over. Nick showed him through the house and the property in back, then described to the broker what he had in mind.

"What you're talking about is called a life estate," the broker said as they walked through the house. "It's not all that uncommon."

"Oh," Nick said, disappointed, having thought he had invented the concept. "So how does it work exactly . . . I mean, I want to get the money right away."

"Well, the best way," the broker said, "is you get an appraiser to price the house, then you look at what are called actuarial charts, figure out approximately how long the, ah, owner is expected to live, then you discount—"

"But I don't have time for all that, just tell me what it's worth, I'll show you papers that prove I inherit it, then we'll draw up an agreement. Like if you say it's worth, I don't know, $20 million—"

"A little less," the broker said.

"Okay, fifteen . . . then I discount it by 50 percent, so that's $7.5 million, then I sign an agreement selling it to a buyer for that and they give me 20 percent now—" Nick said, gesturing wildly with his hands—"the rest after my grandfather passes away and it closes."

"That's a huge discount," the broker said; "you sure you want to do that?"

"Yes, I'm sure. I want to make a quick deal."

The broker nodded. "Okay, you're going to need your grandfather to sign off on it, you know."

"Yeah, no problem."

Forgery was child's play compared to the other things he had pulled off.

"If that's what you want to do, Mr. Robertson," the broker said, "I'm sure I can make a few calls and . . . make a quick deal."

Nick nodded to the broker as they walked to the front door. "That's exactly what I want to do. Make your calls, get back to me as soon as possible."

"You got it," said the broker, turning and shaking Nick's hand.

Nick said good-bye and closed the front door.

He was on to his next project now, a man who had a lot to get done. No one was around so he figured it was a good time to take the big Bacon in the front closet over to his storage unit on Okeechobee.

He called Yellow Cab on his cell, figuring it was safer than taking Spencer's Rolls Cloud Three or Alcie's Corolla. It wasn't likely, but what if he got a flat? Palm Beach cops were so damn accommodating. He could just picture a cop trying to help him, then recognizing him from the flyer. Why take a chance? Just in case the cabby had seen one of the flyers, he'd wear his wraparounds and Spencer's yellowed Poinciana golf cap.

He told the dispatcher to have the cab there in twenty minutes. That would give him time to bubble wrap the big picture from the closet.

He turned to the closet and flipped on the switch. He didn't see the picture right away. He pulled out Spencer's big golf bag, then the canes and the two umbrellas that it had been behind. But it was nowhere in sight.

In a panic, he turned the whole closet upside down, yanking raincoats and heavy jackets off their big wooden hangers, pulling out a folded-up card table, then grabbing a big cardboard box and dragging it toward him. It was heavy and went crashing to the floor. Nick heard glass shatter inside, but didn't care.

It was then he realized the Bacon was gone.

FIFTY

Donnie jammed the accelerator to the floor and was doing sixty down Worth Avenue. Thing was, Worth Avenue was a one-way street, going the other way. Fulbright watched as they blurred past a red-faced guy pointing frantically in the other direction. He looked back and saw a big white car two blocks behind them.

"Shit, they're comin'," Fulbright said.

"I see 'em," Donnie said, totally cool, as he yanked the wheel hard to his right and skidded onto South County Road. "We're gonna be fine."

That was the soldier side of Donnie that Fulbright loved. Solid ice.

Ott was behind the wheel two hundred yards back and Crawford was on the radio. He had alerted the dispatcher about their pursuit; problem was that the three other cops on duty were all up at the north end in Zone Four, five miles away. He told the dispatcher to get them down to the north bridge and block it.

BOLO for a black Navigator, he said.

Then he got a call from Misty.

"You okay?" he asked.

Dominica's coded warning to Misty had been the signal for Misty to slip over the far side of the drug boat and swim to safety at the south end of the docks.

"Yeah," she said, "never swam so fast in my life. Wrapped my phone in a baggy I found on the reefer boat."

"Good girl. Call you later." He clicked off.

The Navigator, after hanging a hard, tire-burning right, was going in the direction of the Southern and Lake Worth bridges.

"This is 322, headed down South Flagler," Crawford heard the voice on the radio say.

Ott glanced over. Shit, it was Dominica.

"Three minutes north of Southern," she said.

"McCarthy," Crawford shouted into the radio, "don't get anywhere near the Southern bridge. You saw what they did to the boat—"

"Blew it into another zip code," Ott mumbled.

But there was no response from Dominica.

"McCarthy?"

Nothing.

Crawford turned to Ott. "I know damn well she heard me."

"Girl wants to join in the fun," Ott said, pedal to the metal.

They flashed by the Everglades golf course off to their right. Ott had the Crown Vic up over eighty now, but wasn't gaining.

"Dispatch," Crawford said into his radio, "try to get West Palm to block the Southern bridge. If we got anyone down south, same for Lake Worth."

"Got it," the dispatcher said.

Crawford doubted whether dispatch would be able to get anyone there in time.

The Navigator blew through a stop sign on South Ocean, barely missing a gray Porsche it would have T-boned into the ocean.

"Son–of–a–bitch can drive," Ott said, eyes wide, sweat glistening on his face.

He slowed at the stop sign on South Ocean—barely—then gunned it. Ott kept the pedal down and within ten seconds had it back up to eighty, then ninety. Fifty-five miles over the speed limit, still not gaining.

The Navigator was at Mar-a-Lago now. Its brake lights flashed, a hard right ahead, a choice whether to go through the roundabout and due south or straight across Southern bridge into West Palm.

Crawford looked up and saw the chopper he'd phoned in for. A moment later the Navigator disappeared around the corner—going close to sixty.

A few seconds later they were going into the hard right turn.

"Hang on, man," Ott said.

Crawford knew that Crown Vics were too fat for good cornering even with their Police Interceptor suspensions. It went into a big slide. He hoped like hell nobody was coming the other way.

A midnight blue Audi 8 was.

It was halfway through the roundabout. Ott had to cut the turn even tighter. Crawford prayed they wouldn't flip. The tires squealed and the Vic clipped the Audi's bumper. Then, as if nothing had happened, Ott stomped on the pedal again.

"Hammer time," he yelled.

"Crazy bastard," Crawford said, looking back.

He hoped the Audi driver hadn't gone into cardiac arrest. Then, he turned back and saw the Navigator roar up over the top of the Southern bridge.

Crawford knew if the driver got to West Palm, he could be gone. At least the helicopter was on him. But the hitters had a hundred options. Their best play was probably to go onto a side street. Ditch the car and disappear.

Crawford had his Sig Sauer out and was bracing himself with his left hand on the dashboard. They got to the top of the bridge, then saw the Navigator, a Christmas tree of red brake lights in front of them. Past it, Crawford saw a Chevy Caprice sideways on the far side of the bridge, blocking the road. It was Dominica's Caprice.

"What the hell's she thinking?" he yelled.

He stuck his head out the window and aimed his Sig. The driver of the Navigator suddenly accelerated hard. Tires screaming, it was headed for a spot between the Caprice's ass-end bumper and the north side of the bridge. Crawford didn't shoot, worried a ricochet could hit Dominica.

"Fucker ain't gonna make it through," said Ott.

Then Crawford saw Dominica's head pop up from behind her Caprice. She ducked down fast as he heard a burst of automatic gunfire come from the Navigator. He saw the windows on the Caprice get blown out like ice falling off a roof. He couldn't see Dominica. The Navigator blew past the tail of the Caprice with no more than six inches to spare. Crawford suddenly heard loud pops, and saw the Navigator fishtail and go into a slide, heading straight toward a telephone pole. There was nothing the driver could do and Crawford heard the crash, then saw a shower of sparks. The pops were the Navigator's tires getting blown out. Somehow Dominica had managed to throw down tire-puncturing stop sticks. The big spikes probably blew out all four tires.

Ott flashed through the same space the Navigator had just gone through. Crawford was looking everywhere for Dominica. He didn't see her, then checked the rearview. Nothing. Ott stood on the brakes with all his 220 pounds and skidded to a stop fifty feet behind the Navigator.

Then in a sudden screeching cacophony of steel wheels on pavement, the Navigator started coming at them, jammed into reverse. Crawford and Ott, leaning out their windows, started firing and in seconds the Navigator's back window was a fringe of glass shards. It stopped dead twenty-five feet from them.

Through the blown-out back window, Crawford could see the bloody, unmoving head of the man in the passenger seat. He didn't see the driver and thought maybe he was hit, slumped down on the seat.

Ott reached in his pocket for another clip for his Glock, when suddenly the driver's side door swung open and a skinny guy staggered out. An RPG Stinger was pressed up against his shoulder.

Crawford had counted three bullets left in his clip. He sighted the guy in and fired three times.

Two in the chest, one in his forehead. The man stumbled, then fell forward.

Crawford looked over and saw the other guy's head, wire rim glasses dangling from one ear. He was behind an inflated air bag, white powder splotched all over his clothes.

He heard the dispatcher say in his earpiece that they'd have a roadblock set up on the Southern bridge in five minutes.

"We won't be needing it," Crawford said. "Just send a couple body bags."

Crawford jumped out of the car and ran back toward Dominica's Caprice.

He got to within ten feet of the Caprice and bent down to see if she was under the car. But all he saw was shattered glass.

He heard sirens in the distance and smelled burnt rubber and gas. He walked up to the Caprice and looked inside. Dominica was facedown in the backseat.

He yanked the door open and crouched over her, not sure he should touch her. He didn't see any sign of a wound.

Then he saw her move imperceptibly, like she was exhaling.

"Dominica? You okay?"

"Oh, thank God," she said, turning to him and sitting up. She hugged him. "I thought you were one of the bad guys."

He stroked the back of her head gently.

"You mean . . . the former bad guys."

FIFTY-ONE

(O)tt had a grin as wide as the Crown Vic as he and Crawford walked up to Ward Jaynes's house. It was five forty-five on the damp, humid morning and the sun had just poked up over the ocean. He and Crawford had covered a lot of ground since the shoot-out. Crawford was on his cell phone.

"—tell you what, Barrett, old buddy, if you make the headline big enough, maybe the lawsuit'll just go away," Crawford said, then clicked off.

"Jesus, Charlie, how many reporters you got comin'?" Ott asked.

"As many as I could scare up," Crawford said, walking up the steps. "Wonder who gets this place after Jaynes moves his operation to a cell at Starke?"

Ott thought for a second.

"One of those poor girls in Bangkok, maybe?"

They hadn't been to sleep yet and were in that zone somewhere between punchy and wired, partly because of the Box O' Joe they had shared with a man named Dan Rumbough. Rumbough was Jaynes's subcontractor, meaning the guy who had hired Fulbright and Donnie. They had gotten his number from Fulbright's cell phone, looked up his address, and had gone there to take him in. They found him zonked out and wild-eyed, leaning over a small mountain of crystal meth. He was sharing it with a woman who claimed she didn't know him and had no recollection of how she got there. They turned her loose, pumped a quart of Dunkin' Donuts into Rumbough and sobered him up. Last thing they wanted was the charge overturned because Rumbough was too high to know what he was saying.

After they double-teamed him for over an hour, telling Rumbough about the various bad options available to him, the assistant district attorney, who they had rousted out of bed, offered Rumbough a deal. Faced with a long prison stretch, Rumbough agreed to cop to an accessory charge and, promptly, gave up a guy he called "the lawyer." Turned out the lawyer, a man named John Rhodes, was an old friend of Ward Jaynes's.

When they brought him in, Rhodes acted all innocent and told them all he had done was make a few phone calls. The ADA informed him that those phone calls—conspiring to commission two murders—were going to cost him twenty years unless he fingered his "client." After weighing that option for about ten seconds, Rhodes suddenly got very loquacious. Said how he used to be a lawyer, but was disbarred for life eight years before. Something to do with a major insider trading charge and—as Rhodes explained it—him "taking a bullet" for Ward Jaynes. Ended up losing his license but said Jaynes owed him big time. Not only that, trusted him, too. So much so that Rhodes became Jaynes's confidant. The ADA said, "That's a very nice story, John, but you're still looking at twenty years at Marion County, unless you give us something big."

John Rhodes apparently had heard of Marion County correctional, because it took him about three seconds to flip. He ID'ed Jaynes as the man who not only ordered the murder of "the sisters," but then, he gave them the really big prize: how Ward Jaynes had boasted to him on several occasions about strangling the "greedy little redneck bastard," Darryl Bill.

Confession signed, Ott and Crawford went straight to Jaynes's house down on South Ocean.

Ott leaned hard on the doorbell.

A few minutes later a man in his sixties and a bathrobe opened the door. He looked bewildered at the sight of two seemingly sober, but disheveled, men standing there. Crawford had a rip on the left sleeve of his shirt and Ott was a particularly sorry sight. His hair, which normally had a neat swept-back wave in front, was matted down and looked like a deflated mole. His big Windsor tie knot had slipped down to his upper sternum.

"Yes?" the man asked.

"We need to see your boss," Crawford said.

"Is he expecting you?" the man asked.

"Not exactly." Crawford flashed him his badge. "Just get him. We got a warrant for his arrest. Might want to tell him it's Murder One."

The man reeled back a few steps.

Crawford stuck his foot between the door and the jamb.

The man glared at him.

"I was just going to awaken him," he said.

"So what are you waiting for, Pops," Ott said, stepping inside, " 'awaken him.' "

The man shuffled off toward a circular staircase.

Crawford heard the thumping of a helicopter and shot Ott a smile.

"Here they come," Crawford said, looking up. "I just love the press."

Ott flashed him a thumbs-up. "Yeah, me too."

After a few minutes of waiting for the old man, Crawford got twitchy.

"Come on." He went in and headed toward the staircase, jerking his Maglite out of his pocket.

He shined it upstairs and pulled his Sig Sauer out of his shoulder holster. Ott had his Glock out and his Maglite, too. Their beams of light crisscrossed.

"Jaynes, we got a murder warrant for you," Crawford yelled up the stairs. "Come on down *now*."

But there was no response.

Crawford ran upstairs, taking the steps three at a time. He saw the old man coming out of a bedroom. He ran toward it.

"Where the hell is he?" he asked, hearing Ott a step behind him.

"He wasn't in his bedroom," the old man said with a shrug.

"Bullshit," Crawford said, shoving the old man aside, and running into the bedroom. It was twice the size of Crawford's whole apartment. The covers on the bed were pulled down. There was a huge semicircular porch off the master and the french doors were open.

Crawford ran through the doors out onto the porch, Ott right behind him. He heard two helicopters now.

Crawford looked down to the ground below. It would have been a twenty-foot jump. No way Jaynes was going to make the leap.

He motioned with his Sig to Ott.

"Back inside, Mort," he said.

Ott nodded and turned.

Crawford ran back in and opened the first door he came to. It was a Gatsby-size walk-in. Ott opened another door. It was the master bath. Crawford opened a third. It was an empty closet, but with steps going down from it.

"Bingo," Crawford said, charging in and running down the steps.

"This is where he went," Crawford yelled back to Ott.

At the bottom was a long, straight, dimly lit tunnel about five feet wide. Crawford started running at full speed and heard Ott's footsteps close behind. A dank smell was suddenly replaced by a salty ocean scent as Crawford saw light fifty feet ahead.

He got to the end and saw a six-inch-thick steel door with a large slide bolt on it. He ran out through the door, onto the beach and stopped. It was as bright as if a bank of Klieg lights was shining down from above. The tunnel was built into a dune. Crawford looked down the beach in one direction and saw nothing. He looked the other way and saw a man.

It was Jaynes, in bright red pajamas.

Crawford looked up and saw three helicopters now.

"Okay, Mort," Crawford shouted at Ott, "pretend he's O.J. and we gotta stop him from making a touchdown."

Crawford started sprinting, though loafers were hardly ideal footwear. He heard Ott right behind him. The helicopters were louder as they got lower.

Then, suddenly, Ott passed him. He was breathing heavily but Crawford spotted a faint smile on his face.

Crawford tried to see if Jaynes had a gun, then saw Ott throw it into another gear up ahead. Ott was just thirty yards behind Jaynes now. Jaynes looked back, the panicked look of a cornered animal on his face.

One of the helicopters had landed and was ahead of Jaynes. Crawford saw a man with a TV camera and the letters of the local CBS station on the side of the helicopter.

Then he saw Jaynes swing around again and—just as he did—Ott dove.

It was a tackle worthy of the NFL.

The two went down in a heap. Ott reached back for his cuffs and slapped them on Jaynes's wrist. It reminded Crawford of a cowboy tying up a steer.

Crawford was standing above Ott and Jaynes now. He saw four men and a woman running toward them a hundred yards down the beach. He recognized one of the men.

"Nice goin', Mort," he said. "You made the six o'clock news."

Ott was gasping for air, breathing too heavily to say anything.

Crawford went over to one of the helicopters that had landed twenty feet away.

"Okay, you got your shot, this is a crime scene," he said. "Now don't get any closer. No interviews, no nothing."

"What are your names?" a reporter with a mike shouted.

"That's Detective Mort Ott," Crawford said, pointing. "And Wardwell A. Jaynes, III, is the one with the sand all over his face."

"And you are?" the reporter asked.

"Irrelevant," Crawford said.

He walked over to Jaynes and Ott. The reporter with the mike followed him. Crawford swung around.

"What the hell did I just tell you? Back off."

The reporter did as he was told.

The four men and the one woman were in a huddle ten feet away from Jaynes and Ott now. They all had their recorders out.

"Okay, people, back up, there will be no interviews with me, my partner or Mr. Wardwell A. Jaynes, III. Thank you . . . oh, and you in the bad shirt," Crawford pointed to one of the men, "can I have a word with you?"

The man walked up to Crawford.

"Like I said, Barrett, the whole lawsuit thing goes away if you get a front-page picture of your boss . . . along with a big headline that says something like, WARD JAYNES, BILLIONAIRE PEDOPHILE, ARRESTED FOR MURDER . . ."

Barrett Seabrook seemed at a loss for words.

"What the hell you waiting for?" Crawford asked. "Go write the damn story."

Crawford walked back to Ott and Jaynes, both on their feet now. Even in handcuffs and with sand coating his face, Jaynes's arrogance was undiminished.

"You're going to sorely regret this travesty, Crawford," Jaynes said.

"Not this time, Rainmaker," Crawford said. "All your rats jumped ship. By the way, those red PJs . . . very photogenic."

FIFTY-TWO

The afternoon before, Alcie had walked in on Nick packing his bags.

"Goin' somewhere, partner?"

"How 'bout knocking next time," Nick said, then all buddy-buddy, "don't worry I was going to settle up with you before I left."

Sure you were, Alcie thought.

"I never had any doubt of that," he said.

"Hold on, I'll write you a check," Nick said.

"I gotta better idea," Alcie said. "How about us going down to the bank, you do a nice little wire transfer. That way you don't need to waste a check."

After the money was in his account, Alcie shook Nick's hand, thanked him and told him it was a pleasure doing business with him. It was the end of a short-lived, but highly profitable, relationship.

✳ ✳ ✳

EARLY THE next morning, Alcie called the Palm Beach Police Department and asked for Mort Ott, the detective who had given him the sketch with Nick's likeness. He figured he'd just leave Ott a message, but to his surprise, Ott picked up. They had patched him through to Ott's cell.

"Ott here," he answered, sounding way more chipper than most people did at that hour of the morning.

"Yes, hello, Officer, I am calling you to inform you that the man in that flyer you're looking for currently resides at 101 El Vedato."

Ott motioned frantically to Crawford next to him as he hit the speaker button on his cell. They had just booked Ward Jaynes and put him in a six-by-nine cell.

"Who is this?" Ott said into his cell. "Who am I speaking to?"

"Just a concerned citizen, Officer," Alcie said, "trying to make sure Palm Beach is a safe place again. That address—in case you neglected to jot it down—is 101 El Vedato."

Click.

Ott put his fist up and Crawford bumped it with his.

"Guess we can forget about sleeping," Crawford said. "That guy's voice . . . what'd he sound like to you?"

"Like a black guy trying to sound like Prince Charles."

"Exactly."

Ott spun the car wheel so hard Crawford almost slid into his lap.

"The hell you doin'?"

"Going to get the guy at El Vedato, whataya think?"

Ott took a skidding left turn onto Congress.

Crawford grabbed the dashboard for support.

"Mort, for Chrissake, lose the Skip Barber driving school shit. It gonna matter we get there two minutes faster?"

"Sorry."

"You *do* understand we got nothing on the guy?"

Ott thought for a second.

"I mean, not a damn thing," Crawford said, shrugging. "We go to the house . . . then what? We got probable cause?"

Ott scratched his head. No sleep in a long time wasn't helping his thought processes.

"I mean," Crawford said, "charge him with what?"

"Suspicion of murder. Cynthia Dexter," Ott said, scratching his head harder.

"Based on what?"

Bloodhound creases sliced across Ott's forehead.

"Okay, well . . . what's the guy doing living in a $10 million house?"

Crawford shook his head. "That illegal, Mort?"

"Sure as hell is suspicious. Bet we can nail him for art theft."

"And whataya got for proof?"

"Fucking A, Charlie," Ott said, tapping his fingers on the wheel, "work with me here, will ya."

"You're too damn eager; we jump the gun, we hand some defense asshole a way to get him off."

"So what are you saying?" Ott asked.

"We get a warrant," Crawford said. "We'll come up with a reason for it between now and when we see the judge."

"Okay," Ott said, accelerating on the green light. "In the meantime, what if the guy flies?"

"We'll put guys on the house," Crawford said punching seven numbers into his cell.

"Who the hell you calling at this hour?"

"The judge."

"Christ, it's six fucking thirty in the morning."

Crawford let it ring. He waited. Someone answered.

"Sorry to bother you, judge, it's Charlie Crawford. I got a murder suspect at a house on El Vedato. I need a warrant. Can—"

Crawford listened for fifteen seconds, then clicked off his phone.

"What'd he say?"

"Same thing you did, but we're meeting him at ten. He must have an afternoon golf game."

FIFTY-THREE

Fifteen minutes later, Crawford and Ott were parked two doors down from 101 El Vedato.

"How do you want to play it?" Ott asked, over the engine that idled too loud.

"Two guys, front and back." Crawford gestured toward the house.

"I'll call the station, get the guys. Then what?"

Crawford looked at his watch.

"Then . . . we go catch some Zs."

"Really?"

"Yeah, if Greenleaf's in there, he's not going anywhere. Got three hours 'til we see the judge. What do you want to do? Sit around and drink coffee?"

"Guess I could handle a nap."

Ott then lifted up his foot.

"Hey, by the way, you never asked me about the secret of my speed." He pointed at his shoe. "Right there, waffle soles."

"Is that what it was?" Crawford laughed. "I gotta hand it to you, you showed me some wheels. Helluva tackle, too."

"Just a little FYI, Charlie," Ott said as he put his foot back on the floor, "you can't catch anyone on a beach in Bass Weejuns."

Crawford raised his foot.

"Never catch me dead in Bass Weejuns . . . Skechers, man."

※ ※ ※

THEY DROVE back to the station.

Problem was, Crawford couldn't get to sleep there. He kept thinking about Dominica. How he could've gotten her killed. She was probably back at her place now, he figured, having bad dreams about large cars hurtling toward her.

His adrenaline was surging. His exhaustion no match for it. His mind jumped to Greenleaf. Leaning back in his chair, he watched the sun rise from his office window. He was churning through Greenleaf scenarios. Lil hadn't given him much, but enough to get him speculating. He knew she was holding back. By the time the sun had cleared the four-story condominium building to the east, Crawford had a pretty good working theory. Why Nick Greenleaf had killed Cynthia Dexter.

Still, it was hard wrapping his head around the idea that the guy in funny-looking devil slippers could hurt a fly.

At nine thirty, Crawford got out of his chair and walked down to the soft room.

He opened the door and heard snoring, then saw the unmistakable super-sized body of Mort Ott with the orange and brown striped tie still around his neck. His calf-length socks had slid down below his ankles and Crawford saw his hairless skin the color of dead fish. The small room smelled a little ripe. But then, it usually did. With or without Ott in it.

"Two feet on the floor, fat boy," Crawford said, shaking Ott's shoulder.

"Fu—uck," came the muffled protest from Ott.

Ott sat up, straightened his tie and hiked his socks up over his calves. Then he reached into his pocket, took out a roll of Certs and threw down three of them. Crawford went into the can and splashed water on his face and combed his hair. Then they drove over to the judge's office. The judge was not impressed with their appearance but gave them the warrant anyway.

On their way to the house on El Vedato, Crawford got a call on his cell. It was Jim McCann, one of the detectives who was covering the house. He checked his watch. Ten thirty. He put McCann on speaker.

"Yeah, Jim?"

"Car's leaving here, big old Rolls Cloud Three."

"Who's in it?"

"Can't tell, windows are tinted."

"Follow it."

"I'm on it."

"Check back when he stops."

"Will do," McCann said. "Hey, I heard there was a whale sighting in the soft room a little while ago."

Ott rolled his eyes.

"Yeah, wearing a stylish orange and brown tie and waffle-sole shoes," Crawford said, ducking Ott's slap to the back of his head.

FIFTY-FOUR

"I remember this place," Ott said, as Crawford pressed the buzzer on the front door of 101 El Vedato. "When I was handing out those flyers, this is where I met that civic-minded African American gentleman who, I'm guessing, placed the call earlier."

Crawford nodded and hit the brass knocker three times.

Finally, the door was opened by a woman around fifty in a light blue uniform.

"I'm Detective Crawford, this is Detective Ott, Palm Beach police . . . Mr. Greenleaf here?"

"Who?"

"Nick Greenleaf, blond hair, around twenty-five years old, six feet or so."

The woman squinted and her head tilted to the side.

"That sounds like Mr. Avery."

"Excuse me but . . . who are you?"

"Regina," the woman said with a smile. "Mr. Robertson's cook."

Crawford had looked up 101 El Vedato in the reverse directory and saw who owned it.

"Spencer Robertson's the owner, right?"

"Yes."

"And who is Avery?"

"Avery Robertson," she said. "Mr. Robertson's grandson. Just drove off a little while ago."

"Is Spencer Robertson here?"

"Oh, sure, he never leaves."

"We'd like to see him, please."

She hesitated.

"He's . . . watching TV."

"Can you take us to him?" Ott asked.

She hesitated again. "Ah, sure, he's in his library."

They followed her down a long wide hallway, through the dark formal living room and into the library.

Spencer Robertson was in white pajamas with blue piping. Crawford could see the outline of something lumpy in the back of his pajamas. The old man—Crawford figured he had to be way into his nineties—was watching a cartoon. Crawford heard Barney Rubble's voice.

Robertson didn't hear them come in.

"Mr. Robertson," Regina said.

The old man turned and his face brightened as he looked up at Crawford.

"Ruby," he said to Crawford, like they were old buddies. "Game of backgammon?"

Crawford caught the cook's eye.

"Sorry, sir, I'm kind of busy," Crawford said.

Robertson looked hopefully at Ott.

"Ah, maybe some other time, sir," Ott said.

Crawford nodded to the old man and walked out, just ahead of Ott.

Crawford went into the hallway.

"Pretty easy pickings here," Ott said.

Crawford nodded.

Then he turned to the cook.

"Regina," he said, showing her the paperwork, "this is a search warrant. We're going to go through the house."

The woman's eyes blinked. "Oh, okay . . . sure."

"Don't worry," Ott said, with a reassuring smile, "we won't mess things up."

She nodded.

Crawford pulled out his cell and dialed.

Jim McCann answered.

"Jim, where's our guy?"

"He just pulled into a little yellow house up on Arabian."

It was a hard kick in the gut.

Crawford knew the house. He had been there quite a few times.

"Green shutters, gray paver driveway?"

"That's the one."

Crawford knew Greenleaf wasn't picking up Lil for brunch at Green's.

"Let me know if they go anywhere."

Crawford hung up and glanced at Ott, who looked as eager as a bird dog on point.

"Where's Avery's bedroom?" Crawford asked Regina.

"Take the stairway up, turn right, end of the hallway. The blue one."

"Thank you," Crawford said, heading toward the dark wood stairway.

He turned to Ott. "Lots of pretty pictures on the walls."

"I noticed. Expensive looking, too."

They walked up the stairway and down to the blue bedroom.

The first thing they saw was a bureau across from the bed with two empty half-open drawers. Crawford walked over and pulled out the other two drawers. They were empty, too. Ott opened the closet door. There was nothing inside but wood hangers and a pair of brown loafers.

"Looks like Nick's history," Ott said.

"From Nick Greenleaf to Avery Robertson," Crawford said. "A rags-to-riches tale."

"Wonder why he'd give up the good life."

"Heard footsteps, maybe," Crawford said, pulling open a drawer. "I bet if we got here a day ago we'd find a jacket missing a button with a Z on it."

He spotted a yellow piece of paper and a card at the back of the drawer and reached in and pulled them out.

"Well, now, isn't this interesting," he said, showing Ott a deposit slip, "Avery . . . Nick . . . just had $3 million wired to his bank on Friday."

Ott looked at the slip while Crawford picked up the card and read it.

It was a cosmetic surgeon in Boca Raton. The time and date of an appointment the day after tomorrow was written on it.

"Our boy Nick's a little young for a nip and tuck," Crawford said.

"What are you thinking?"

"A wild guess, maybe he wants to look like someone he isn't? Let's go have another chat with Regina."

Crawford headed for the stairs, then turned back to Ott.

"I got a hunch we might find a few paintings missing," Crawford said.

His cell rang as he started down the steps.

"Hello."

"Charlie, woman with a bunch of suitcases just got into the Rolls," Jim McCann said, "young blond guy's driving."

Crawford didn't need to ask him what the woman looked like. He looked at his watch. It was ten forty-five.

"Just follow 'em, headed to the airport is my guess."

"I won't let 'em out of my sight."

Crawford clicked off and turned to Ott.

"After we have another chat with Regina, we're going to the airport."

Ott nodded.

Regina was in the laundry room.

"Regina, does Mr. Robertson have another bedroom. Upstairs maybe?" Crawford asked. "One he used to use?"

She was folding big, fluffy towels with blue "R" monograms.

"Yes, he couldn't get up the stairs anymore, so we put him in one down here. But his old one, the master, is upstairs. Opposite end from Mr. Avery's."

"Thank you . . . ah, Mr. Avery . . . anyone ever call him any other name?"

Her lips pursed in thought. "No."

"Besides you, Mr. Robertson and Avery . . . another man lives here, right?"

"Well, yes, Alcie, Mr. Robertson's butler. Except . . . he just retired."

"An African American gentleman?" Ott asked.

"Yes, he is."

"And where is he?" Crawford asked.

"Out shopping, I think."

Ott looked at Crawford.

"Let's go back upstairs," Crawford said.

"I just remembered something," Regina said. "I over-heard Mr. Avery say something to Alcie about someone coming to visit."

"Who was that?" Crawford asked.

"I didn't hear a name."

"Coming to stay here?"

"I think so."

"Thank you very much, Regina."

"Have you noticed any paintings missing, by any chance?" Ott asked.

She nodded and took them to the powder room near the front door.

Crawford spotted three holes on the wall.

Then she pointed out a discolored rectangular area on a wall above a banquette just off the kitchen. As he got closer Crawford saw the same triangle of little holes.

"I don't get it," Crawford said.

"What?"

Crawford ushered Ott over, out of earshot of Regina "Only these two missing. And in places where you'd hang the third string. Why wouldn't he have sold the big ones in the living room?"

Ott shrugged.

"And how'd he get $3 million for those two little ones?" Crawford said.

Crawford turned to Regina.

"Thanks again," he said, then to Ott, "let's go back upstairs."

Crawford was halfway up the stairs.

The master bedroom was like a small museum. It had old rifles, Japanese swords, models of boats, pictures of famous golf courses in Scotland, old stock certificates of defunct airline companies. In a glass display case was a baseball card collection of the Milwaukee Braves including a valuable one of Hank Aaron as a rookie, and a stack of stamp collection books about five feet high.

"You could spend all day going through all this shit," Ott said.

Crawford nodded absently, his eyes scanning the cavernous master bath.

Then he walked over to the walk-in closet. He flipped on the switch. It was huge but completely empty. He saw another door on the other side of the room. He walked over to it and opened it.

Everything was hanging perfectly. A row of double-pleated tan slacks, probably twenty pairs, exactly the same. Another long row of blue blazers, each one with shiny silver buttons. He took one off its hanger and studied it. It had a breast pocket patch from Seminole Golf Club. He looked at another one, then another. Each had a patch from a famous club. Then he scanned a row of close to thirty black belts. Crawford turned one over and saw the size. Forty-two. He saw another row of brown belts, all of them either crocodile or alligator. Crawford turned to Ott and pointed to a space between two of them. One was missing.

"The one around Cynthia Dexter's neck," Ott said.

"Yup," Crawford said. "Remember McCarthy's write-up: 'Size 42, expensive-looking brown alligator belt.'"

Something had caught Ott's attention. He was looking at the black belts.

"See near the end," he said, pointing.

Crawford looked over. Another one was missing.

FIFTY-FIVE

Lil, sitting in the passenger seat of the Rolls, knew that everything Nick had told her was complete and total bullshit. But at least he was consistent, so she played along like an infatuated girlfriend. No point in letting on she knew.

They were talking about where Nick said he was jetting off to. Cap d'Antibes, he had told her.

"I think of Cap d'Antibes as strictly a summer place," she said to Nick, "but it's nice in winter, too?"

They were pulling up to Signature, one of the private jet terminals, two miles south of Palm Beach International Airport.

"Oh, yes, Cap is fabulous this time of year. The expat crowd is there year-round. But no tacky tourists now."

Nick had no idea what he was talking about. Fitzgerald only wrote about summer there. But he thought it sounded plausible.

He slowed down as he drove up to the front entrance of Signature.

"Wheels up at what time?" Nick asked, opening his door.

"In about twenty minutes," Lil said, " 'course since I'm the only passenger . . . they can wait until I'm good and ready."

"Gotta love flying private, huh?" Nick asked, never having had the privilege.

"Yeah, it's the only way to go." She hadn't either. "You going through Paris?"

She knew he wasn't going anywhere. She had checked on flights, pretending to be his wife. No reservations to anywhere for Avery Robertson or Nick Greenleaf.

"Yes, Paris, then down to Nice," he said, turning to look at their bags in the back seat. "Tell you what, Lil, you go on in, I got a little surprise waiting for you in there. I'll get the bags."

She smiled. She loved surprises.

"Thanks. See you inside."

He watched her walk inside, and as soon as she was out of sight unzipped her blue canvas T. Anthony bag. He dug down beneath the black thong underwear on top, and felt a soft bag. She had made the mistake of telling him that she had gone shopping at Cartier after getting Ward Jaynes's wire transfer. He opened the bag and saw a diamond necklace that had a Cartier logo on it. Bingo. There were two expensive-looking rings and a brooch in the bag, too. He grabbed the three items and put them on the car seat. Then he paused, eyeing her black thong. How better to remember her? He grabbed it and jammed it into his pants pocket.

Then he unzipped the heavy leather suitcase that he had taken from Spencer's closet, containing his clothes, and put the jewelry underneath one of his shirts, right next to the black belt he'd pilfered from Spencer's closet.

He had the belt on top for a reason.

He figured Lil would be pouring her first glass of Cristal champagne now from the bottle he'd had delivered earlier to the private terminal.

He opened another of her suitcases and felt around.

Nothing. He was hoping for a thick wad of cash maybe. He zipped it back up and, making two trips, carried all six of their suitcases inside. After Lil got on her plane, he was going to take a cab to the Chesterfield hotel where he'd made a reservation. He'd hang out there until he paid his final visit to 101 El Vedato and took care of business. He had it all perfectly planned. Sneaking back in, in the middle of the night. Taking the belt with him. His new cosmetically reconfigured face. A patrician nose, instead of the pathetic, mashed-in mound he was born with.

※ ※ ※

"You were right about the airport, Charlie," Jim McCann said, "but you got the wrong one."

"The private one, huh?"

"Yeah, Signature . . . you get off at Southern, go down to Military and double back on a little street running parallel."

"We're fifteen minutes away," Crawford said, flooring it.

Ott looked over at Crawford.

"Man, this bartender, $3 mill in the bank, private metal, guy doesn't fuck around."

※ ※ ※

The Cristal had been a nice touch, but that was not all. Nick had ordered caviar to go with it. Lil checked her watch as she polished off the champagne.

He refilled her glass and poured one for himself. Nick raised his glass and clinked hers.

"To the options," he said.

"To the options," she said.

"You leaving the Bentley here?"

"Rolls," he said and smiled. "Alcie's picking it up."

He reached for a cracker, dragged it through the caviar like it was salsa dip, then wolfed it down. He chased it with Cristal.

Lil grimaced at the sight then checked her watch again.

"Well, I've got a flight to catch," she said.

She stood up and walked over to Nick.

Lil was going to reward him with a kiss for having given her the opportunity to become a very rich woman, but changed her mind when she saw globs of sturgeon eggs on both corners of his mouth.

"Well, Avery, it's been a pleasure doing business with you."

"Lil," he said, raising his champagne glass, "you are truly one of a kind."

He leaned toward her to give her a kiss but she turned her cheek and he grazed her diamond ear stud.

"Well," she said, with an extravagant sweep of her hand, "good-bye, Avery . . . my G-5 awaits."

She walked toward the door and went out on the tarmac. Within minutes, her jet was streaking down the runway going 200 miles an hour, then the shimmering G-5 split the sky at a sixty-degree angle.

※ ※ ※

Nick didn't notice Crawford and Ott come in. He was too busy pigging out on caviar.

"Nick Greenleaf," Crawford said, looming over him, "you're under arrest for first-degree murder."

Greenleaf's head jerked up, caviar glopped on his chin and upper lip.

The two employees at the counter looked over, bewildered.

"Where's Lil Fonseca?" Crawford demanded, as Ott went for his handcuffs.

"Her plane . . . just left," Nick said.

His lip quivered as he eyed the cuffs.

Crawford ran up to the counter and flashed ID to the two employees.

"Blonde woman, Lil Fonseca," he said to the older woman at the counter, "her plane took off?"

The woman nodded.

"Five minutes ago," she said.

"What's her destination?"

"San Francisco."

"Thanks," he said and walked back to Ott and Green-leaf.

Greenleaf, cuffed now, looked scared enough to have had an accident in his pants.

"If you want to look at something less than 2,000 volts," Crawford said, getting in Nick's face, "better figure out a way to get her back on dry land."

FIFTY-SIX

The copilot asked Lil to come up to the cockpit. She had an "urgent call" from the terminal.

"Hello."

"You left so fast," Nick said, "I forgot to give you your 'going away' present."

"'Going away' present?" she asked.

"Rabbit is the clue," Nick said, struggling to sound casual.

She was so done with him and his fake blue eyes.

"Thanks, but I'm halfway—"

"Lil," Nick said, his heart racing, "Ed-ward fuck-ing Hop-per?"

"What about him?"

"I'm looking at a twelve-by-eighteen oil, one of his houses on the Maine coast. There's no provenance problem 'cause there's no record of him painting it."

A small one . . . but still, $2–$3 million easily, she figured. She pulled the phone almost into her ear.

It was definitely worth a U-turn.

"That's my present?"

"Yes, if you hadn't run off so fast. With the champagne and everything . . . I just forgot all about it."

Lil turned to the pilot and gestured.

"Meet me on the tarmac in fifteen minutes, Nick."

FIFTY-SEVEN

One thing sure, Dominica cleaned up nice.

She had traded in her blue Ripstop pants and polyester gray shirt with the official Palm Beach town emblem logo for a short skirt and a robin's egg blue T-shirt. Her long, athletic legs and full physique were nicely displayed. She looked more like a woman who hung out on South Beach than one who analyzed blood splatters at South County Road.

On his way to pick her up, Crawford reflected on the lame expression, "don't dip your pen in company ink." That widely unheeded warning about not dating someone you work with. He found he could rationalize his way around it pretty easily, even better, ignore it altogether. Hell, it wasn't like he was going to go and flaunt it—skip past Rutledge's office hand in hand with her.

But, if people found out—and they always did—well, then, screw it.

Dominica had chosen the restaurant. It was up in the Northwood section of West Palm, on the corner of Dixie and Twenty-Second Street. It was an area that had struggled to gain respectability back when gentrification came to the area in 2004, but fell off a cliff in the crash. Café Grappolo was still hanging on, though, getting four-star reviews in the *Press*'s TGIF section.

Crawford had taken Nick Greenleaf to Gun Club Road and decided not to stick around when Lil came back to get her Harper, or whatever the painter's name was. He just thought it would be too damn painful seeing her, reading her her rights. They did have a thing, after all. Ott told him about arresting her—how she went crazy, pleading, raging, screaming all at once. Crawford called her later, said he was sorry about all that happened. It didn't calm her down much.

He and Dominica were seated in wicker chairs. He studied Dominica across the table and suddenly it hit him like a mule kick: what could have happened to her if things had gone off the tracks even just a little. The whole Jaynes setup was not one of his all-time great plans. Even though it got the job done, he wouldn't be trying it again anytime soon. Rutledge found out about it and started to go ballistic, but what could he say? The bad guys were dead or behind bars.

He put his hand on Dominca's and remembered the terrified look in her eyes the night before on the Southern bridge.

"You know, with everything going on, I never asked . . . are you okay?"

She leaned back in her chair.

"You mean . . . after my little breakdown in the back of the car."

"Are you kidding . . . you're gonna get decorated for what you did."

"Chest full of medals, huh?"

"Yeah, probably offer you my job."

She laughed. "Ah, no thanks."

"I'm serious," he said, leaning forward and taking her hand again, "how many times you think I've been there? Come off this huge adrenaline rush, then it smacks you in the face, 'Christ, I coulda been dead ten different ways . . . blown up, shot, hit by a car, you name it.'"

Dominica leaned across the table and kissed Crawford.

"Thank you, Charlie," she said and took a sip of wine. "So come on, fill in the blanks."

"What do you want to know?"

"Start with the art scam."

He was a little sheepish describing it, seeing how it involved his old girlfriend.

"Well, my . . . ah, friend got herself in a little jam. This guy Greenleaf killed Cynthia Dexter—then he sold my friend a few stolen paintings, then they came up with a plan to make a pile of money. I talked to her a little while ago, recommended she get herself a really good lawyer."

He went on to explain how the option thing worked, how—he theorized—Lil and Nick split the money fifty-fifty.

Dominica nodded. "But I still don't get why Greenleaf killed that woman."

Crawford leaned back and put his arms behind his head.

"Neither did I at first. All we had was that he knew her. Greenleaf stonewalled for a while, completely denied killing her. Until I told him you found his DNA all over Dexter's condo. I could see the wheels turning. 'Did I touch anything? Was anything on the belt? My clothes?' I finally said it was his call—life if he cooperated; the chair, if he didn't."

"But I still don't get his motive, why he killed her."

"See, the guy was looking to make a major lifestyle change, start climbing the social ladder, the Poinciana Club being the highest peak. But Cynthia Dexter knew him back in his humble bartender days. And unlucky for her—"

"—that's where she worked."

"Exactly, but the big thing was she found out he had wormed his way into Robertson's house, knew whatever he was doing there had a real bad whiff to it."

Dominica just shook her head and pushed a strand of hair over her ear.

"Then his plan was to kill the real Avery," Crawford said.

Dominica's mouth dropped.

"See, what happened was . . . the real Avery called, told Greenleaf he was coming to Palm Beach. Like he could smell his inheritance. So first Nick figures the jig was up. Then he goes, 'Wait a minute. I'd be leaving a ton of money on the table if I let this guy just waltz into town.'"

"Wow, so he figured if he got rid of Avery, he could get the whole shootin' match when the old man died?"

Crawford nodded.

"Exactly. Not to mention the old man's impressive collection of blazers, ties, belts, you name it. Speaking of which, Nick had a really nice belt picked out for Avery."

"You mean . . . to cinch around his neck?"

"Yeah, this beautiful black croc."

Crawford signaled the waitress. She came over and they ordered.

"So before I picked you up tonight," Crawford said, "I went over to Spencer Robertson's house, met the real Avery—"

"What was he like?"

"A jerk," Crawford said. "Wanted me to drop everything and go find the two paintings that Greenleaf sold Lil Fonseca."

Dominica just shook her head.

"I hope the old man lives forever," she said. "Did you tell Avery you saved his life, taking in Greenleaf?"

"Nah. Why bother? Guys like him . . . not real big on 'thank yous.'"

Dominica nodded. Then she broke into a wide smile.

"What?" Crawford asked.

"I was just thinking about Ward Jaynes."

Crawford moved closer to her.

"Yeah, what was it about Jaynes anyway?"

She looked down at her dessert for a while, not saying anything.

"I used to go out with a poor version of him," she said, then looked up at Crawford. "Took me awhile to figure out he had serious . . . *issues.* Some warped mommy thing, but first in his class at charm school. Beat me up so bad once I spent three days in the ICU. A lot of guys like him get away with it."

Crawford decided to leave it at that, not pepper her with his usual twenty questions. They finished dessert and Crawford suggested a nightcap at the Hard Case.

On their way over, Dominica got a call on her cell phone. She looked down at the number.

"It's my sister," she said, then pushed the green button. "Hey, Misty, what's up?"

Dominica just listened and nodded for a solid minute.

"Like I told you at the station," she said finally, "I think you'd be really good. Gotta get your GED first . . . and, yeah, a little college wouldn't hurt."

She listened for about ten seconds.

"Yeah, you definitely gotta clean up your act, though," she said and laughed. "I'll be keeping an eye on you. No more cigarettes, you got a curfew . . . the whole deal."

Crawford heard Misty's voice through the phone.

"Yeah, I'm *dead* serious," Dominica said. "Come on down tomorrow, I'll give you a little tour. Let you wear my 'Crime Scene' jacket."

Crawford pulled into the parking lot at the Hard Case and turned to Dominica.

"So you recruiting now?" Crawford asked.

"Yeah, well . . . she's basically a good kid," Dominica said. "How do you think you'd end up if your role models were a guy in prison, an alcoholic mother who bailed on you and a brother . . . well, you know."

Crawford held up his hands.

"Hey, I totally agree. I can see it. She ever wants to be a detective, I'll be her rabbi."

He put his arm around Dominica and kissed her.

They got out of the car, walked into the smoky dive and Sonny Johnson was the first person Crawford saw.

He gave Crawford a sheepish grin. Crawford thought he saw Do-rag at a table, his back to them. He could tell from the looks that everybody knew about what happened. Then he realized, most of the looks were just guys checking out Dominica.

They went to a table, Dominica sat down and Crawford walked up to the bar.

"Nice goin', man," Jack Scarsiola said.

"Thanks," Crawford said.

Crawford took a beer and glass of wine back to the table and sat down.

A few minutes later he heard someone shuffle up behind him.

"I gotta hand it to you," said the voice.

Crawford turned. It was Johnson.

"Nice work," Johnson said, then nodded to Dominica.

"Thanks," Crawford said, gesturing, "Dominica this is Sonny Johnson, one of West Palm's finest."

Johnson nodded and shot her a smile that was missing a tooth.

"Hi," she said.

"You're the . . . CSEU chick?"

Dominica nodded.

He raised his glass.

She nodded and smiled her dazzler.

"Well . . ." Johnson turned to go.

"Appreciate you stoppin' over, Sonny," Crawford said.

Sonny nodded and walked back to his table.

"What's the connection there?" Dominica asked.

"Oh, we had a . . . little disagreement once," Crawford said, "all patched up now."

Dominica had never been to the Hard Case before. She scanned the room, taking in the ripped felt on one of the pool tables, the blinking beer signs, her eyes stopping at the big, dirty glass jar containing pickled eggs.

"So, this is where you take your girls . . . to impress 'em, huh?"

He looked at her for a second, smiled and shook his head.

"I got news for you . . . you're the first."

She cocked her head.

"So . . . that would be a compliment?"

He nodded. "Oh, yeah, the highest."

She reached out for his hand as they heard something behind them.

Crawford turned.

It was Do-rag with a Bud and a glass of wine.

"Truce," he said, handing Crawford the Bud.

Crawford laughed and took the bottle.

"Truce," Crawford said.

"I just wanted to say good job," Do-rag said.

Crawford looked down, trying to conjure up his modest look.

"Thanks," he said.

Do-rag snorted a laugh.

"Not you, numbnuts," he said, handing Dominica the glass of wine, "your lady friend."

EPILOGUE

Alcie was on Interstate-95 just past Jacksonville. He had exchanged the plates on the Rolls with the ones from his Corolla. The Rolls was riding lower to the ground than usual because of all the gold bars and coins Alcie had just bought. Alcie didn't trust the stock market, which had turned out to be exactly what he suspected all along: a scam perpetuated by rich, white guys who graduated from places like the University of Goldman Sachs.

After buying the gold bars and coins, he spent the afternoon going around to every pawnshop he could find. He had a big wad of cash, a Saturday night special—just in case—and went on a massive buying spree. He had read in the *Palm Beach Press* that local pawnshops were long on inventory because people who had lost fortunes on Wall Street were desperate for cash. Cash was king and Alcie had stacks of it. So he bought anything and everything made of gold. Rings, watches, earrings . . . even sprung for a huge gold filling.

Then with more than $2 million dollars in gold—along with his pride and joy, the big, beautiful Francis Bacon painting of the guy with the funny head—he was on his way back to his ancestral shack in the mountains of North Carolina. He still wasn't exactly sure what he was going to tell his mother. Maybe he'd won the lottery?

Hell, did it really matter? It wasn't like she'd be grilling him too hard.

A broad smile washed over his face as he thought about his time in Palm Beach. People went there for a lot of reasons. Sun. Golf. The ocean. Marry someone rich. Reinvent yourself. But Alcie, he had just gone there to earn enough to pay his mother back. For keeping him off the street . . . off the crack pipe.

Not to mention, all his life he had dreamed of motoring down the interstate in a big-ass Rolls, people nodding and thinking, dude did all right for himself.

Well, no question about it, he surely had.